A NARROW VICTORY

Previously published Worldwide Mystery titles by
FAITH MARTIN

A NARROW RETURN
A NARROW MARGIN OF ERROR
WALK A NARROW MILE

A NARROW VICTORY

FAITH MARTIN

WORLDWIDE®

TORONTO • NEW YORK • LONDON
AMSTERDAM • PARIS • SYDNEY • HAMBURG
STOCKHOLM • ATHENS • TOKYO • MILAN
MADRID • WARSAW • BUDAPEST • AUCKLAND

A Narrow Victory

A Worldwide Mystery/November 2016

First published by Robert Hale, an imprint of The Crowood Press.

ISBN-13: 978-0-373-27963-0

Printed in U.S.A.

A NARROW VICTORY

ONE

HILLARY GREENE ROLLED over in bed, looked out of the porthole window onto the canal bank beyond and blinked lazily in the mid-August sun. A glance at her watch told her that it wasn't yet seven o'clock, so she allowed herself the luxury of a stretch for a few moments before climbing out of the narrow bed.

Yawning, she stood up and walked a bare step to her wardrobe, where she ran a critical eye over the tiny space and the mostly sombre work-orientated suits that hung there. Surely on a summer's day, when you were going back to work after a fortnight's holiday, you could be forgiven for donning a colourful summer dress?

Or maybe not.

Her lips pulled into a small smile as she contemplated her boss's reaction if she walked into Thames Valley Police Headquarters dressed like someone from an M&S advert.

Detective Superintendent Steven Crayle would probably be delighted.

Then again, she *had* just spent the first week of her holiday with him, on board the *Mollern*, her narrowboat home, cruising around the Gloucestershire canal system. The weather had been good, and they'd managed to avoid most of the usual tourist spots, in between testing out the limits of the small confines of her bed.

Yes, Steven might be happy to see her arrive for

work dressed in something more feminine, but professionalism—even in a now retired and still very much ex detective inspector—was too ingrained in her for her to give in to temptation. Instead she reached for a pale beige skirt and jacket combo, and made do with a multi-coloured blouse in gemstone colours to mark the lovely summer's day outside.

Habit had her in and out of her minuscule shower in three minutes flat, and after a sparse breakfast of brown bread toast and three cups of coffee, she stepped off the boat with a definite spring in her step.

Slinging her large black leather bag over her shoulder, she walked along the towpath to where Puff the Tragic Wagon was parked in his usual spot in the neighbouring pub's car park. As she unlocked the car door, she thought she could just distinguish the first hint of autumn's approach. There was that slight coolness in the early morning air, and the housemartins skimming the canal had that frantic look about them that told her they were desperate to see their second brood fledged.

Her mind went back briefly to that moment some time ago when she'd been standing in almost this very spot, and had been dragged off into the bushes by a man holding a knife to her throat, but she refused to let the image linger.

That was all sorted, and didn't need any re-hashing.

With a mental shrug, she opened up the car and got in. Puff, a somewhat ancient Volkswagen Golf, started after his usual nominal grumble, and from the tiny hamlet of Thrupp the commute into Kidlington on the outskirts of Oxford took her barely five minutes.

As she was idling at one of the many sets of traffic

lights that Kidlington had to offer its happy motorists, her mind was still on her final week's holiday.

Because Steven had only been due one week's leave, she'd spent last week abroad on her own, in a pleasant little mountainous spot in northern Spain's Basque region, where the tourists were few and the frogs were many. (The amphibians, that is, not the French.) Her nights had been serenaded by so much chirruping, croaking, and singing by the nocturnal males that by the time she'd become used to the racket and could get a full night's sleep, it had been time to come home.

The next time she was going to bloody Benidorm and be done with it.

But she had managed to enjoy herself, in spite of being that butt of all jokes, a single, middle-aged English woman abroad. No Spanish waiters had dared to pinch her backside, she thought with a brief grin—none of them would have dared!

For all that she had a curvaceous hour-glass figure, and her long cap of bell-shaped hair was still a rich and glorious chestnut colour, there was something about her that warned off many contemplative males. Perhaps the copper in her came through, in spite of the fact that she no longer actually held a warrant card. But although she now worked in a civilian capacity as a consultant to the Crime Review Team, where she helped work cold cases, somehow she was always going to be DI Hillary Greene.

Or perhaps the fact that she and Steven Crayle were now such a firm item, thus making her officially no longer available, sent off some kind of invisible signal that, alone and abroad or not, warned others that she was no desperate female seeking sun, fun and sangria.

Most likely, she thought with an inner snort, it was just the usual, habitual piss-off look that was generally to be found in her sherry-coloured eyes that did it. It was a look that many a villain had seen in their time, and most of them had known instinctively not to test it.

Now as she turned into the car park fronting Thames Valley HQ, Hillary sighed as the familiar building greeted her. Monday morning and back-to-work ennui battled against a more upbeat sense of anticipation. Who knew what cold case would be coming her way next? Or just how pleased would Steven be to have her back?

As she parked and turned off the ignition, Hillary Greene allowed herself to contemplate those two questions. The first was by far the easiest to deal with. Work had always been her mainstay. It gave her life purpose and definition and her career had always been the driving force of her adulthood. So whatever case was on her desk, it would get her best efforts.

The second question was far more worrisome. The cruise with Steven, in the intimate confines of the *Mollern*, had been wonderful, and had gone far better than she'd ever allowed herself to hope. She'd hesitated long and hard before asking him to go out on the boat with her for such a long period of time. A narrowboat, by its very nature, is a very intimate space, and she'd half-expected them to find it too much. She wouldn't have been surprised to find niggling arguments arising, or for them to have to acknowledge that so much time spent together had been a mistake.

After all, they'd only been together as a couple for a matter of six months or so.

But it simply hadn't happened. In fact, rather the opposite. Their week together had only drawn them closer. They'd spent lazy days cruising, before tying up in some out-of-the-way spot and sunbathing. They'd spent hours just talking about anything and everything, before cooking something simple but delicious al fresco and then sleeping rolled up together, ridiculously closely, in her narrow bed.

They'd learned so much more about each other, and seemed to like whatever they'd learned.

And for some reason, she found it almost worrying.

Perhaps because her life, up until Steven Crayle had come into it, had been largely predictable and, if not exactly uneventful, then at least manageable.

When she'd retired from the police force just before her fiftieth birthday, she'd cast off in her boat and chugged out to explore the canal system, and never thought to see her old haunts again. But after a year, she'd been back. And her canny boss, Commander Marcus Donleavy, who'd predicted just such an event, had had a place all lined up ready and waiting for her.

It was not possible for her to get her old position back, of course, even if she'd wanted it. But in an offshoot of the Crime Review Team (or CRT as it was known), one very good-looking Superintendent Steven Crayle worked with a small team dedicated to cases that needed tried-and-trusted methods, and an SIO with experience in murder cases.

Old crimes, by their very nature, were notoriously hard to close, and Hillary, of course, had gone for the bait like a trout rising to the fly. Just as Donleavy had so smugly predicted. And so, a year after thinking that she'd left the police service for good, and that her days catching villains were totally behind her, Hillary found herself once again back in the thick of it, this time working as a civilian consultant in a new team.

And her first day on the job, she'd been introduced to her new boss.

Hillary's first thought was that the man was a walking cliché—tall, dark and handsome, he was also a good six years her junior. Long divorced, with children that he hardly ever saw, he had not been at all happy to have her more or less forced on him by Donleavy.

Which was, Hillary had had to admit, not altogether surprising, since no one could deny that she came with baggage. A lot of it. And both good and bad.

The bad began with her late and extremely unlamented husband, Inspector Ronnie Greene. As bent and corrupt as a three pound note, she'd been on the verge of divorcing him when he'd died in a road traffic accident. And whilst subsequent investigations into his activities had proved that he'd run a very lucrative animal parts smuggling operation, it had also cleared her of all involvement.

Fortunately for Hillary, Marcus Donleavy knew a good detective when he saw one, and her success rate for collars, especially when it came to murder investigations, had been second to none. Her relationships with some of her immediate superiors, however, had always been strictly chequered.

The time she'd spent working with her best friend and longest-serving boss, Phillip 'Mellow' Mallow, had been very successful. They'd become very tight-knit, and she had even taken a bullet for him, and won a bravery award because of it. Between them they had put away half the local big-time villains.

And then, just a few years ago, he'd been shot dead in front of her eyes, in this very car park.

One of Philip's predecessors had openly fancied her and pursued her, until finally admitting defeat and heading back north to lick his wounds. Yet another boss had stolen her husband's ill-gotten gains and scarpered with them overseas, whilst one had very unwisely tried to ruin both herself and her ex-sergeant, Mel's widow, and get them thrown off the force. *Him* she had promptly out-manoeuvred and sent packing off to Hull, where he'd been forced to await his own retirement in chilly solitude.

All of which had been station-house gossip for years, and none of which could have helped to endear her to one Superintendent Steven Crayle. He'd simply listened to Commander Marcus Donleavy extolling her solve rates, and nodded obediently when he'd pointed out her experience with murder investigations. He smiled through gritted teeth and agreed readily when admitting that the rank-and-file rated her, not least because rumour had it that she'd gone above and beyond the call of duty in protecting her ex-sergeant, Janine Mallow, when she'd killed the man who'd murdered her husband.

The moment she'd arrived, he had handed her the coldest, most dead-end unsolved murder case he could find, and then had been forced to watch her as she solved it. And all the while, as he had finally been forced to admit, fighting the urge to keep his eyes (not to mention his hands) off her.

Hillary was still smiling at the memory of how very good he was with those said hands as she walked into the main lobby of the building and instantly fell foul of the desk sergeant.

'Bloody hell, the wanderer returns. Where's the suntan then?' he jeered amiably.

Desk sergeants, as Hillary had very quickly learned as a raw recruit and a still-wet-behind-the-ears WPC, were a breed apart. They knew every last drop of station-house gossip, had seen it all and done it all, and took flack from nobody. In the instances where they had first contact with the public, they had an almost supernatural ability (or the good ones did) to sift the wheat from the chaff. And they had no respect for authority at all. And the latter was probably one of the main reasons why Hillary had always liked them and got on with them so well.

By way of reply to this first wave of witty banter, she gave a pretty standard two-figured reply and, without breaking stride, headed for the stairs that led down into the bowels of the building.

With the sound of the desk sergeant's pithy riposte about Steven's mating habits still ringing in her ears (which would, incidentally, have been legally answerable in a slander case), she headed down to the labyrinthine underworld where the CRT hung its hat.

The vast bulk of the department was desk-bound and computer-based, of course, but she had very little to do with that. They dealt with the majority of cold cases that were solved due to the advancement of DNA profiling and the improvement in forensic science. These colleagues of hers brought villains to book for past crimes by comparing old samples of DNA taken from unsolved cases, and matching them with more recent crimes. Rapists who'd long thought they'd got away with it suddenly had their collars felt when the CRT computer programmers ran their names through the database and matched their DNA to, in some cases, decades-old crimes.

But Steven Crayle ran a unique (not to say very small and totally under-funded) department that was dedicated to reopening cases where only good old-fashioned detective work would do.

Which was where Hillary came in, and why Donleavy had been so insistent that Steven include her. So far, she'd been working here less than a year, and had already successfully removed three unsolved murder cases from the files, as well as put away a very dangerous individual who had stalked a number of women and almost killed one of their own.

His big mistake had been in trying to add Hillary Greene to his list of victims.

Now, as she pushed open the door to her tiny office (it had literally once been a stationery cupboard), Hillary didn't even reach up to touch the now almost invisible scar on her neck. Nowadays, she very rarely had nightmares about feeling the cold slice of the knife blade on her skin, nor did she any longer have flashbacks to the attack in the pub car park.

With a sigh, she flung her bag under her desk, booted up her computer and checked her emails. Time to get on with the daily grind. Nothing much stood out, but after two weeks away she spent a couple of hours dealing with the inevitable admin, before, at just gone ten, taking a break and heading for the slightly bigger office where her team worked.

Not that they could really be called her team, Hillary mused, as she walked down the gloomy corridor towards the sound of voices.

It was hardly like her glory days, when as a fully active and accredited DI, she had a whole bunch of people at her command—specialists, subordinates, and not to mention a whole range of old-pal networks that helped her to get the job done.

When she'd first arrived at CRT, this change had been something of a culture shock for her. As Donleavy had explained, the current economic situation meant that police forces everywhere were downsizing, and new recruits were few and far between. And since cold cases were inevitably low down on the totem pole, it was hardly surprising that Steven's small unit-within-a-unit would be the least well funded of all.

Consequently, Steven Crayle had been the sole working, official police presence. After him there came Hillary Greene and another ex-copper, Jimmy Jessop, a grey-haired former sergeant who had quickly become her right-hand man. Apart from them, there had been two youngsters who were gaining 'work experience' and who might, at some unspecified point in the future, join up and become regular coppers.

Of these, Sam Pickles was a student at Brookes University studying for his BA, and the other, Vivienne Tyrell, had been a precocious little madam, job-hopping and seeking her place in life while simultaneously (and unsuccessfully) trying to seduce her boss, the gorgeous Steven Crayle.

But after the events of their last case, when Vivienne's life had, for several long hours, hung in the balance, she had not surprisingly taken the decision to leave the team, and had headed instead for the bright lights of London and a career in the media.

Which suited all of them much better.

Now, as she paused in the doorway and looked

around, she expected to see two new faces, and did so. Donleavy had told her before her break that he would be interviewing for two new placements.

Jimmy saw her first and grinned across at her. 'Morning, guv. Had a nice holiday?' The small room was, as usual, crammed with two shared desks, telephones, laptops and assorted, ill-matched chairs. A lone spider plant battled for survival under an ultraviolet-light-producing lamp. It looked like it was losing.

As he spoke, Sam Pickles looked up from his computer and nodded hello at her. Sandy haired and freckle faced, he was shaping up nicely, Hillary thought, with some satisfaction. He'd worked well with her on the previous cases, and since uni was out for the summer, she knew he'd been working (unpaid and on a strictly voluntary basis) full time, helping out the computer-based team whilst Hillary had been away. She'd considered it time well worth spent toughening him up a little and showing him the ropes and she was quietly confident that, once he'd graduated, he would apply to join up and have no trouble being fast-tracked up the ranks.

'Lovely, thanks,' Hillary said, 'apart from the noisy bloody frogs.' Her eyes went thoughtfully to the two newcomers, who no doubt instantly had her pegged as a raving Francophobe.

Donleavy had personally chosen them both, and she had just been going over their files to familiarize herself with their circumstances. What she'd read had certainly been interesting, and she'd instantly been able to tell why the commander had chosen them.

'Guv, this is Zoe Turnbull and Jake Barnes,' Jimmy introduced them briefly. 'Zoe, Jake, this is Detective

Inspector Hillary Greene—listen to what she says and do it.'

'Hardly the Battle of Agincourt speech, Jimmy,' Hillary said with a grin. 'And it's ex DI, actually. Welcome to the team.' Zoe Turnbull, Hillary knew from her personnel file, was twenty-four years old but looked more like a teenager. This might have had something to do with her style of clothing, hair and make-up, which distinctly leaned towards the goth. Her short somewhat spiky hair was jet black and had scarlet-coloured tips, and was the perfect foil for a rather gamin-shaped face. Her eyes had the inevitable black gunk liberally applied, and her lipstick was a matching scarlet. She was wearing black denim jeans that fit her lean frame well, and some sort of faded black T-shirt with a logo that was now indecipherable.

Hillary knew, again from her file, that she was an only child, born of middle-class parents, and had gained a sociology degree from Reading University. What she was doing working in the CRT, Hillary had yet to determine.

As she met a rather challenging pair of dark brown eyes, Hillary wondered what made her feel that the police service might be for her. A sociology degree tended to indicate a certain personality type, of course, but one look at Zoe Turnbull's rather ironic gaze left Hillary doubting that this woman had ever considered becoming a social worker.

Perhaps she was attracted by the prospect of power? Some people, Hillary knew, were drawn in to uniform by the desire to wield control over others. But these usually got weeded out during the training process. Of course, neither Sam nor the other two new recruits had gone through such a process, and Hillary hoped that Donleavy knew what he was doing.

In normal circumstances, Hillary had no doubts that she could rely on the commander's bullshit meter firing on all four cylinders. But as she and Steven knew only too well, when resources were sparse, you had to take what you could get. And with the low pay on offer by the CRT for its civilian consultants, what you could get might not amount to a hill of beans.

'So, are we supposed to call you guv, too?' Zoe Turnbull asked, with a wry and genuinely amused twist to her lips that took much of the sting out of the question.

Hillary, cautiously, decided that she liked her.

'Oh, take no notice of Jimmy. He's old school, as you've probably already realized,' Hillary said, holding out her hand to shake Zoe's. 'And since I'm not an active police officer, technically I'm not a guv at all. It's just what Jimmy's comfortable with. You can call me Hillary, or ma'am if you like, or even your royal highness if I really get on your wick. But since it's easier to work cases if you have a formal structure, and a clear chain of command, guv is just easiest.' Zoe Turnbull thought about that for a moment, then nodded her head and grinned. 'Suits me. Besides, I always wanted to call someone guv. My dad's favourite old telly show was *The Sweeney.*' Jimmy coughed back a laugh and turned back to the report he was reading, and Hillary's eyes swept across the small room to the other stranger.

A more marked contrast to Zoe Turnbull was harder to imagine.

For a start, at thirty-three years old, John Barnes was a generation older. And despite the fact that he was also dressed in jeans and a top, he might as well have been wearing a three-piece suit, so marked was the contrast with Zoe's goth-style attire. His denims were strictly high end, bore a very discreet label, and had an almost knife-like crease running down the length of them. Similarly the T-shirt he was wearing was pristine white and bore a famous brand mark discreetly on the right-hand shoulder. At just on six feet tall, with thick, short brown hair and attractively wide, grey-green eyes, he was almost as good-looking as Steven, Hillary mused dispassionately.

She eyed him thoughtfully as he smiled and stepped forward, hand outstretched. She took it with a friendly smile, all the time wondering just what his game was. From the moment she'd read his file, Hillary Greene suspected that he had to be up to something.

'John, isn't it?' she asked pleasantly.

'I prefer Jake, ma'am,' he said, with an open and engaging smile that somehow effected to be just a touch shy. 'My friends at pre-school started to call me that and it just stuck.'

Oh yes, Hillary thought instantly. Definitely a game player.

'Only my mother still sometimes calls me John, and that's usually when I'm in the doghouse over something,' he added, with a self-effacing shrug.

Zoe laughed dryly. 'I can't imagine the Boy Wonder ever being in the dog house,' she said, and again, something innately friendly in her voice stopped the comment from being uncomfortably sharp.

Jake Barnes rolled his attractive eyes at her. 'Ignore her, ma'am. She thinks she's being funny.' Hillary nodded. But Boy Wonder, she thought with an inner smile, in many ways, suited him. For, according to what she'd read in his file, wasn't Jake Barnes nothing less than that?

Coming from a strictly working-class family, he'd attended a local comprehensive school with a bad reputation and left with hardly any academic qualifications worth mentioning. And yet at the age of twenty-four he became a multi-millionaire when he sold off his dot.com business just ahead of the bursting bubble.

Since then, he'd spent his 'retirement' dabbling in this and that, as he'd put it in his rare interviews with the press, inventing wildly successful apps for mobile phones and tinkering around with some internet-based ideas that had paid off even more handsomely. He was currently investing his money in property, taking advantage of the deflated property market to buy, buy, buy. He now owned buildings all over the country and was sitting on a fortune in assets.

He had married in his pre-boom years but had recently divorced, his ex-wife Natasha getting a surprisingly low alimony settlement. True, there had been no children involved, and he'd obviously taken the precaution, even then, of getting her to sign a pre-nup.

All of which told Hillary a great deal.

The man had brains. He'd been lucky. He could be ruthless. He had a good grasp of his personal finances. And he was imaginative but also astute.

So what the hell was he doing here, in the sub-basement of Thames Valley HQ, working for peanuts in a cold-case unit?

Because one thing was for sure: Hillary did not buy his explanation. Even though Donleavy—and presumably Steven as well—had both taken it at face value.

On his application, Jake Barnes had said that, having earned his fortune, he wanted to 'give back something' to his community. He wanted to stretch himself by exploring new horizons and doing something more useful than simply making money, and loaning his expertise to the police had seemed like the ideal opportunity to do all of that, and more.

Hillary could see why his application had appealed to the top brass. As a rich man, he had no need for a working salary and was therefore unlikely to fall prey to corruption by accepting bribes. He was obviously intelligent, and understood the modern world and how it worked. And in the CRT, his apparent bleeding-heart liberalism wouldn't be allowed to do much damage. Besides, they were all probably hoping that some of his wealth might come their way by various convoluted means. And failing that, someone with his influence and clout had to be a good proposition to have in your corner.

Oh yes, Hillary could well see why they'd snapped him up. Perhaps it was just her pessimistic nature that was making her predict problems where they might not exist?

Yeah, right, Hillary thought grimly.

'So, how have you both been settling in?' she asked now with a friendly smile, and leant one shoulder more comfortably against the doorframe.

She was looking at Zoe as she spoke but she didn't miss the slight relaxation in Jake's shoulders that told her that he'd been tense—which in itself struck her as rather odd. Why should a man with more money than he could possibly spend in his lifetime worry about making a good impression on someone as unimportant as herself? It was not as if he needed a job so badly that it was vital he made a good impression on the boss, was it?

'Well, it's still early days,' Zoe said. 'But Sam and Jimmy have been showing us the ropes. We're up to speed on the computer systems now, and have a good idea of what we'll be doing. While you've been away we've been following up on some old burglary cases that match the MO of some new cases in Summertown.'

Jimmy grunted and gave Hillary a quick résumé of their progress so far. Hillary listened attentively. 'So I reckon it's Knocker Clarke and his old gang back at it,' Jimmy concluded. 'You're not telling me it's a coincidence that all this has kicked off again three months after he's let out of Bullingdon.'

Hillary nodded. 'From the sounds of it, you and Sam seem to be closing in on them,' she said, knowing that she didn't really need to offer encouragement or valediction, but aware that Sam, especially, appreciated it. 'You two should keep on to it, and make sure you're allowed in on the collar at the end.'

Since neither of them were police officers, she knew that when the time came, the CRT would have to hand over their work and any evidence to uniform to enable them to make the actual arrests. But that didn't mean that they shouldn't get their share of the glory.

Jimmy grinned wolfishly. 'Don't worry, guv. I've got mates in Robbery that'll be happy to take the file off me and will see us right.'

Hillary nodded and then smiled at the two newcomers. Part of her remit, she knew, was not only to solve cold cases but also to train the wannabes up. 'So, it looks as if it'll be just the three of us taking on the next case together then.'

She straightened up in the doorway. ‘Speaking of which, I’d better go and see what the super’s got for us.’

Zoe Turnbull grinned secretly. From what she’d been hearing on the grapevine, the super-sexy Steven (as she’d instantly dubbed him the moment she’d first clapped eyes on him) had quite a lot to give to Hillary Greene, one way or another. What the desk sergeant had been telling her about them had made her ears burn.

As she watched her new boss turn and walk away, Zoe felt a brief twist of regret that Hillary Greene was so clearly heterosexual.

Fifty or not, she was definitely a babe.

Jake Barnes too watched Hillary Greene leave, but whatever thoughts might have been going through his head were definitely not readable behind his attractive, grey-green eyes or handsome face.

HILLARY KNOCKED ON the door to Steven’s office and walked in.

The man seated inside looked up at her from behind his desk and beckoned her in with a smile, whilst simultaneously speaking into the telephone. ‘Yes, sir, I can.’ Pause. ‘Yes, tomorrow will be fine.’ Pause. ‘That’s fine, sir. Yes, goodbye.’ ‘Donleavy?’ Hillary guessed with a wry grimace.

She and Commander Marcus Donleavy had either a very complex or a very simple relationship, depending on how you looked at things.

Although he’d always been the boss that her boss reported to, almost from the moment that she’d first come to HQ, they had soon come to regard each other with a wary but mutual respect that rendered them, in some odd way, equals.

In Donleavy, Hillary had quickly come to recognize a ruthless efficiency that she admired. Nor had it taken her long to realize that she and the commander had quite a lot in common. They both despised those who preyed on the weak, who bullied and destroyed, ruining lives in the process, indulging in the arrogant belief that they were above the law.

Hillary and Donleavy delighted in proving them wrong. Donleavy, in turn, had quickly come to realize that in the unlikely guise of the crooked and despised Ronnie Greene's wife was that rare and much prized asset, an astute and clever mind, allied to a strong sense of what was right and what was wrong. Someone who neither despised nor worshipped money and mammon, who could keep a clear head when all around her was chaos, and keep her eye firmly fixed on one goal. Nabbing collars.

In short, the perfect detective.

And the fact that she had been able to follow his lead over the years without in any way brown-nosing him, or compromising either of them, was a much-appreciated added bonus for them both. But if all of this had led them to regularly performing a curious kind of dance around one another, neither of them were willing to acknowledge it, either to themselves, to each other, or to anyone else.

Certainly the rank and file had always been intrigued by the way they interacted. At first, and almost inevitably, the more jealous of her male colleagues had assumed that they were having an affair, but that particular hare had very quickly run its course when it became apparent, even to the most ribald male psyche, that that had never been the case.

Others had always contested that it was strictly professional between them. When Hillary Greene had risen through the ranks the hard and honest way, via plenty of hard work resulting in a record second to none, they had simply assumed that Donleavy had done as he'd always done: realized the detective gem he'd discovered in-house and right under his nose and cannily used her to the best advantage.

As was his wont.

But others, his secretary included, knew that it went much further than that. On the rare occasions when DI Hillary Greene requested a meeting with the great man, she was under strict instructions to agree at once, and to fit her in. Many a time she had sensed ructions in the air, and the advent of something that smelled bad and which interfered with the smooth running of Marcus Donleavy's remit. And almost inevitably, after the appearance of DI Hillary Greene into her boss's office, the ructions had ceased—sometimes in a somewhat spectacular and unexpected manner, as in the banishment to Hull of a certain superior officer, other times with barely a whisper.

It had got to the point where the guardian of Donleavy's office had come to think of the DI as her boss's secret henchman. (Henchwoman?) Throughout the rest of HQ, the rumours that persisted about them sometimes clashed and overlapped, or contradicted themselves. They were friends; their relationship was tense. He liked her; she didn't particularly like him. He trusted her; she was wary. It was, however, widely agreed that Donleavy listened to Hillary Greene whereas he very often didn't listen to his peers. Which was true, but it didn't necessarily do Hillary any favours.

Others insisted that Donleavy gave her far more headway than most, and backed her up when perhaps he shouldn't—which both of them would probably have reluctantly admitted was true but Hillary would have very quickly pointed out that it occurred only when it suited him.

It was certainly true that, when it came to managing problems strictly and quietly within the force, she and Donleavy were firmly on the same page.

And so, while the exact nature of their relationship endlessly fascinated everyone from the chief constable down to the bobby on the beat, nobody really understood it, and this included Steven Crayle.

Now, as he hung up the phone, he nodded, and looked at her curiously. 'He wants to meet me to discuss "matters of interest". Any ideas what's on his mind?'

Hillary looked briefly amused. 'Don't have a clue. The commander hardly keeps me up to date on his daily doings. Especially now that I'm strictly a civilian.'

Steven believed that as much as he believed in the tooth fairy, but he held up a hand in a show of surrender. 'OK, OK. I just thought I'd ask. In case I needed a head's up.'

'Got a guilty conscience, have you?' Hillary shot back with a smile.

Steven smiled a very slow and sexy smile at her. 'Always. But nothing that need concern the commander.' At just over six feet tall, he was slender in that way that spoke of masculine elegance. This somewhat sophisticated air was enhanced by the well-tailored cut of the dark suits he wore. He had short dark hair and dark brown eyes, and was good-looking in a way that wasn't particularly rugged but was hardly feminine either.

Now, as he smiled that devastating smile at her, Hillary felt her toenails curl.

She curled her lip briefly at him, like a terrier sizing up which bit to bite first, and demanded flatly, 'I've just been talking to the two new recruits you've lumbered me with. I think the goth fancies me.'

Steven blinked. 'Really? She didn't strike me that way. In fact, I rather thought that she fancied *me*.'

And who wouldn't, Hillary thought, somewhat despairingly. Her lip snarled up a little more. 'And what's with the Boy Wonder?'

Steven grinned. 'Now if I'm not mistaken, that's Zoe's pet name for him. Who do you think she sees as Batman?' he asked.

Hillary sighed, knowing when she was beaten. 'All right, all right. At least tell me that you have a case for me.' Although she liked this new and easy way they had with each other, and she had been delighted to discover that they had very much the same irreverent sense of humour, their growing closeness worried her.

'Back, what—' he glanced at his watch '—barely three hours, and already you're a glutton for punishment.'

But as he spoke, he reached down his desk to pull open a drawer, and an indulgent look crossed his face, like a parent about to bestow a special Christmas gift on his favourite offspring. He withdrew a thick dusty file and dropped it theatrically on the top of the desk. 'As it happens, I do have something that should interest you.'

He opened the file and glanced dispassionately at the top page. 'It's a murder case, naturally. This is the preliminary report and findings only. There's more boxes in the archives that'll have to be gone over.'

Hillary fought the urge to roll her eyes and make some spurious comment invoking grandmothers sucking eggs.

As she reached out to take it from him, his hand came out and rested on hers. She looked at him, surprised for a moment, and then tensed as he smiled somewhat stiffly. Instantly, her suspicious nature made her wonder what was coming now.

'I really enjoyed our week on the *Mollern*.'

Hillary blinked, utterly wrong-footed. It took her a moment to drag her mind from the contemplation of whatever was in the files and back to the personal again.

'Oh, right. Yes, so did I,' she agreed, wondering why her words came out sounding so stilted and uneasy. Because she *had* enjoyed their time together as much as he apparently had. In fact, perhaps a shade too much? Was that what was making her feel suddenly tense?

After the disaster that was her first marriage, she had, not surprisingly, been very unwilling to let any man get too close again. And so far, none had. Until now?

The thought slipped in like a snake in the grass, and she almost literally took a step backwards. Steven Crayle, watching her closely, sighed very softly, and to cover the give-away little sound, pushed the file firmly towards her.

His voice turned businesslike again. 'It's a bit of a sod, actually. Hardly any decent leads, too many suspects with not enough meat on their bones, and the forensics is a nightmare. It's hardly a surprise the SIO at the time couldn't close it.'

Hillary snorted, feeling a sense of relief as she found herself once more on familiar ground. 'So what's new?

You only ever give me the stuff nobody else would touch with a bargepole.'

'Oh. You noticed.'

Hillary Greene was still smiling appreciatively over that snippy little rejoinder when she left the office, the precious file clutched to her chest.

Once the door was shut behind her, however, Detective Superintendent Steven Crayle leaned slowly back in his chair and sat perfectly still. For several minutes, he was lost deep in thought.

Then he gave a small sigh, a barely perceptible nod, and reached for the next file in his in-tray.

TWO

WHEN SHE GOT back to the communal office, Jimmy and Sam had already left to follow up on their burglary cases, so Hillary took Jimmy's seat and put the file on the desk.

Zoe watched her alertly, looking a bit like an eager terrier at a rabbit hole. When she'd been interviewed for the job, Marcus Donleavy had made it clear that, if she was serious about joining the police, she needed to learn the ropes, and in that respect Hillary Greene was definitely the best one to watch.

So Zoe intended to do just that.

She'd always considered herself to be a good judge of character, and the commander had mightily impressed Zoe. So the fact that the commander clearly rated the ex DI so highly was enough for her.

Besides, she'd done some research on Hillary Greene for herself, and what she'd learned had been an eye-opener. The disastrous marriage was intriguing, but it was the success rate that Greene had maintained over the years that had really caught Zoe's attention. Plus, she'd never met someone who'd been given a medal for bravery before, and right now she had to fight back to absurd instinct to ask her if it had hurt to get shot.

Of course it must have bloody hurt. Zoe gave herself a mental head slap as she watched Hillary Greene take a seat and drop a dusty file on the desk top.

Her new boss certainly had a poker face because Zoe couldn't even begin to guess what she was thinking. She'd been a little disappointed on her first day at Thames Valley Police HQ to find that the investigative driving force behind the team was away on annual leave. She'd wanted to get started! But she had to acknowledge that it had at least given her time to find her feet and suss out the lay of the land before things really kicked off.

She was beginning to think that she'd need to be well up on her game in order to keep in the ex DI's good books. You didn't need to have much about you to see that she wasn't going to tolerate sloppy work. And any woman with a conviction rate like hers deserved respect with a capital 'R'.

Steven Crayle, the sexy super, was clearly the man who held it all together and was the only one with the power to make an actual arrest. And it hadn't taken Zoe long to realize that Jimmy Jessop, wrinkly or not, firmly held the reigns (for the moment anyway) as the guv's right-hand man. And while Sammy Pickles was a nice enough lad, and had already been in CRT for a while, she didn't really regard him as much competition.

Her fellow tyro, however, Zoe had to admit, had her a bit stumped.

She'd Googled Jake Barnes, of course, the moment she learnt they'd be working together, which had only served to confirm the jaw-dropping truth. He really was filthy rich, single and had applied to work in CRT. On their first meeting, when they'd done the usual get-to-know-you thing, she'd thought he'd been pulling her leg.

Zoe had expected to have some inkling by now as to why a man like Jake wanted to be a cop, but so far it eluded her. With his money he could travel the world, dabble in Hollywood producing films, sail a yacht, go into racehorse breeding, learn to play polo or indulge in any number of the things that the idle rich found time to do.

Not that she'd let the enigma that was the Boy Wonder worry her now. She had far bigger things on her mind.

Hillary Greene was finally back—the woman who'd put away more murderers than anyone else. And, unless Zoe was totally off her game, it was now her turn to get up close and personal with a murder case at last.

Zoe was suddenly aware that Hillary Greene was watching her with a somewhat wry smile playing on her lips, and she grinned back. Busted! OK, so the boss had guessed that she was eager to go. No point in denying it.

Hillary nodded. 'Yes.'

'A murder?' Zoe pressed, fingers crossed.

'It is.' Hillary glanced casually across at Jake Barnes as she spoke, and found him watching her with level, assessing eyes.

If it was now clear why Zoe Turnbull was here, it was far harder to read the expression on the Boy Wonder's face. Whilst Zoe was clearly in love with the idea of solving crimes, and had probably watched far too many crime shows on television when she was a kid, Jake Barnes, she could have sworn, felt far less excited at the prospect of taking on his first serious case.

It had been made clear to both of them that, as civilians, their powers were strictly limited. Also, that they would be closely monitored at all times by either Hillary herself, Jimmy or Steven. Even so, she had expected them both to feel a certain sense of kudos at a moment like this. They'd hardly have been human otherwise. But Jake seemed.... What? She could see by a certain amount of tension in his shoulders that she had his undivided attention but there was none of Zoe's eagerness in his body language. If anything, he seemed more...resolute? More determined to do well, as if Hillary was a professor who was about to set him an important assignment.

It was hard to pinpoint exactly what it was about him that bothered her so much.

Hillary sighed. It was early days yet. Besides, what did she really expect from this pair? Maybe Zoe's gung-ho attitude would harden into a more realistic acceptance of what police work was really all about; in which case she might make a decent enough officer when she'd gone through training and been given a few years' experience on the beat. Or (and which was sadly far more likely) her enthusiasm would simply flare up and then die when she got bored. And then she'd move on.

So perhaps Jake Barnes' more careful interest was the better bet for the future. Once she'd found out just what he was up to, that is.

'Right then, I've just been handed this by Superintendent Crayle.' She reached in and separated the paperwork into two halves and handed them each a fistful. 'Make five photocopies. I'm going to arrange for the rest of the evidence to be bought up from storage. When I get back, we'll read through it together and then we'll make a start.' Zoe was a little surprised to be given such a mundane task but quickly set to, nabbing first dibs on the sole photocopying machine in the office. Jake grinned and said he'd wander down to the computer rooms to find a machine there, and Hillary did what she'd said she'd do, and took a walk down into the vaults.

There she spent a pleasant ten minutes chatting with the records officer, and after handing over her new case file number arranged for the boxes to make their way to the main office. She then detoured to her own cupboard space to make a decent mug of coffee, before returning with it to the communal office where she found her new recruits reading in silence.

It was already nearly lunchtime but she doubted that anyone would be stopping to eat.

Hillary took one of the photocopies for herself then sat down with a gentle sigh, experiencing that vaguely pleasant sensation she always got when starting on a new case. Years of experience with paperwork had allowed her to fine tune the skill of quickly sifting the salient points from the mountains of routine information, and would, she knew, allow her to grasp the essentials of the case long before either Zoe or Jake.

For the first time, she looked at the name on the file.

The murder victim was one Felix Edward Olliphant. He'd been thirty-two years old at the time of his death, which had occurred either in the dying hours of 1999 or in the first hour of the brand new millennium, according to the pathologist.

Hillary, knowing the sense of humour that abounded in the mortuary, could well bet that the poor medico had had his leg endlessly pulled by his colleagues about not being able to place time of death down to the nearest millennium.

She quickly skimmed the hard-to-understand medical language, and boiled it down into simple English.

Felix Olliphant had been found stabbed to death in a

spare bedroom of the house where he'd been attending a New Year's Eve costume party. From the crime scene photos, the house had clearly been large, and a quick check of the relevant pages told her that it had been owned by a wealthy divorcee. The bedroom in question had obviously been designated as the one where the guests deposited their coats, hats, gloves and scarves, for his body had been almost hidden by a mound of outer garments.

The senior investigating officer—or SIO—in charge of the case, one DI Ian Varney, had theorized that the killer had deliberately heaped the coats around him before the attack, in order to keep any blood spatters from getting on to his or her own clothes. Certainly, they hadn't been able to find any signs of bloodstains on the guests that they had questioned, but then, as Varney had pointed out, the killer could well have left the party before the body was discovered.

He wasn't even able to say with any confidence that they'd been able to track down all the guests either, since the party was a costume party and that inevitably led to confusion. There had been, for instance, either three or four Elvis Presleys, according to which witness you talked to. They had found only two, and the other or others couldn't be traced. To make matters worse, the guest list was extremely fluid, as the hostess had invited all and sundry to bring friends. Consequently, friends of friends had come and gone, known to some and not to others, and could have looked like anyone or anything from a giant stuffed teddy to Marilyn Monroe.

Just the thought of trying to make a decent witness list from that mayhem gave Hillary a giant headache.

A blood-alcohol test had come back showing that

Felix Olliphant, probably in common with a lot of the people at the party, had been extremely drunk, of the falling-down, unable-to-walk variety. No doubt a lot of people at the party had been in a similar state, which meant memories would have been hazy at best.

Hillary herself had attended a New Year's Eve party that night, and she could vividly remember the frenetic, drunken revelry that the countdown to midnight, and not only a brand new year or a brand new century but a brand new millennium, had wrought in the people surrounding her.

She could well see why a killer might find it the ideal time to strike. And why the SIO in charge had an uphill battle to fight, right from the very get-go.

DI Varney had hypothesized that one of two things might have happened. A well-meaning friend might have helped Felix to the bedroom and left him there to sleep it off, and the killer had either seen what had happened or later discovered Felix alone and incapacitated, and had decided more or less on the spur of the moment to kill him.

Or the killer had been responsible for taking Felix into the bedroom with the express intention of killing him.

Either way, it had been a clever idea to heap the coats over the prone man before parting them just enough to get a hand through and stab him a number of times in the chest.

The pathologist had stated that the weapon used had been very sharp and narrow, and even speculated that a knife may have been deliberately honed and sharpened specifically for the job. Which would definitely smack of premeditation.

Or it was just possible that the killer had, perhaps unexpectedly, found a suitable weapon somewhere in the house, realized that his victim was lying in a drunken stupor, and taken the opportunity to kill?

Hillary, on reading through Varney's reports, thought it unlikely that it had been a spur-of-the-moment thing. Mainly because nobody at the party had come forward to admit to helping Felix into the bedroom in order to sleep off his excesses.

True, people were often not willing to come forward in circumstances such as these. Even the most innocent of people sometimes got too scared to own up to their actions when they found themselves in the middle of a murder inquiry. Nowadays, sadly, miscarriages of justice happened often enough to give people pause to think. So Hillary could well see why even a good friend of the man might not be willing to bring himself to police attention.

It was also possible, of course, that any friends of Felix's who might have helped him to the bedroom could themselves have been very drunk as well, and simply not have remembered the incident.

It was something to bear in mind. Always supposing that he hadn't managed to stumble his way there on his own, of course.

Also, Hillary didn't much like the pathologist's description of the murder weapon. True, it was only educated guesswork on his part, but from the pictures of the incision even Hillary could see that it was unlikely that a common-or-garden steak knife, or the kind you'd find in the average kitchen, would have fit the bill.

And indeed, the hostess of the party, the unlikely named Querida Phelps, had been adamant that no such thin-bladed sharp knife belonged in her kitchen. According to her interviews, she was not much of a cook and her kitchen rarely got used. And as such, collecting fancy equipment—including a large and esoteric range of knives—was never going to be a top priority for her.

No, to her mind, the killer had come prepared.

Hillary got up and refilled her now empty mug, using the instant coffee that Jimmy preferred. She took a sip, glanced at her watch, and returned to her chair thoughtfully.

'So, anything in particular strike you as interesting?' Hillary asked, looking first at Zoe.

'Wasn't it all rather risky, guv?' Zoe asked tentatively. She hated to look like a fool, and, after being so keen to start, had found herself floundering a bit in the morass of information. Worse, now that the great woman herself had asked her a question, she wasn't sure, exactly, what was required of her.

'I mean, don't most people get killed in lonely, out-of-the-way spots? Or in their own home? To kill someone, to stab them, when a hundred people were dancing and partying just a few feet away... I dunno. It strikes me as really... weird.' She shuddered.

Hillary nodded gently. 'But the house, according to DI Varney, was a big place, with lots of rooms. The noise would have been tremendous. Even if the victim had been conscious and had managed to call out, who'd have heard him? Even if they didn't have loud music playing in all the rooms, the noise of that many people just talking would have been deafening.' She sighed.

'And don't ever discount human nature. Even if somebody *had* heard a bit of a struggle, or some strange noises, is it likely that they'd have even investigated?

Supposing they were sober, and in the mood to actually care what was happening, wouldn't they think it more likely that something of a love spat was going on and be inclined to keep well out of it?' 'Yeah, I suppose so,' Zoe agreed. 'When you put it like that, the killer didn't really stand that much of a chance of getting caught, did hc? Not unless the victim fought back and got in a few blows of his own. He might have managed to get away and find help then.'

'The pathologist doesn't think that was the case though,' Jake Barnes put in. 'There were no defensive wounds on his hands or arms, so they reckon he was just lying there. Asleep.'

Hillary nodded. 'At least the poor sod never knew much about it.'

'Where was his girlfriend?' Zoe asked.

'Around,' Hillary said dryly. 'According to her statement, she danced a lot, drank a fair bit, and didn't realize he was missing until she couldn't find him for the countdown to midnight.'

'Very careless of her,' Zoe said. 'And why were they there anyway? I mean, at that particular party?'

'The victim and his business partner owned an interior decorating company, and they had just recently revamped the whole house for this Mrs Phelps woman,' Hillary said. 'That's why she invited Felix and Greer Ryanson, the other half of Olligree Interiors to the party—the girlfriend came along as Felix's guest, I suppose.'

Hillary stretched and took another sip from her mug. 'From the scene of crime photos the bulk of the party was taking place downstairs, spilling out into the conservatory and on to the patio and the indoor pool area.

Upstairs, there were—' She quickly checked the notes '—eight bedrooms, including the one where Felix was found. Even if we take it for granted that one or two of the other rooms had been...commandeered, shall we say, by the odd amorous couple or two, the killer wouldn't necessarily have been running that much risk in killing Felix the way he did.'

'And even if he had been seen leaving the area, anyone noticing him might have thought he was just coming out of a loo, I suppose,' Zoe conceded.

'Or her,' Hillary corrected mildly, and when Zoe looked at her blankly Hillary smiled. 'Don't automatically assume that the killer is a male. Statistically, of course, it's more likely, but if you read the medical report again, you'll see that the pathologist concluded that it wouldn't have taken any great strength for the killer to stab Mr Olliphant. A woman could have done it.'

Jake Barnes checked the file as well. 'He was stabbed five times in the chest—twice the blade slid along his ribs, not doing much damage. But on three occasions the blade penetrated the chest cavity. Two of these blows managed to puncture his heart, which would have resulted in death within minutes.'

'Which suggests what?' Hillary prompted him.

Jake looked up at her, his grey-green eyes narrowing thoughtfully. 'Well—the killer wanted to make sure he or she got the job done, I suppose. But it wasn't really what you might call frenzied either, was it? I mean, I don't think the killer could have been feeling out-of-control rage or anything.'

'No, I agree,' Hillary said. 'It was a thorough job, but not over the top.'

Zoe looked at Jake thoughtfully. It was a good point.

She was going to have to keep her eye on the Boy Wonder. *She* was the one who wanted to shine in this outfit.

'What about the suspects, guv?' Zoe asked, bringing the spotlight firmly back her way. 'DI Varney really fancied this man Brandt for it, didn't he?'

'Or failing that, the business partner, Greer Ryanson,' Jake added.

Hillary held up a hand. 'Let's not get ahead of ourselves. And remember, what we're reading here is the result of DI Varney's work, done nearly fifteen years ago. Which is useful, but it's only our starting point.'

Hillary took a sip of coffee and held up a warning finger. 'Working a cold case isn't like working a new case, where everything has an urgency to it, and a sense of time running out. As you may have heard, most fresh murder cases are either solved within the first three days, or week at the most, if they're going to be solved at all. After that, solve rates diminish rapidly. So DI Varney would have been under immense pressure to produce results right from the start, and of a necessity he had to do things in a rush. That's not to say that he skimped things, or necessarily missed anything. So far I haven't seen any signs of that. But we have the luxury that he didn't, of being able to take things much more carefully, to check out the things that he thought irrelevant, and to tie up any loose ends that he disregarded. And generally to use the passage of time to take an overview that was denied to him.'

As the other two solemnly acknowledged the wisdom of these words, Hillary took another sip of her coffee and rubbed her eyebrow thoughtfully. 'Tell me what you make of the forensic evidence.'

Zoe laughed helplessly. 'Where do you start? There

was so much of it! I was beginning to get cross-eyed trying to keep track of it. There was the different blood spatter patterns on the different coats, for a start. And all that that proved was which coat was lying where, and in relation to other coats, when he was stabbed. And then the owners of the coats had their own DNA and hairs all over them, as you might expect.' She rolled her eyes and took a breath. 'Then there were fingerprints all over the bedroom—some from the party guests, some from this Querida Phelps woman, by the Phelps woman's cleaner, for Pete's sake. I mean, there were over a hundred people at the party. It must have been a nightmare.'

Hillary nodded.

'And then there was the fact that the victim had been partying all night as well. How could they say what hairs or fibres were relevant to his murder, and what he'd just picked up during what was obviously a boisterous party?' she demanded.

'In fact,' Jake Barnes put in quietly, 'there was so much forensic evidence, you might as well say that there was no forensic evidence at all. At least, none that helps us.'

Hillary gave him a quick approving glance. 'Exactly. And that was the first of DI Varney's problems. Speaking of which, we need to talk to him. I daresay he's retired long since but, Zoe, check with personnel and see if you can find a current address for him.'

'Guv.'

'You said that was one of his problems,' Jake said cautiously.

'What would you say was another?'

'You tell me,' Hillary said quietly. He was obviously

a bright boy—it would be interesting to see how long it took him to figure it out.

Zoe shifted restlessly on her seat, not liking the way the Boy Wonder seemed to be taking over.

'Well, the witness statements aren't helpful, are they?' Jake Barnes said, a shade tentatively. 'I mean, it seems everyone was shocked by what had happened, and all that, and nobody seemed to be acting out of character, or had anything to hide. But it was a big, lavish New Year's Eve party. A lot of the witnesses were sloshed. And those that weren't had been milling around, dancing, chatting and what have you. It's not surprising that nobody seemed to be able to give a coherent answer to when was the last time they'd seen the victim. And the fact that nobody noticed when he left the room, or who with, isn't really surprising either, is it? I mean, why would they notice? It's not as if they knew beforehand that the poor sod was going to get murdered and so kept track of him. Not only that, but with so many people at the event it's almost inevitable that everybody's eyewitness evidence gets mixed up with everybody else's, making it almost impossible to make sense out of the jumble. And that's not really helpful either, is it?'

He took a huge breath and gave another of his semi-shy smiles. 'Sorry, that was a bit of a ramble, wasn't it?'

'Again, it's like we've got so many witnesses that we might as well not have had any at all,' Zoe chipped in, paraphrasing the Boy Wonder's previous words with a cheeky grin.

It was nice to see that even Jake Barnes could fluff things sometimes.

'And the costumes don't help,' Hillary said wryly.

Zoe laughed. 'Yes, it was a costume party, wasn't it? I keep forgetting that. I mean, who does that nowadays? Or even back then? Aren't they a bit naff?'

'The upper classes at play,' Jake said with a smile.

Zoe snorted. 'Hardly that. True aristos probably wouldn't be caught dead dressed up as highwaymen or Marie Antoinette. No, this was strictly a middle-class jolly hockey-sticks affair. Ugh! What was our victim dressed as again?'

'Lord Byron, or some other romantic poet,' Jake said, again taking a quick sneak at the crime scene photos.

Hillary pulled one out and looked at it thoughtfully. Felix Olliphant had been a very good-looking man when alive. Six foot one, according to the pathologist, and a healthy twelve stone, he'd had a full head of honey-blond hair and big grey eyes. The hair, on the night of the party at least, had been covered by a dark wig with bangs, and his costume had consisted of tight-fitting black leggings and knee-high boots, and the sort of loose, white blouson-style shirt that had supposedly made him look Byronic.

'He was a looker, wasn't he?' Zoe echoed Hillary's thoughts, but she was looking at a head-and-face shot of the victim, taken at the morgue, in which Felix Olliphant looked as if he was asleep.

'Right,' Hillary agreed. 'Which suggests what?'

'A lover killed him?' Zoe said at once. 'A man who looks like that, single—well, not married at any rate—and running his own business with presumably plenty of lolly to splash around, he must have broken a few hearts. And how likely was it that he was faithful to the girlfriend anyway? If he had been playing around, it could be reason enough for someone to want to kill him when they found out.' If there was one thing that Zoe understood, it was passion. Sexual passion, emotional passion—she didn't really differentiate.

'Unless the motive was money, like DI Varney thought.' It was Jake Barnes who spoke. 'It seems his business partner Greer Ryanson came into both his half of the business and a substantial insurance payout when he died.'

'Oh, trust the Boy Wonder to think about the cash,' Zoe said, with a grin. 'My money's on a crime of passion every time.'

'Yeah, but male or female? According to the reports, it seems the victim might have been gay,' Jake shot back quickly.

Zoe cocked her head to one side. 'Something wrong with that?'

'No, of course not. I'm just saying—from the interview notes with his friends, there seemed to be a strong suggestion that he was in the closet.'

Hillary coughed gently. 'He had a girlfriend of some years standing at the time of his death,' she pointed out. 'And other friends didn't believe the gay rumour.'

'Perhaps he wasn't either gay or straight, but bi,' Zoe put in nonchalantly. And fluttered her heavily mascara-clad eyelashes camply, first at Jake, who grinned at her, and then at Hillary, who likewise grinned at her.

'We're getting ahead of ourselves again,' Hillary remonstrated gently. 'Let's stick to what we know, as of this point. Time of death?'

'Sometime between the hours of 11.30 and 1.15 when the body was discovered,' Zoe said smartly. 'It seems odd that nobody can say for sure whether he was there when they counted down to midnight though. Surely you'd remember who you were with when the New Year came in?'

'You're forgetting the costumes,' Jake pointed out. 'Even the victim, who wasn't wearing either a full face mask or anything even more outlandish, looked different in a wig. And if you were standing next to some bloke with a Bill Clinton mask on, would you necessarily know who it was underneath?'

Zoe grimaced. 'Oh yeah, right. I forgot. I'm beginning to feel sorry for the original team. It must have been a nightmare sorting out what was what and who was who and who saw what and who. Er...if you see what I mean.'

Hillary laughed. 'OK, enough. We need to keep on reading and sorting. I've ordered the boxes up. This is just the tip of the iceberg. I need you both to go through what we've got and get sorting. Jake, I want you to follow up and report on the financial aspects of the matter since that seems to be your area of expertise. Go into the partnership agreement Felix had with his business partner, and see if there's anything dodgy about it, as well as the other financial leads DI Varney came up with.'

'Guv.'

She took a breath and turned to Zoe. 'Zoe, I want you to make up a list of all the main witnesses. I want to know their current whereabouts, addresses, phone numbers and jobs. Plus I want to know what they've been doing since the time of Felix's death and how they've all got on. When we get around to interviewing them again, who knows what you might have discovered. Sometimes the seeds of a crime can take a long time to grow, and it's only a long time after the event that you begin to get a clearer picture of what went on back then. I want to know how everyone's coped since Felix Olliphant died. I'm guessing psychology is more your thing?'

Zoe's eyes shone. 'Yes, guv. Where will you be?'

Hillary smiled wryly. 'Oh, I don't know, getting my nails done, perhaps, or having a massage down at the spa. Perhaps I'll do a bit of window shopping or grab lunch at Browns.' Jake Barnes, for the first time, laughed out loud. Zoe, abashed, grinned.

Hillary went back to her office and dived into the files. Time to open a new murder book and start making a to-do list. Before the day was out, she needed to know all that the dry and dusty paperwork could tell her about the living and once-breathing man known as Felix Olliphant.

Only then could she begin to set about finding who it was that had wanted him dead.

THREE

IT WAS NEARLY 4.30, and Hillary had just read the last of the preliminary files on the Felix Olliphant case. Her mind was still on DI Varney's joint favourite for the killing, William Jeffrey Brandt.

Brandt had been sixty-one at the time of the murder. From his rap sheet photograph, he'd been a heavy-set, balding man with small brown eyes and a somewhat florid complexion. The broken veins on his nose had clearly shown up the man's weakness, which had always been booze.

Married at twenty-five, the man had blamelessly worked as a building labourer for all his life, and with his wife, Margaret, had produced three children, who'd likewise all been raised as good solid citizens with not a black mark between them. Well, none that would make the law sit up and take notice, anyway.

From what Hillary could tell, the Brandt marriage had been happy and straightforward enough, with no signs of domestic violence. Usually, when booze was involved, violence wasn't far behind, and Hillary knew that paperwork could only tell you so much. Just because his wife had never reported abuse didn't mean that abuse hadn't taken place. And neighbours could be very selective in what they heard and saw.

One day, in the summer of 1998, William had been taking his grandson out to see a local football match when he'd lost control of his car on a corner and crashed into Felix Olliphant. Felix had been driving a rather old but sturdy Range Rover at the time, and Brandt, in a small Skoda, had not surprisingly come off the worst.

When the ambulance and fire brigade services extracted him from the crumpled wreck of his car, Brandt had broken his right leg in several places, fractured his collarbone and jaw and lost a considerable amount of blood.

But he'd lived.

The same, tragically, could not be said of his 10-year-old grandson, Billy, who'd been declared dead at the scene.

In the hospital, a blood test had shown that William Brandt had been well over the legal driving limit. Moreover, the traffic investigation team were able to calculate that at the time of the accident Brandt must have been driving at well over fifty miles an hour, which would have been all right on a straight bit of road but highly dangerous on a sharp bend. It was not surprising, then, that he'd taken the corner far too wide, and had clearly been on the wrong side of the road when he'd collided full on with Olliphant's Range Rover.

From the skid marks and various measurements taken, the accident investigation team had had no hesitation in confirming that Brandt had been in the wrong. Not that too much technical evidence had been needed, for the whole incident had been witnessed by another driver, just behind Olliphant, who'd seen the whole thing.

Colin Harcourt, a 48-year-old who owned his own modest double-glazing company, had been on his way back from seeing a potential customer and confirmed Felix's account in his police statement.

Felix had stated that he'd been driving at about thirty miles an hour, on the correct side of the road, when he'd approached the bend and found a red car bearing down on him very fast. He said he didn't have time to do much, except to start, instinctively, to try and turn the wheel to run his Range Rover up on the side of the road to get out of the way. But it was by then way too late to avoid the other car. This was confirmed by the positioning of the impact itself, which had Brandt's car clearly colliding with the Range Rover not quite full on but at a slight angle.

Moreover, Olliphant, who'd been shaken up but not seriously injured, had agreed to take a breathalyzer test there and then at the accident scene, and had passed it with a zero reading. He'd been released after being treated at the local hospital for cuts and bruises, shock and a slight shoulder injury.

Not surprisingly, Brandt had been convicted of dangerous driving while under the influence of alcohol. The fact that he'd been badly injured himself, spending nearly six months in hospital, helped marginally at his trial. His legal team pointed out vociferously that he'd suffered a great deal already, being responsible for the death of his beloved grandson, which had left him and the rest of his family utterly distraught. Obviously the court to some degree agreed with this assessment because Brandt was given just a short prison sentence plus a lifetime driving ban.

But it was what had happened after this tragic tale that had attracted the attention of DI Varney, and now, nearly fifteen years after the event, caused such thoughtful contemplation from Hillary Greene.

For, far from admitting to his guilt and trying to

come to terms with it or seeking therapy or psychiatric treatment, William Brandt had consistently and with increasingly angry desperation insisted that he had not been to blame for the accident.

Faced with the results of the blood tests, he'd been unable to deny that he'd been drinking but he'd claimed, as so many heavy drinkers did, that he could handle his booze and that six pints of bitter had not affected either his hand-eye coordination or his driving abilities. He'd flat out denied that he'd been speeding, saying that he'd been doing thirty, if that—the same as Felix Olliphant. This was in direct contradiction to both Felix Olliphant's and Colin Harcourt's eye-witness testimonies. It also flew in the face of the skid marks on the road, the measurements taken that proved the speed of Brandt's car, and the report of the very experienced accident investigation officer. Even the computer-generated programme that allowed the accident investigation team to re-enact the crash proved that Brandt had to have been travelling at speed, and had been on the wrong side of the road at the time of the collision.

Of course, it wasn't much of a surprise to anyone that Brandt had been unable to accept responsibility for what had happened. By all accounts, he'd adored his eldest grandson, who'd been named after himself, and had gone to pieces after his death. After serving his prison term, things had only gone from bad to worse for him. Brandt's son, the boy's father, Matthew, had cut off all contact with his father. Brandt, unable to drive, lost his job. His wife suffered a physical breakdown and required hospitalization for a short while.

And William Brandt publicly and repeatedly blamed Felix Olliphant for it all. He started by accusing Felix of lying, and when he wasn't believed, insisted that Colin Harcourt had been paid off by Felix to support his version of events. From there, he'd accused the accident investigation team of bias, and threatened to sue.

And on more than one drunken occasion, he had, in front of a variety of witnesses, threatened to 'get that bastard Olliphant for killing my Billy'.

DI Varney had suspected that Brandt also made abusive and threatening phone calls to Olliphant, and left similar text messages, but Olliphant had never lodged a complaint. Hillary didn't find that particularly surprising. Innocent of blame or not, being in a car crash where a 10-year-old boy dies is going to leave anyone with a whole shedload of unresolved guilt. And no doubt Felix hadn't had the heart to make things worse for the dead boy's family by dropping his grieving grandfather in it with the police.

So it was not surprising, therefore, that once Felix had turned up stabbed to death, DI Varney had been very keen to question Brandt.

Unfortunately, his alibi for the night of the murder had been one of those that was neither too elaborate nor too non-existent to be of much use.

Being New Year's Eve on such a momentous date, Varney might have expected Brandt and his wife to be at a party of their own, in which case dozens of witnesses could have vouched for them. Alas, that was not the case.

In no mood to celebrate a new millennium that would not see their grandson Billy growing up in it, the couple had spent a quiet night indoors, watching telly. Brandt had avowed that he was trying to stop drinking and that going to a party where booze would be flowing like water wasn't exactly a good idea. His wife, Margaret, had confirmed quietly but firmly that she and her husband had been together all that evening and night of 31 December and that they'd gone to bed at about one o'clock in the morning.

Since the Brandts lived a good half an hour from the house where Felix had been killed, there was no way Brandt could have done it. Even if you took 1.15, when the body was found, as the very outer limit of when the crime had been committed, and accepted the possibility that Felix had been killed only moments before being found, Brandt wouldn't have had time. To wait for his wife to fall asleep, leave the house, illegally drive his wife's car, gain admittance, and find and kill Olliphant would have taken him at least an hour. According to Varney's calculations anyway—and he'd had a DC go through the motions to make sure.

Of course, Varney hypothesized that an alibi provided by a spouse was virtually worthless anyway. Margaret Brandt could easily have been lying, and if she were a browbeaten wife, lying on command on the orders of her spouse would have been second nature to her anyway. Or she could even have been complicit in the crime. She could have driven her husband to the house, waited for him to do the deed and then taken him back to their home.

No CCTV cameras had managed to pick up the Brandt family car en route to the murder scene but again that meant nothing. Either one of them, acting alone or together, could have made their way there via other means—bus, or taxi, or even by borrowing a friend's car. And although neighbours of the Brandts, when questioned, had admitted that they'd seen lights on in the family home all that evening, that in itself meant very little either. None of them had admitted to seeing or talking to the Brandts during the time in question—most had been either hosting parties of their own or going to or from a party themselves. And how hard was it to leave a light on in the house to mimic occupancy?

On the other hand, you couldn't disprove such an alibi either. And with no eye witnesses to put either of the Brandts at the house—and here Hillary found herself, not for the first time, damning those concealing costumes—and with no forensics to place them at the crime scene, Varney had been stumped.

Hillary firmly added an interview with the Brandts to her list and closed the file.

It was time to go home.

She grabbed her coat and stuck her head in the office on the way out. Sam and Jimmy were back, and seemed excited about a lead they'd run down on their vast pile of unsolved burglaries. And she could see why. If they succeeded in bringing in Knocker Clarke and his gang to answer for the whole lot, they would do their solved-crime statistics a power of good, which would earn brownie points for everyone all round.

Hillary added her own encouragement and good wishes to the mix, then told the Boy Wonder and the goth to pack it in for today, and that she'd see them bright and early tomorrow.

STEVEN CRAYLE DIDN'T get home until gone seven. Although he spent about half his time nowadays with Hillary on the boat, the rest of the time he spent in the neat semi he'd finally finished paying for, in the area of Kidlington that ran beside the Oxford canal.

As he let himself into the house, he paused for a moment in the kitchen to listen to the silence, which nowadays felt more oppressive than ever. Then with a sigh he opened the freezer and cast a weary eye over the array of frozen ready meals.

He'd been divorced for nearly six years before Hillary Grcene had joined his team, and his life had slowly changed. Now, the silent emptiness of the house seemed depressing, whereas before he'd simply never noticed it. Now it felt almost too big, and he found himself missing the enforced but cosy intimacy of a narrowboat.

As he opened the microwave and chucked in his beef stroganoff dinner, he found himself wondering what Hillary was doing. Then he wondered what Donleavy wanted to see him about tomorrow—although he thought he could guess.

Steven frowned. If it was what he thought it was, what should he do about it? His options were limited to a simple yes or no. But nothing in life was as simple as that, as he well knew. He just wished things with Hillary were a little more clear cut. A man liked to know where he stood.

He sighed, loosened his tie, and set about making a pot of coffee.

He was going to have to have a serious talk with Hillary. And he was not at all confident that things would go well. Perhaps she did not see their relationship as he did? Perhaps he'd read it all wrong? What if he ended up making her mad, or worse, hurting her? This morning it hadn't just been in his imagination that she had mentally and emotionally pulled away from him. The growing strength of their relationship was clearly confusing her.

But then he couldn't really jib at that. He'd known from the first that that bastard Ronnie Greene, her bent, womanizing first husband, had really done a number on her. No wonder she didn't trust men. So, looking at it from her point of view, why should she trust Superintendent Steven Crayle?

But if she couldn't get past her issues…well, where exactly did that leave them? He was too old to be messing about playing silly buggers. The week they'd spent together on the boat had been a bit of an eye-opener, and for him, at least, had started to make him seriously question the nature of their future together. And the only realistic conclusion, to him at least, had been obvious.

But what if she didn't feel the same? And what if his meeting with Donleavy tomorrow changed everything about their working relationship, as he feared that it might?

Where would that leave them then?

He was still staring sightlessly out over his rather overgrown back garden when the microwave pinged that his dinner was ready.

HILLARY AWOKE EARLY, unaware that her lover had spent a long and predominantly sleepless night thinking about her and the precarious nature of their future together. If she had, she probably wouldn't have been feeling so pleasantly cheerful and upbeat as she drove into HQ and entered the building on the dot of nine.

There were, after all, perks to being a civilian. And having proper holiday time, and no unpaid overtime, were right up there with the best.

In her office, she checked her mail—electronic and

otherwise—and then grabbed her notebook and a large concertina file and went to check on the new recruits. Both were in, of course, and looking bright eyed and bushy tailed, as they should be.

'Right, first things first.' Hillary held aloft the concertina file.

'This is the murder book. A bit dramatic, I know, but it has a solid purpose. Every time you complete a task, dig out some data or have a thought, you make a copy of it, and leave it in here. The murder book is to be kept updated at all times, and available for any of us to read at any time,' she stressed firmly.

'Investigations can get very complicated very quickly, leads get tracked down and dead ended whilst other things can get forgotten or overlooked. This way, we don't repeat ourselves and everyone knows what everyone else is doing. Also, if one of us misses something, there's a good chance another member of the team will pick up on it. So, Jake.' She looked up as Jake stiffened to attention. 'Today, I want you to concentrate on the financial aspects, like I said yesterday, and when you've done make a report for me, and one for the file. And as well as finding out about how Olliphant's business dealings stood, I want you to check out how a Mr Colin Harcourt is doing now.'

'This is the witness in the Felix Olliphant/William Brandt car crash, right?' Jake said. 'I saw from the files that he'd accused our murder victim of paying him off. You want to see if I can find any trace of evidence that he might have done so?'

Hillary nodded. It was the one thing she'd found that DI Varney hadn't bothered to follow up on. She could understand why it wouldn't have been high on his priorities but a cold case was all about checking down the paths not followed in the original investigation. And the fact that the Boy Wonder had picked up on it too was impressive. The man had done his homework and was thorough—but then, what else could you expect of someone who'd made their first million by the age of twenty-one or whatever?

'Right,' Hillary said. 'I want to know how Harcourt's company is doing now, how it was doing then, and anything else that catches your eye as being off or interesting. You're a man of business—your nose should twitch if something isn't right. Trust your gut.'

'Guv.'

'And Zoe, this morning, you're with me. We're going to start with Felix's immediate family. A victim's loved ones are nearly always where you start—statistically, they're the most likely to be either guilty of the crime, or be able to point you in the right direction. And besides any of that, they're the ones who knew the victim the best—and getting to know the victim thoroughly, and working out what made them tick, is the first step in finding out who wanted them dead.'

'Guv. Felix's mother died eight years ago. His father's still alive though—I've got his current address. Oh, and by the way, DI Varney is now deceased. He died two years ago—lung cancer. And his sergeant isn't in the job any longer, and has moved to Scotland. I've got his address and phone number if you want it.' As she spoke, Zoe shot a quick, smug look at the Boy Wonder, just making sure that he'd seen that he was not the only one who'd been doing his homework.

'Good work,' Hillary said, somewhat dryly. Although she wasn't about to discourage competition between her two new recruits—after all, a little competition was healthy, and would ensure they were kept on their toes and producing their best work—she was not sure that Zoe needed to worry. If Jake Barnes felt at all threatened by his co-worker, he was doing a damned good job of looking indifferent. 'But I think we'll leave off talking to the sergeant just yet. This is our investigation now and it doesn't always do to pick up the preconceived ideas and prejudices of the original team. We'll wait and see what we can come up with that Varney didn't, and only talk to his right-hand man if we get desperate.'

'Right, guv,' Zoe said.

When Hillary and the jubilant Zoe skipped out of the door, the younger woman on her way to conduct her first ever interview with a witness, Jake Barnes was already tapping away with expert and ferocious speed on his computer keyboard, and barely seemed to register their leaving. Once they were gone, however, he paused for a moment and leaned back in his chair thoughtfully. Then he gave a mental shrug.

He had a mountain to climb, he knew, but it was early days yet.

FELIX'S IMMEDIATE FAMILY still lived in Woodstock, so as she sat in the passenger seat of Zoe's trendy little new Mini (painted a glossy black, naturally) Hillary assessed the goth's driving ability. Which was surprisingly good. The 24-year-old drove with that deceivingly relaxed and laid-back air coupled with full alertness that only seriously competent drivers displayed. So although she chatted, and sometimes even gesticulated, Hillary slowly relaxed as she became convinced that they were not about to get wrapped around any lamp posts or rear-end the car in front.

'Felix's mother died not quite a year after he did,' Zoe informed her now, as they approached the famous market town where the Duke of Marlborough and his Blenheim Palace hung out, attracting tourists year round. 'I reckon—' Zoe neatly dodged a car full of Japanese, who seemed to be slightly bemused by the roundabout system '—that she died of a broken heart. Although the doctor's report I tracked down said that it was a heart attack,' she admitted more prosaically.

Hillary, now coming to expect the dramatic from her newest recruit, didn't bother to comment, except to say mildly, 'And of course you'll copy that report and put it in the murder file when we get back.'

'Uh? Oh, yeah, sure,' Zoe said. 'The Olliphants have lived in the same house for, like, forty years or so. Don't you think that's a bit weird?'

'Not everyone moves about like a cat on a hot tin roof,' Hillary said, amused. 'Perhaps one of the Olliphants inherited it from one of their own parents and didn't want to sell it for sentimental reasons? Or maybe they just liked it too much to move. And once their son was dead, they might not have wanted to move because all their memories of him growing up were in the house.'

'Right. So now the old man's a widower as well, he won't want to move because the wife's memories will all be there as well. Poor old sod.' Hillary glanced out of the window as Zoe, using the sat nav with imperious ease, pulled them up outside a small cul-de-sac of substantial, between-the-war houses, built in the local pale stone. With grey slate roofs, and generous and mature gardens, the detached residences had that air about them that spoke of respectable money—not vulgar new money, or aristocratic old-time money, but that middle-class comfortable money which was becoming much rarer to find in these days of austerity.

'So this is where our murder victim was brought up?' Hillary said. 'He went to the local school, I take it?'

'Yes, guv. Then on to Birmingham University, where he studied art,' Zoe added dismissively.

Hillary couldn't help but smile. With her own BA from Reading safely in the bag, it was clear that Zoe wasn't particularly impressed by Felix's credentials.

Hillary had no doubt that Zoe must have checked up on her new boss's educational background, and had thus discovered that Hillary herself had taken a BA degree in English literature from an unaffiliated Oxford college. Just where did that place her in Zoe's strict academic hierarchy?

'So, what do you see, Zoe?' Hillary asked now, considering it high time that Zoe's proper education should begin. If she was indeed serious about making the police service her career, then there was no time like the present to start studying for it. 'And from what you see, what does it tell you about our victim?'

Zoe realized she'd been put on the spot and took a quick breath and looked around, her dark-lashed and elaborately black-smudged eyes darting about and taking it all in.

'Well, the Olliphants were always well off,' she began cautiously. 'Felix didn't really want for anything. He was an only child, and they had him late in life, so he was probably a little spoiled. And growing up around here, there's nothing that would have had the chance to toughen him up, would it?' She gestured around the genteel surroundings. 'No street gangs, no drug dealers, no other harsh realities of life. He left uni and set up his own business straight away with someone who obviously knew what they were doing—which was probably very smart—and as far as we know, this Olligree Interiors outfit always turned a decent profit.'

She paused for breath, and began to wish she'd studied psychology instead of sociology. 'Perhaps that tells us he was cautious, not one to take risks? He always did what was expected of him, paid his taxes, and all that. And he was a good-looking fella.' She suddenly grinned. 'Perhaps that's where he let his hair down a little? Pushed the boat out, experimented a little? Made him feel brave, perhaps?' Then she sighed. 'All in all, I'd say he'd always had things pretty easy.'

'Except for the car crash when young Billy Brandt died.' Hillary, somewhat bemused by all the theorizing, had to put in a bit of blunt reality.

'Oh yeah. Except for that,' Zoe said bleakly.

'And for the fact that someone stabbed him to death,' Hillary pointed out.

Zoe shot her boss a quick look and grinned. 'OK, OK,' she said, holding out her hands and crossing her fingers. 'Pax. I know I can get carried away sometimes. I'll try to rein it in in future.' Hillary grinned. 'Well, I did ask for your opinion. And a little speculation can be helpful. Just don't get so caught up in your own theories that you miss significant details.' 'Right, guv. Engage eyes and brain before operating mouth. Got it.' Hillary laughed. Zoe Turnbull certainly had an open and engaging way about her that boded well.

'Right, let's see if Mr Olliphant is in then. And Zoe,'

Hillary said quietly, 'I want you, this time, to just observe and learn. If you think of something I've missed tell me what it is later and we'll talk about it. You can always go back and interview a witness, many times if you have to, but if you do or accidentally say something that puts them off, or makes them feel antagonistic or humiliated right at the outset, then you may never gain their trust again. OK?'

'I get it, guv,' Zoe said, and mimed zipping her lips closed. Hillary was still smiling wryly when they walked up the neat, flower-bordered path to Gordon Olliphant's front door and rang the bell.

FELIX'S FATHER WAS a tall, slightly stoop-shouldered man, with wispy white hair, watery grey eyes and skin like old parchment. He was dressed in grey trousers, white shirt and one of those baggy, curiously colourless cardigans that seemed to be the province of old men. He seemed surprised to see them, as well he might after all these years. But if Zoe's dark pseudo-Victorian skirt and ragged-style bodice complete with the complicated goth make-up disturbed him, he gave no sign of it. Indeed, even after Hillary had painstakingly explained who they were, and what the Crime Review Team was all about, he looked neither excited nor unduly worried or fretful by their presence, but simply stood wordlessly aside to let them in.

He must, Hillary gauged, have been in his early eighties, and as he beckoned them to follow him and led them through a spacious and airy hall into the main lounge, he shuffled his slipper-clad feet carefully along the parquet flooring as if not quite steady on his legs.

The heating was full on, in spite of it being August,

no doubt because his blood was thin and he felt the cold, but Hillary found her own face becoming flushed by the heat. Beside her, she saw Zoe looking around avidly, as if trying to fix the interior of the room into her mind.

Hillary quickly did the same but rapidly came to the conclusion that if Felix, as an interior designer, had had a hand in his parents' house, there was no sign of it now. The room was bland, comfortably furnished and predominantly beige, with not a decorator's focal point anywhere to be seen.

Unless his parents had asked him to do it and had given him that brief?

'Please, sit down, Inspector,' Gordon Olliphant said, and himself sat down, with evident relief, in a large and upright armchair. Hillary didn't bother to correct him on his instinctive use of her title. Besides, she always felt better when people used it anyway. Being called Mrs Greene was always guaranteed to put her in a bad mood.

She chose the sofa opposite him, and gestured for Zoe to sit beside her and get out her notebook and take notes.

'So, what can I do for you exactly?' Gordon Olliphant asked. His voice had a raspy wavering quality to it that wasn't unpleasant on the ear.

'We just wanted to talk about your son for a bit, Mr Olliphant, if you don't mind,' Hillary said, careful to pitch her voice clearly and a shade more loudly than she would otherwise do. Although she couldn't see her witness wearing a hearing aid, she assumed that his hearing probably wasn't the best. 'Felix was a very talented man, I understand?' she began with a carefully innocuous question.

Gordon Olliphant surprised her by smiling slightly.

'I wouldn't know. I was never what you might call arty myself. My wife was, and she said Gordon had "the eye", whatever that meant. Myself, give me a ledger sheet or a business plan any day.'

Hillary smiled. 'But his company, Olligree Interiors, did well, I understand?'

'Oh yes,' Gordon said, with evident satisfaction. 'I may not have understood the company product, so to speak, but his spreadsheets were always satisfactory.'

Hillary nodded. 'He was an only child?'

'Yes. My wife couldn't have more. It was a surprise when she had Felix—she was in her forties, you see, and we'd given up expecting...well, expecting!'

Hillary smiled dutifully at the pun. 'It must have been a wonderful time when he was little. Alas, they grow up so quickly, don't they?' she led him on gently.

'Yes.'

'You must have wished he'd got married and had grandchildren. That would have been a comfort when the worst happened,' she continued.

'Yes. It might have saved Alice if he had. Given her something to live for, that is. But after the boy died, all the life just went out of her,' he said simply.

Hillary nodded sympathetically. 'He had a girlfriend at the time though. Was that serious?'

'Don't know. Might have been. But Alice always said that she was far more keen than our Felix, and that nothing would have come of it. Alice knew stuff like that. Women do, don't they?'

'Yes,' Hillary agreed simply. In her experience, they usually did. 'So Felix wasn't in any hurry to settle down then?'

'No. My generation, by the time we were thirty, we'd

been married for a good few years already, with children well on the way. But nowadays, it seems, things are different. If the youngsters bother to get married at all, that is.'

Hillary nodded. There was no easy way to ask the next question, and now that she had the measure of her man, she wasn't sure that too much delicacy was even needed. Gordon Olliphant struck her as the kind of man who would call a spade a spade. But you never knew. Although he seemed comfortable enough talking about his dead son, and time had clearly helped soften the edges of the worst of his grief, appearances could be deceptive.

It was probably just best to get it out there and see what reaction she got, Hillary mused, and took a slow breath.

'At the time of the original investigation, it seems that the question arose that Felix might have been in the closet, Mr Olliphant,' she said calmly, and then wondered if the old man would understand the euphemism. She opened her mouth to further elaborate, but she needn't have worried for Gordon Olliphant merely waved a hand in the air in a dismissive gesture.

'What, that he was a poofter, you mean?' Gordon's face creased into a smile, as did Zoe's, as she imagined the scandalized reaction from some of her friends at the extremely politically incorrect language.

You had to hand it to the oldsters! They were fearless.

'Rubbish. Even I would have recognized that, if the boy had been that way inclined,' Gordon said simply. Then he shrugged.

'He always had girls hanging around him, ever since he hit puberty.' Hillary nodded but didn't push it. Beside her, she could almost hear Zoe bite back the laughter. Either one of them could have told the old man that having girls buzzing around didn't necessarily mean anything.

Hillary decided to change tack slightly. 'That car accident he had was nasty.'

'Oh, I'll say.' Gordon's face fell slightly and he sighed heavily.

'It affected him badly, that did. Even though he wasn't to blame. We told him, Alice and me, over and over again, there was nothing he could have done. It wasn't his fault that poor little boy died. But he had nightmares for years. And it stopped him drinking as well. Not that he ever was much of a drinker in the first place, mind,' the old man said flatly, giving them a gimlet glance. 'Alice and I were always worried about that sort of thing, you see. Drink and drugs and that AIDS thing that was around back then. But in the end, we were lucky. He never got into that sort of trouble, our Felix.' He sighed again. 'But he felt things more than most, I have to admit. When he had to go to the funeral of that friend of his, he was upset and down for weeks afterwards. But that was just Felix. He was a good boy.'

The almost inevitable last sentence made Hillary's heart ache in a familiar way. How many times had she heard parents say just that about their children—either when she'd just informed them of their death or injury, or after arresting them for causing death or injury to someone else?

He was a good boy.

Well, perhaps Felix Olliphant had been. In which case, someone had wanted a good boy dead.

'I'm sure he was, Mr Olliphant,' she said gently. 'Do you have any idea who may have wanted to kill him?'

Gordon Olliphant seemed to shrink in his chair, and suddenly looked every minute of his age. 'I wish I did,' he said heavily. 'And don't think I haven't wondered about it, every day. But Felix just wasn't the kind to make enemies. Oh, I know what you're thinking,' the old man said, rallying a little and shooting them a rueful smile. 'I bet you hear it all the time. But Felix really *wasn't* the sort to get into fights or cause aggravation. He was a talker not a doer. He liked to see the best in things. His job was typical of him—he liked to make dull things beautiful. He was always reading as a lad, couldn't play football to save his life. He used to sit drawing for hours. If his friends started arguing, he'd be the peace-maker, you know?'

Hillary thought she did. Already a picture of their murder victim was beginning to form in her mind. Of course, as they spoke to others who knew him, that picture would be added to, and shift in focus. But slowly, Felix Olliphant would be resurrected, and then they might have a chance of finding out who needed to kill him. And why.

Hillary talked to Gordon Olliphant for another hour or so, smiling over the photo albums he produced and discussing different aspects of his son's life. Inevitably, most of Gordon's insights had centred around his early years—his boyhood and teens. The more adult he grew, the less Gordon knew about his son, which was only natural. When he left home at eighteen to go to uni, contact became even less, and when he started his own business and bought his own home, the contact became even more sporadic still.

So although he'd been a dutiful son, coming back once a month for Sunday lunch, and never forgetting Mother's or Father's Day, family anniversaries or Christmas, it became clear that Gordon hadn't known much about what was going on in his son's life by the time he died. Eventually, they thanked him and left him in peace.

Outside, Zoe was unusually quiet as they walked back towards her car and Hillary could easily guess why. She slipped into the passenger seat and watched Zoe start the ignition.

'He was a nice old boy, wasn't he?' Hillary said calmly, as she buckled up her seatbelt.

'Yeah, he was,' Zoe agreed, sounding subdued. 'He reminds me a bit of my own granddad.'

'And he loved his son. And his wife.'

'Yeah, you could tell.'

'And it's suddenly hit you that his life was torn apart by what happened,' Hillary said softly. 'That nice old man, and his wife, who clearly doted on them both. Their world was shattered when someone stabbed Felix to death that night.'

Zoe bit her lip, then burst out, 'I really want to get the sod that did it!'

Hillary grinned and nodded approvingly. '*Now* you're thinking like a copper,' she said with deliberately bracing cheerfulness.

FOUR

HILLARY AND ZOE got back to HQ at lunchtime. As they descended the stairs Hillary glanced at her watch and nodded to herself. It was time to start drawing her worker bees into a cohesive unit, which meant just one thing.

It was time for a team pint.

'Why don't we all go down to the Black Bull?' she asked, once she and Zoe had negotiated the bowels of the labyrinth and were back at the main office.

She saw Jimmy glance up with a quick grin. 'You know me, guv, never say no to a lunchtime pint and pie. Whose treat is it?' he added cannily.

Hillary grinned. 'The kitty's. I'll take it out of petty cash.' She saw the Boy Wonder open his mouth and then close it again without speaking, and guessed that he'd been about to offer to pay and then had second thoughts. She tucked away that particular snippet for later thought. Did people who were rich perpetually feel obliged to pick up the tab? And if so, why had Jake Barnes fought the impulse?

'Right, then. Sam?' She glanced at the sandy-haired lad, who was still poring over his keyboard. Before the freckle-faced youngster could enthusiastically consent, Jimmy quickly put his oar in.

'Sam's up to his eyeballs in some research for me,' he said, clearly guessing that Hillary wanted to spend some time getting to know her new team members, and neatly paving the way.

Sam groaned but good-naturedly nodded when Jimmy promised to bring him back a pork pie and pickled onion if he were good, then grinned at Zoe when she crossed her eyes at him.

THE BLACK BULL was a pub close enough to reach easily but not so popular with the police at HQ that it could be considered strictly a hangout for coppers. In the week, it wasn't that crowded, and Jimmy was easily able to get their orders in while Hillary nabbed a large table next to a somewhat grimy window with an uninspiring view of Kidlington's main street.

'So, how's it feel to be working your first case, Jake?' Hillary asked, once their food had been deposited on the table.

Jake shrugged. He was wearing a light fawn pair of slacks with a matching sports jacket, and a plain white open-necked shirt. He wore no jewellery of any kind, not even a watch. But his shoes, Hillary bet, had been handmade in Northampton, and the cologne he was wearing probably sold for some three-figure sum by the ounce.

'It's early days yet, guv, but it's exciting, of course,' he replied cautiously.

Zoe nodded, and gulped at her virgin bloody Mary. 'I'll say.' She went on to expound, at some length, about her first interview experience. Hillary saw Jimmy fighting back a smile in the face of such eager enthusiasm, and let her wind down before continuing her own agenda.

'As you can see, Zoe's all in favour of field experience, so I think it's time we got you out of the office as well,' Hillary said to Jake, sipping at her own lemon and lime and eyeing her Ploughman's without much enthusiasm. 'I thought we'd start with some of the victim's friends. Try and build up a general picture of our murder victim.' She'd made sure that Jake Barnes had brought his own car to the pub since she'd always intended to leave with him, and send Zoe back to HQ in Jimmy's car, with orders to write up their notes on the Gordon Olliphant interview.

'Sounds reasonable to me, guv,' Jake agreed amiably. He was no mug, and knew when he was being sounded out. And it was important that he didn't blow it.

'I read from your file that you're recently divorced,' Hillary said matter-of-factly. 'Everything all right on that front, is it?' Subtlety was a tool she could handle as deftly as she chose, but there were times when only plain speaking would do. Besides, she wanted to see how the Boy Wonder handled a full-frontal assault.

Jimmy, a little surprised by the suddenness of the attack, paused with his beer glass halfway to his lips, then glanced at Jake, realizing that the guv'nor was testing his mettle. And he was rather curious himself to see how someone who must have been used to calling the shots took to being forced into a secondary role. A man as rich as Barnes surely wasn't forced on the defensive very often.

Jake met Hillary's mild glance with a meaningless smile.

'Things between the ex and me are fine, guv. Tasha owns her own travel agency. I helped her set it up but I didn't mind her getting it in the settlement. We still see each other from time to time.' He paused and took a sip of his Diet Coke. 'I'm not saying we're still friends, exactly, but we're not enemies either.' He thought for a moment of Natasha, and the moment he'd first set eyes on her when he'd been a young and know-nothing 20-year-old. Tall, cool, blonde, a keep fit fanatic like himself, they'd jogged the same route through Oxford's parks. He'd been intimidated by her beauty at first, and then later spellbound by her physical passion. They'd married a few months after his business had had its first major success.

They'd bought a flat together in the centre of Oxford with a stunning view of Keble College and the park—one of those large lofty Victorian house conversions, and had partied long and hard for nearly a year before settling down.

Jake had assumed they'd have children after a year or two, but Natasha, unbeknownst to him, had always had other ideas. When she'd said she wanted to run her own business, a keep fit gym, perhaps, or a travel agency, he hadn't thought twice about it. His company was raking it in in those early days and a quick scan of the markets made it clear that whilst a gym might not be very economically viable, a travel agency certainly was.

And when Tasha had put her heart and soul into it, finally taking over full control and building it up, Jake had been happy, because it had made her happy.

It was only when he began to mention that, at twenty-five, it was a good time to start thinking about having a family, that the cracks finally began to show.

Now he made sure his face was bland as he sipped his drink and met the calm, beautiful sherry-coloured eyes of his new boss. He wasn't fooled for one instant by the gentle, questioning look on her face.

'The divorce was amicable enough in the end, guv,' he told her truthfully. 'Well, as amicable as things can be with two sets of lawyers involved,' he added, and Jimmy grunted a laugh.

'So why did you decide you wanted to join the police?' Hillary asked flat out. 'I would have thought a young guy like you, footloose and fancy free, with plenty of readies to spend, the world was your oyster.' Jake smiled and again sipped his Coke calmly, forcing himself to relax. So, she wasn't altogether buying his altruism act. He wasn't particularly surprised—someone as sharp as she was, she'd never take things at face value. And if he showed any sign of tension now, he knew she'd be on it like a flash.

He'd researched Hillary Greene thoroughly before applying to the CRT, and after meeting the formidable lady herself, he was not about to underestimate her one damned millimetre.

'Like I told Commander Donleavy, guv, I wanted to do something useful with my life. My business was—' And here he shrugged '—well, almost a fluke really. It was when the dot com boom was just taking off. Me and two pals came up with this idea that just happened to work. I think I must have always known it was too good to be true because I quickly sold out when the money became silly—I mean, ten million for a business that had only been going six months?' Again he shrugged.

'Anyway, I let my pals buy me out, and barely a month later—' He spread his hands '—the bubble burst.'

'They must have loved you,' Zoe snorted over her tomato juice.

Jake sighed. 'Not really. I mean, yeah, sure, it must have smarted, but they couldn't really blame any of it on me. It wasn't my fault it was all so fleeting. Nobody could have predicted it; it was just a fluke, like I said.'

'You must have had some reason for opting out the moment the going got good, though,' Hillary said, careful to keep her voice neutral.

Jake realized that she simply wasn't going to let it go, and reluctantly sacrificed a little bit of his precious privacy to keep her sweet.

'I suppose it was just my pessimism showing, guv,' he said with a wry smile. 'I grew up on one of the big council housing estates in Banbury. My dad died when I was five, and my mum married again. Curtis, my stepfather, was great, and his daughter, my stepsister Jasmine, was three at the time. But times were always hard—Curtis was always in work but even so it was never easy. We never went on holiday, for instance, until Jas was ten. I got a part-time job during the summer holidays the moment I hit thirteen. Mum used to go around the supermarkets looking for the cheapest prices, buying the home brands because they were cheaper, stuff like that.' Zoe began to mime playing a violin, and Jake grinned at her.

'Yeah, yeah, I'm just trying to explain it like it was,' he said defensively. 'Anyway, me and my mates set up this business almost as a bit of a laugh really, but when it became deadly serious, with real money involved… I dunno.' Jake shrugged.

'Things changed.'

'I think I get it,' Hillary said, nodding slowly. 'You were suddenly worth, literally, millions, at least in theory, and you didn't trust it enough not to cut and run?'

Jake drew in a sharp breath. Bloody hell, she was quick.

He was going to have watch his step around her and no mistake.

'That's exactly it, guv,' he agreed. 'I saw the cyberspace version of my supposed wealth, and didn't really believe it could be real. So when my mates wanted to push on, and expand and build on what we had, I just wanted to make it…real somehow. To have the money in my hand, like. Or rather, in a real bank, with four walls. You know, the real, physical thing. To be able to go out and buy the Jaguar, or what have you. So I let them buy me out. Everyone thought I was mad, but as it turns out…'

'You weren't mad at all,' Zoe said. 'The Boy Wonder strikes again.'

'But afterwards. You did stuff with the money you'd got, right?' Jimmy said, not sure that he was following all this. His knowledge of computers was strictly limited to the utterly necessary. 'I mean, normal stuff?'

Jake laughed. 'Yeah. I invested in stocks and shares mostly, and got out just before the economy crashed in 2008.' Now that was something everyone could understand.

'Lucky sod, ain't ya?' Jimmy mused, without malice.

Jake laughed. 'This time around quite a few of us could see the writing on the wall though. It was obvious the bankers were on a wing and a prayer and that it couldn't last for ever.'

'So what are you doing with all your dough now? I mean, any tips for us poor impoverished plebs?' Zoe demanded.

'Well, at the moment I'm buying property while it's so cheap,' Jake admitted. 'I mean, prices are at an all-time low, and if you pick the right area…'

'Yeah, right, like I can afford to buy a couple of houses.' Zoe mimed a huge yawn, and Jake laughed again.

'Want me to give you some tips on stocks and shares?'

'No!' This time they all laughed, but while Hillary let the conversation meander away on to other topics, she didn't lose sight of the fact that the Boy Wonder had very cleverly managed to avoid explaining just what it was about joining the CRT that had seemed so damned attractive.

She picked at her lunch, aware of Jimmy casting her curious glances from time to time. Zoe held forth on her new insights on the Olliphant case, and Hillary was glad, but not surprised, to see that Jake Barnes was taking it all in.

When they'd finished eating, they separated in the car park, with Jimmy and Zoe going back to HQ while Hillary followed Jake towards a long, low-slung, dark green E-type Jaguar parked protectively against the wall at the far end of the car park.

As she stood in front of the iconic car, she let out a long, slow whistle as she eyed the wired wheels, the cream leather interior and the walnut-wood dashboard.

'You weren't kidding about the Jag, were you?' she said, impressed. Like a lot of people who'd grown up watching that British classic film, *The Italian Job*, she'd always had a soft spot for the E-type Jag.

Jake smiled, looking genuinely abashed. 'It was the one boy-toy I always craved, guv. So when I first got the dosh, I couldn't resist it, and treated myself.' 'The wife didn't get the car in the divorce then, I take it?' she teased.

Jake Barnes smiled that bland smile of his. 'She knew better than to try and get it,' he said lightly.

Hillary filed that too, for further reference, and slipped into the passenger seat. When Jake started the car, it came to life with a satisfyingly throaty growl. 'So, guv, where to?' he asked.

Hillary checked her notebook. 'We'll start with Felix's best friend, Mitchell Harris. He lives here in town but he works in Aylesbury. A business park.' She rattled off the name and address. 'You know it?' 'Think so, guv,' Jake said, and set off.

Unlike Zoe, he didn't seem to need a sat nav.

BACK AT HQ, Steven Crayle knocked on Commander Marcus Donleavy's door and was bidden to enter by his secretary. A few minutes later, he sat down in the chair opposite the commander's desk and accepted his offer of a cup of coffee.

Donleavy was wearing his trademark silver-grey suit, which went so well with his silver-grey hair and silver-grey eyes. He was even wearing a stainless steel watch.

'So, Steven, it looks like we weathered the fallout from the Tom Warrington case all right,' he began, and Steven smiled briefly.

'Looks like it,' he agreed dryly.

Tom Warrington had been one of theirs: a uniformed officer who'd taken to stalking girls. He'd also made the monumental mistake of roping Hillary into his nasty little hobby. For a while, Steven and Hillary had thought Warrington was responsible for a string of missing girls and had treated him as a murder suspect. This had turned out not to be the case, but before they'd caught up with him, he'd managed to kidnap Vivienne Tyrell, Zoe Turnbull's predecessor, and holed up with her in a caravan in a deserted little wood. Luckily, they'd managed to rescue her before anything too bad could happen, but it had been a bit of a dog's dinner of a rescue, with Hillary and Jimmy going strictly against orders, and Hillary all but offering herself as bait in order to create a distraction.

Luckily, they'd managed to steer everyone clear of too much trouble in the inevitable shit storm that had followed. The media had, of course, made the usual splash about a cop-gone-bad, but since the CRT had solved two other missing girl cases, plus the murder of a third whilst pursuing the Warrington angle, professionally, at least, it hadn't been too bad. And Vivienne Tyrell had, briefly, been made into a media star, and heroine-of-the-day, so even the top brass had been happy.

'Yes, we were lucky all right,' Donleavy said. 'And the powers-that-be were impressed by the way you handled things,' he added smoothly. Which meant, Steven translated, that they'd never been told the whole story—or at least had been spoon-fed a very edited version by the commander. No doubt Donleavy had managed to stand on the sidelines until he'd seen how things were going, before offering his own endorsement of Steven's actions. Or was he being too cynical? Perhaps he'd stepped in to bat simply to keep Hillary actively employed in the CRT?

He eyed Donleavy warily now and nodded. 'I'm glad to hear things are settled, sir,' he said, just a shade drolly.

Marcus sipped his coffee, his eyes glittering. 'And

how is Hillary these days?' he asked neutrally, catching Steven utterly off guard.

He covered it smoothly, however, by taking a sip of his own brew. 'She's fine, sir,' he said flatly.

Before they'd identified Warrington as the man they were after, he'd attacked Hillary from behind in the car park near her boat, holding a knife to her throat and leaving her with a fine, silvery scar on her neck. She'd managed to talk him out of killing her on that occasion, but Steven, who'd raced to the scene after she'd managed to phone him for help, wasn't about to forget seeing her crumpled body, lying in a pool of blood, in any great hurry.

For a few moments back then, he'd thought he'd lost her, and he didn't like to be reminded of the sick feeling it had given him.

Now he eyed the commander with a brief smile. 'No lasting damage. You know Hillary—I sometimes think she can cope with anything.'

'Yes, I agree,' Donleavy said, and obviously meant it. And once again, Steven, like many others at the HQ, found himself wishing that he understood just how their relationship worked.

'You and she are getting on, I take it?' Donleavy asked next.

Steven instantly bridled. 'Professionally, you mean? Yes, of course we are. She is, as you always said, one of the best investigators we have on the force.'

Marcus nodded. He knew that, at the time, Crayle hadn't been any too pleased to have Hillary Greene foisted upon him and his team, but he was too wise to allude to that now. Especially given the unexpected way things had turned out between them.

'And, I understand, privately too, you're becoming close?' he probed delicately.

Steven shifted a little uncomfortably on his seat. Commander or not, this was straying into territory that was strictly none of Donleavy's business. 'There's nothing against that, sir,' hc pointed out stiffly. 'Hillary's a civilian now.' He was able to tell, from the way Hillary talked about Marcus Donleavy, that they weren't, and never had been, interested in each other in any romantic way. Sometimes she'd sounded positively scathing about him but there was always a note of caution and respect in her voice whenever she mentioned Donleavy, and Steven had never quite had the courage to pick her up on it.

'Oh, quite, quite,' Donleavy said, blandly now, distracting him from his darkening thoughts. 'No, I have no problem with you and Hillary becoming a personal item. But you can see why the top brass might feel a little uncomfortable with it. Which brings me on, as you can probably guess, to why I've called you in today.' Steven made the usual demurring noises.

'You've done wonders within the CTR, Steven. Your progress has been steady and your solve rates are admirable. With Hillary's help, naturally, as I predicted.' Donleavy couldn't resist just a little dig. 'And every little bit helps when it comes to improving the crime figures. But perhaps now would be a good time for you to consider moving onwards and upwards?' Steven kept his face carefully blank.

'Just what did you have in mind, sir?' he asked smoothly.

HILLARY HAD READ in the file that Felix Olliphant's best friend, Mitchell Harris, now worked as the office manager in a supply warehouse that provided storage of dry goods for a major supermarket chain. Jake Barnes was able to find the industrial estate on the outskirts of Aylesbury where their main office was situated with very little trouble. A foreman overseeing an expansive forklift operation in one of the cavernous depths directed them to the boss's office upstairs.

His secretary, a young woman who looked fresh out of college, couldn't seem to make up her mind whether to be impressed, alarmed or excited to have the police call on her boss. No doubt she'd always hitherto considered him to be rather staid and boring, and now she eyed them nervously as she used the intercom to inform him of their arrival. Her voice dropped a theatrical decibel or two when it came to using the words 'the police are here to see you, sir'.

But the voice that came back over the little tin box sounded not a whit theatrical in response as he ordered her to show them right in.

As he rose from his desk, Mitchell Harris was just shrugging himself back into the jacket of his cheap suit that had been lying across the back of his chair. He was a large man quickly running to fat, but Hillary could see the echoes of an old rugby player in his physique. He was losing his hair but a comb-over was valiantly trying to fight back the evidence of the passing of the years.

'Yes? This isn't about the attempted break-in last month, is it? Only I thought the uniformed officers told my MD that they'd signed off on it?'

Hillary held out her ID. 'No, sir. We're with the Crime Review Team, and we're taking another look at the Felix Olliphant case.'

Mitchell Harris frowned, his hazel eyes almost becoming lost in the folds of his face as they distinctly clouded. 'Bloody hell, Felix,' he said flatly, and sat back down, a shade heavily.

'Funny how that never really goes away. I find myself not thinking about him for weeks at a time now, and then something reminds me of him—something not important, you know? Like someone ordering his favourite drink in the pub, and it hits me all over again.' His eyes abruptly focused again and he looked at Hillary levelly. 'It's about time you lot pulled your finger out, I reckon. You never did find out who did for him, did you?' Hillary weathered the accusation stoically. He was, after all, quite right.

'We're going to do our best to rectify that, Mr Harris,' she told him firmly, her voice flat and level. 'Which is why we're here. A case of murder is never closed, and we never give up trying.' Something about the look in her eye made him flush slightly, but then he nodded.

'OK.'

'You weren't at the party that night?' She got straight to the point.

'No, course I wasn't. And he was only there because he and Greer had done the house up a few weeks before. Mind you, Felix *was* the sort who got invited to swanky dos at posh houses anyway. But I never was!' Mitchell Harris suddenly grinned.

'Even back then, I was only a pleb. Oh, go on, sit down, why don't you? Hovering over me like that, you're giving me a crick in my neck.'

'Thank you.' Hillary and Jake selected a couple of generic chairs that were littered around the office and drew them up to the desk. Jake surreptitiously set a tape recorder running in his jacket pocket but Hillary pretended not to notice when she realized that Mitchell Harris himself had not seen what was going on.

She'd have to have a word with the Boy Wonder later. PACE had strict rules and guidelines about taping conversations. Since this was just a friendly chat, and it would be very unlikely indeed that they'd need to use anything from the interview in a court of law, she decided to let it pass.

'You and Felix sound like unlikely friends,' she said pleasantly to Mitchell, as an opening gambit.

Mitchell laughed. 'Sure were. It's only because we sat next to each other in infant school that we even met. I was strictly a working-class oik and Felix was middle-class through and through. But we just hit it off—don't know why. Well, you don't wonder about stuff like that when you're kids, do you? Later we went to the same senior school and just hung out because we didn't really know anybody else there. Besides, Felix was an easy guy to like, you know what I mean? He got on with everybody.'

'Not really, sir, no. That's why we're here. We want you to tell us about Felix,' Hillary said gently, when he looked at her, puzzled.

'Oh. Right. Well, that shouldn't be hard,' Mitchell said with a sigh, and the beginnings of a gentle reminiscent smile. 'He didn't have any side to him, you know what I mean? Some blokes, they're full of bullshit, yeah? Trying to make out that they're smarter than they are, or have more money, or prettier girlfriends, or you name it. It's all about bolstering the old ego, yeah?' Harris shrugged. 'Nothing wrong with that, we all do it, I suppose. But not Felix so much. He just seemed happy to fit into his own skin.'

'Sort of laidback?' Hillary said.

'Yeah. That too. But he wasn't lazy, and he didn't really have any sort of a hippy-like attitude to life—I don't want you to get me wrong.' Harris reached up to scratch his jaw. 'I reckon Felix saw it like it really was. Most people, when they heard he was an interior designer, like, thought… I dunno, that he didn't have much of a clue. That he was all style and no substance, I suppose.'

'And he wasn't?'

'No. I mean, he was good at what he did, don't get me wrong. He could talk colours and fabrics and what have you until I'd go cross-eyed. But he made it pay, see? He was never short of money because Greer and him were always at the top of the game.'

'He was sharp? Yes, his father struck me as being a businessman type. It makes sense he'd have grown up to respect money,' Hillary agreed, being deliberately a shade obtuse. Sometimes you got more out of witnesses by pretending to be just a bit slow off the mark. There was often nothing people liked more than to put you right.

'Yeah,' Harris said, but his frown told her that she still hadn't quite got it. 'But money wasn't his god, either. I mean, Felix wasn't driven to succeed as if that was the be all and end all. I mean, we might have been living in the late eighties, early nineties, yeah? The Maggie Thatcher era and all that, and greed is good and what have you. But Felix had a heart where a heart should be, and a head where a head should be. You'd trust him if you got in trouble to talk sense and see you through, and not give you a load of bullshit.'

'You and he were close,' Hillary said quietly, and with genuine sympathy.

'Absolutely. Hey, no! Not like that. I mean, not in any funny way,' Harris said, going a shade red and sitting up straighter in his chair. 'I've been married for nearly fifteen years and have got two kids.'

Hillary instantly held up a placatory hand. 'You're referring to the suggestion that Felix was gay, right? We've been coming across it from time to time in the course of our inquiries. His father didn't believe it, but then parents don't always know, do they?'

'Huh!' Harris grunted, a shade aggressively. 'His old dad got it dead right, don't you worry none about that. If Felix was gay then I'm a monkey's uncle.'

Hillary smiled. 'You don't look like much of a baboon to me, sir.' Harris blinked at her, and then grinned, instantly settling back down more easily in his chair.

'Right. No, I don't know when that rumour started to get around. I mean, when he died, he'd been with Becky for nigh on two years. And there were plenty of girls before her, believe me. He was a really good-looking bloke, so it just don't make sense, does it? In the sixth form he was a real babe magnet, let me tell you. Being his best friend was a sweet deal for me—I got to go out with more girls than I would have otherwise.'

Hillary smiled. 'Oh, I don't know. I'm sure you did well enough.' Beside her, Jake Barnes listened and marvelled. She had the big man eating out of her hand.

Harris grinned. 'Well, modestly forbids, right?'

'So who do you think started the rumours that Felix was gay?' she asked casually. 'And how did he react to them?'

Harris sighed. 'You know, I'm not really sure. It must have been…what…' He paused, obviously deep in thought and trying to work something out. 'I dunno, a couple of years, maybe three or four years, before he died, that I first heard it mentioned. Some other pal of mine in the pub said that he thought it was weird, me being pals with a gay bloke, and I nearly choked on my beer. I mean, as far as I knew, I didn't have any bent mates. Not that I've got anything against them, mind.' He gave the almost inevitable knee-jerk response without a hint of irony.

'So I asked him what he was on about, and when he mentioned Felix I laughed out loud. Told him he'd been sold a pup.'

'But you heard it from someone else again, later?'

'Yeah. Oh, not that anyone went out of their way to mention it, like. I mean nobody really cared a damn, not really. It just seemed that some people, for some reason, took it for granted that he was. Course, I always put them right.'

'Perhaps people just like a stereotype,' Hillary mused out loud. 'You know, all interior designers have to be gay, just like all male ballet dancers have to be, or hairdressers, or what have you?' Harris thought about this, and frowned, then shrugged.

'Yeah, maybe that was it.' But he didn't sound particularly convinced.

'And how did Felix react to the rumours?' she asked curiously.

'Oh, he'd just laugh, or shrug. Sometimes he'd look a bit miffed, or just long-suffering, you know, depending on his mood at the time, I suppose,' Harris said. 'I don't think he liked it, really, but other than going about wearing a T-shirt with "I'm not gay" written on it, what could he do about it? Why, you think some anti-gay basher had a go at him?' Harris asked, clearly getting angry now.

'Oh no, sir, we have no reason to suppose anything like that happened. We just have to pursue every avenue, you understand? Tell me about Becky. You said they'd been together a few years. It sounds as if it was getting serious.'

'Yeah, it was. Well, sort of. Well, to Becky, maybe. I'm not sure how serious Felix was taking it,' Harris said, somewhat confusingly. 'Don't get me wrong, he wasn't leading her down the garden path or nothing, he wasn't like that. But let's just say I got the impression that Becky was a bit more keen than he was, you know what I mean?'

Hillary thought that she did. 'They weren't exactly planning a lavish white wedding or checking out baby furniture, but she would have liked them to have been?'

'Something like that. I mean, he wasn't seeing other girls or anything. Like I said, he wasn't the type of bloke to do that sort of thing. But I don't think he saw her as the great love of his life, either. He was happy with things the way they were.'

Hillary nodded. And wondered. Just how had Becky felt about that?

'And his business partner, you mentioned her before. Greer Ryanson. You knew her well?'

'Oh no,' Harris said with a grin. 'I mean, I met her a couple of times, at parties. Felix being partners with her and all, we were bound to meet up every now and then in a social situation, like. But, well, like you said, me and Felix were a bit of an odd couple from the start, and I sure as hell didn't mix with the same social set as Greer and that snobby husband of hers.'

'Right. But Felix got on with her OK?'

'Oh yeah. They spoke the same language all right. And especially because Greer liked money and Felix always brought in his fair share of the clients. People just liked Felix, you see? He was good at what he did, and so was Greer to give her due, or so Felix always said, and he should know. And that company of theirs was doing well.'

'No romance there?' Hillary pressed.

'Oh no! I mean, Greer was a looker, I suppose, if you like that type. But she wasn't Felix's type. Besides, I'd have known if he was doing her, and he wasn't,' he added flatly.

Hillary's lips twitched. It wouldn't have surprised her to see the man cross his arms in a 'so there' attitude, so emphatic did he seem.

'You say he never had any money troubles. Did he have any other kind of worries that you know about?' She changed course slightly.

Mitchell Harris sighed heavily. 'You know about the car crash he had, yeah?'

'Yes. That was tough.'

'He had nightmares about that kid that died. Even though we all told him it wasn't his fault.'

'Yes, I'm sure he did,' she agreed softly. 'But apart from that?' Hillary pressed on. 'Had anything been worrying him, do you know? Had he complained about someone hassling him—a dissatisfied client maybe? Did he get odd phone calls that he wouldn't talk about, or did he seem jumpy or nervous about anything?'

'No, not really.'

'You know that he'd had a lot to drink that night? We're all assuming that that was just because the occasion called for it, but could he have been drinking because he was stressed about something?'

'Not that I know of,' Mitchell said flatly and frowned. 'And that's another thing I just don't get. Felix never drank to excess, and I mean never. Like I said, that car crash really shook him up, what with that kid's grandfather being so drunk and all. Well, Felix never had been what you'd call a heavy drinker even before then. He'd been a one-pint man, or maybe a glass of wine with dinner sort of guy, even before that kid died. After that... well, more often than not, he'd only drink orange juice, or one of those non-alcoholic beers.'

'OK. Well, thank you for now, Mr Harris. We may have to come back to you with more questions later. Sometimes when you're investigating a case, you find things out that might need clarification, or elaborating on, so we may be getting back in touch.'

'Hey, any time you need me, just whistle,' Mitchell Harris said earnestly. 'It still sticks in my craw what happened to him, you know. I felt so damned helpless. I still do. So just ask, anything at all. I want to see whoever did it suffer, you know? They deserve to.' There was an implacable hatred in Harris's voice that sent a chill of familiarity down Jake Barnes's back. He knew just how the man felt. He was careful to keep his face averted from Hillary Greene as he reached down into his pocket to turn off the tape recorder. The last thing he needed was for his eagle-eyed boss to notice his reaction.

'Thank you, Mr Harris,' Hillary said, without inflection.

Once outside, they walked back to the car in mutual silence. It wasn't until they'd both got inside the sports car that Hillary told him he was not to record any more conversations without her say-so.

Jake listened to her lecture on the rules of PACE with careful concentration and patience, then apologized.

'It won't happen again,' he said quietly. 'It's just that I'm not any good at taking notes the old-fashioned way. I suppose I'm used to electronics too much. Pen and paper don't suit me.'

'Practice,' Hillary said flatly.

'Yes, guv.'

'Now, what did you make of Mr Harris?'

'Genuine, I'd say. He and the victim seemed to be very tight. He was definitely still hurting over his friend's murder.'

Hillary nodded. 'Yes, I got that too. So, how do you stand on the big debate? Was our victim gay, or was he not?'

Jake shrugged. 'Hard to call, guv. And—' He shot a quick sideways look '—does it really matter?' Hillary's lips almost twitched. He had her down as possibly homophobic, did he, the cheeky bugger?

'Only if we're looking for a male lover who killed him after being spurned,' Hillary said succinctly.

And that puts me in my place, Jake Barnes thought wryly.

FIVE

'WHO ELSE DO we have who was close to the victim?' Hillary asked, buckling up her seatbelt.

Jake reached for his iPad and quickly tapped a few keys.

'There's a Neill Gorman, guv. A chap he played squash with regularly. Works at the Oxford University Press.'

'OK. We'll try him next.'

'Guv.'

Hillary leaned back in the plush leather seat, and for a while was content to just let the scenery speed by. She noticed a lot of people looking at them enviously as they passed, and was not surprised. What must it be like to be able to afford to buy and run a classic sports car like this one? And just what the hell was Jake Barnes doing on her team?

'So, you never really did explain why you joined the CRT, Jake,' she said flatly as they pulled up at a red traffic light. Out of the corner of her eye she saw him stiffen slightly, and then cut off the beginnings of a rueful smile.

'It's like I told Commander Donleavy, guv,' he said with a barely repressed sigh. 'I've had my share of messing about and making money. It was fun when I was in my late teens and early twenties. But everyone grows up eventually. Even me.'

Hillary nodded. Right, that old chestnut. 'And what made you grow up? The failed marriage?'

'I suppose so, guv.'

Bullshit, Hillary thought. She'd gone through a failed marriage herself. And how many countless others had done likewise? It seemed to be almost compulsory in this day and age, she thought cynically. But just how many of us felt compelled to do a complete overhaul of our life and utterly change our direction because of it? OK, maybe we all did a bit of soul searching but to do something as radical as what Jake Barnes had done? No way. She just wasn't buying it.

Was it possible that this ex-wife of his had dealt the man beside her such a serious blow that he'd been totally knocked for six, to the point where he couldn't think straight, or began acting totally out of character? Again, she just wasn't buying it. He was too damned good-looking, too self-confident. Too much the self-made man, the been there, done it and got the T-shirt sort who thought the world was their oyster. As it probably was. And that hadn't been knocked out of him. He was just doing a better than average job of concealing it.

No, if this man had indeed been forced to grow up suddenly, she doubted it was Natasha who had provided the impetus.

Unless he was the sort who, when they fell, fell hard?

But Hillary would have bet her last pay cheque that he just didn't have that broken-hearted vibe.

'Right. So you thought you could be of use to society by helping to catch the bad guys?' she pushed on blandly.

Jake Barnes managed to chuckle. 'I'd like to think I'm not quite that naïve, guv,' he said modestly. 'But yeah, I think the police service is a good place to be. I have skills, I'm young and fit. Why not? Why did you join up, all those years ago?' He managed to lob the ball neatly back into her court.

Hillary, however, was too wily a player to even bother hitting it back.

'Tell me about Neill Gorman,' she said instead, wrong-footing him yet again.

Jake blinked, but quickly rallied. 'Er, he and Felix met at their local sports centre. From what I can gather, they both liked to keep fit but they weren't fanatics about it. They played squash every Tuesday and Thursday night. Met occasionally in a social environment. According to Gorman's original statement, he and Felix had dinner a couple of times with their other halves. That was about it.'

'He wasn't at the New Year's Eve party?'

'No, guv.'

'Right. After we've spoken to Gorman, we'll start with those who were actually at the party, beginning with those who knew him best.'

'I don't think there'll be many of those, guv,' Jake warned her. 'Most of the guests were close friends of the hostess, and didn't really know Felix all that well. Greer Ryanson and her husband and the hostess herself are probably the only ones who knew him at all.'

Hillary already knew that. She'd read and re-read practically every interview Varney had taken from the witnesses at the party. She was just checking to see if the Boy Wonder had done the same. Obviously he had. So whatever it was that had brought him into CRT's orbit, whatever game he was playing, he was willing to work hard at it. Which was good to know. He might just turn out to be useful yet—in spite of himself.

'Right,' she said neutrally.

Jake shot her a quick look. 'You OK, guv?'

'I'm fine. But doesn't that strike you as odd?'

'Guv?'

'That someone chose a party where the victim wasn't particularly well known to kill him? Doesn't that immediately put the onus of attention on those few that *did* know him?' 'What, the Ryansons and the Querida Phelps woman? You think they were set up?' Jake asked, startled by the idea.

Hillary gave a dry laugh and held up an admonitory hand.

'Whoa, not so fast. Let's not get into the realm of conspiracy theories just yet.' Jake smiled briefly, wondering if he'd sounded a bit like Zoe. He liked the spiky-haired munchkin well enough but he didn't appreciate being lumped into the same category as her. He needed to impress Hillary and gain her trust, not have her laughing up her sleeve at him. Time to start earning some brownie points, he thought uneasily.

'But DI Varney wasn't able to find any reason why the hostess might want him dead, was he? Until she hired Olligree Interiors to decorate her house, she hadn't met either Felix or Greer. And the original team couldn't find anyone who'd witnessed them falling out, or any reason why they might have done so. So Querida Phelps would seem to be in the clear.'

'It was her party,' Hillary pointed out flatly.

'You seriously suspect her?'

'I'm just pointing out it was her party,' Hillary insisted. 'So she was by far the one best placed to have done any pre-planning that might have needed doing. By all accounts, she was so happy with the job they'd done that she invited them to her swanky new millennium bash—but who's to say that was the real reason for the invite?'

'OK. So you're saying she did it all to set Felix up for murder? But I don't think even the pickiest of customers would kill her interior designer because she wasn't happy with the wallpaper, guv,' Jake said with a grin, hoping this was a test and that he was passing it. 'Not unless she was well and truly cuckoo, and Varney would surely have spotted that.'

Hillary smiled. 'True—most officers can easily spot the seriously insane. So who does that leave?'

'Greer Ryanson, or her snobby husband,' Jake said quickly.

'Right. Now, tell me, if you were going to kill someone, would you do it at a party of strangers, where only you and your nearest and dearest would turn out to actually know the victim, and thus, presumably, be the only ones who might have a motive?' Jake thought about it for a while. 'No. It would be a bit stupid, wouldn't it? It would be like painting an arrow on your chest, saying "I did it". Unless it was a spur of the moment thing, guv. They literally just had to kill him then and there because something unexpected came up that was so utterly desperate that they had no other alternative.'

Hillary leaned back in the lavishly upholstered seat. 'Go on,' she encouraged.

'Perhaps Felix said something to the Ryansons that put them in a panic? He'd caught them cooking the books or something and was going to turn them in?

No, wait, that wouldn't really be enough, would it?' he instantly contradicted himself. 'I mean, any bad publicity surrounding the company would hurt Felix as well. Sorry, I just instantly think financial—embezzlement, fraud, that sort of thing. It was more likely to be something personal, wasn't it? Perhaps he found out something far more serious about them, and they needed to shut his mouth quickly? Her husband was into child pornography, or she was blackmailing him about something, and the worm finally turned. If he threatened to leave the party and act instantly, then they'd have no choice but to do it then and there.'

Hillary let the scenario sit for a moment or two, then said, 'So they planned on the spur of the moment how to get him drunk, manoeuvre him into the bedroom, find a knife with which to kill him, and do so without getting any blood on their clothes?'

Jake frowned, but wasn't about to let it go so easily. 'Well, it's not beyond the realms of possibility, is it? I mean, it wasn't a particularly high-tech murder—it could have been done on the hoof, as it were. It was New Year's Eve, 1999, so even if Felix didn't normally drink it wouldn't be hard to keep pressing the drinks on him under the excuse that it was a once-in-a-lifetime occasion, would it? And then help him up to the bedroom—well, who else would he trust more than his business partner or her husband? And although the pathologist's best guess is that a specially sharpened knife had been used, it isn't certain, is it? One or the other of them could have found something suitable in the kitchen. And anyone with a bit of common sense could figure out that if you piled clothes on top of the victim, it would reduce the likelihood of you getting blood on your own clothes.'

Hillary conceded it all. 'Maybe. Have you found any evidence of something being off at Olligree yet?'

'Not yet, guv. And if the motive wasn't a financial one but a personal one, I'm not going to find it in the books anyway.'

'Agreed. So start asking around the Ryansons' circle. See if you can dig up any old scandals or any whiff of trouble roundabout 1999, 2000 or so. Something that Felix might have been able to stumble upon.'

'Right, guv,' Jake said, and hoped he sounded more confident than he felt. Just how the hell did you start tracking down something as nebulous as that, even when it hadn't happened nearly fifteen years ago?

Hillary, quietly aware of his dilemma, smiled gently to herself and said nothing more until they got to Oxford and were driving down Walton Street towards the University Press.

'Traffic's bad,' she offered unhelpfully. They might have been in a bottle-green Jag but Hillary was curiously satisfied to note that that didn't help them find a parking space in a city notorious for its lack of them.

The Boy Wonder finally found a not-quite-legal spot near Worcester College, leaving them with a five-minute walk to Neill Gorman's office, which they completed in a mutual, thoughtful silence. There was something off about the whole murder-at-a-party thing that Hillary couldn't quite put her finger on. She sighed as they dodged the usual tourist-packed pavements and the bicycle-riding undergrads that seemed to perpetually clog the famous city.

And found herself wondering just what Marcus Donleavy had wanted to talk to Steven about.

STEVEN CRAYLE RETURNED to his office a thoughtful and ever so slightly worried man. Although his conversation with Donleavy had all been, theoretically at least, good news, there was an element to it that had that certain tension which comes with a ticking bomb.

He shrugged off his jacket, poured himself a cup of coffee and sat at his desk, aware of the tight sensation of tension in his shoulders. He rolled his head on his neck in several loosening rolls, and sighed.

After work, he'd buy a couple of steaks, some salad and a bottle of her favourite red wine and invite Hillary round to his house. He felt like cooking and he wanted to put her in a good mood.

Any serious talk about his future had to include her, and whatever part she wanted to play in it. He felt himself tightening up again as the thought flashed across his mind, as unbidden and unwelcome as lightning, that that might not be a very big role at all.

Then he leant back in his chair and rubbed his eyes, gently cursing Donleavy. Although the man was helping him to achieve his ambitions, right now he could have kicked the commander in the seat of his immaculate, silver-grey trousers.

NEILL GORMAN, WHEN they finally got to meet the man, was almost the polar opposite of Mitchell Harris. Although both men were probably around the same age, Gorman looked nearly a decade younger. And whereas Harris was running to fat, Gorman had the wiry, lean frame of a dedicated jogger. He also had a full head of hair and a rather aesthete sort of face. He was dressed in a dark blue suit and blood-red Oxford loafers.

If these were two examples of Felix Olliphant's friends, Hillary instantly thought, then they certainly added to the picture of a man who could be very varied in his tastes. She couldn't see either Neill or Mitchell having anything at all in common without Felix Olliphant there to provide a bridge.

'Hello, Della said you were police?' Gorman was on his feet and holding out his hand, and Hillary took it, again going through the speech about who they were and what they were doing.

When she'd finished, Gorman echoed Harris eerily when he said, with that same mixture of genuine grief and anger, 'Felix? Oh Lord, Felix. I still can't get over what happened to him. I couldn't understand then, and I still can't, why anyone would have wanted to kill him. Please, sit down. Anything I can do to help. Anything at all.' Hillary and Jake accepted two well-padded leather chairs and sat down in an office lined with books and with a view of the city of dreaming spires that was as far removed from Mitchell Harris's warehouse office as Xanadu was from Charing Cross Station.

'Thank you. You said you didn't know who might want to kill Felix,' Hillary began briskly. 'I take it then that he never mentioned any enemies to you?'

'Not at all. Felix just wasn't the sort to have enemies.'

'Perhaps that's not the right word,' she temporized. 'By enemies I don't mean anything so dramatic really.'

Hillary soothed him with a smile. 'He never said anything more innocuous, say? Like a dissatisfied customer withholding a payment because he wasn't happy about his new study or someone keying his car late one night, or getting weird phone messages, or anything like that?'

'Oh no, nothing like that,' Neill said. He had a neat, nononsense, short back and sides haircut of a mousey brown-grey, and wide brown eyes, topped with dark brows. A shadow of a moustache touched his upper lip and his skin had that well moisturised look that spoke of a man who took care of himself.

'He used to get telephone calls sometimes, you know, on his mobile, that made him look sort of angry. But I think that was because they were interrupting us when we were about to play squash. That's where we spent most time together—at the squash courts.'

Hillary nodded. 'I understand. And he never said who these calls were from?'

'No. Just a friend, he said. Mind you, from the way he said friend I'm not quite sure that's the word he really wanted to use. I got the feeling sometimes that they were being more of a pest than a pal. But sometimes friends are, aren't they?' Neill shrugged philosophically. 'And besides, when we got together we really liked to play, you know? We weren't just mucking around—Felix was a good squash player, and so was I. We improved each other's game, and when we met we liked to get down to it. So neither one of us was in the mood for interruptions.'

'Would you say he liked to win?' Hillary asked, curious. 'I mean, he was competitive?'

'Oh yes. But so am I. But neither one of us had the John McEnroe temperament or anything like that! We never swore at each other or came to blows or had tantrums or anything.' Neill Gorman laughed. 'But we were both serious about our games—we stuck to the rules, we played hardball, as the Yanks would say, and we both wanted to win. Like I said, we were well matched, and playing like that helped us both to up our games.'

Hillary nodded, as yet another side of their victim was revealed. Felix Olliphant might well have been a nice guy but he was also one who liked to play hard and win.

'He had a steely, determined, resolute side to him then?' she asked.

Neill Gorman looked a little surprised, then said slowly, 'Yes, I suppose you could say that. But he wasn't a prat with it, you know? He wasn't the sort who liked to bully or boast or brag. But when we got on the court, we were both there to win. Yes, definitely.'

Hillary nodded. So Olliphant might have been an even-tempered guy who made friends across the spectrum easily but he wasn't the sort who would let himself get pushed around either. Interesting. 'And who won the most?' she asked brightly.

Neill gave a soft laugh. 'I like to think the honours were about even. But I suppose, if I were honest, Felix sometimes had the edge. Which only made beating him feel all the better. But win or lose, we were both sportsmen about it. That's what I meant about him being a bit impatient with whoever it was on the other end of the phone calls. His mind was on the game.'

'You didn't ask him who was on the phone, or what the problem was?'

'Oh no. We didn't really have that sort of a relationship.'

'But you got the feeling that it was just the one person? Or did you think it was just people in general bugging him?'

Neill Gorman shifted a little uneasily on his seat. 'You know, it's funny you asking that. Before, I think I just assumed it was people in general, you know. Clients, perhaps, or his business partner, or a mix of other people. But somehow, now I think about it, for some reason my gut instinct is to say that I think it was just one person calling him every time. Mind you, I only ever saw him at the sports club, so, perhaps… I don't know. You'd better not rely on that.'

Hillary's nose distinctly twitched. 'But you feel as if he was being pestered by just one person?'

'Yes. I suppose I do,' Neill said, somewhat slowly and a little reluctantly. 'It was just the sort of look that he'd get on his face, you know. The tone of voice. It was always a sort of longsuffering patience. A sort of oh-it's-you-is-it kind of attitude. I don't think he'd be like that with everybody, if you see what I mean.'

'Yes, I think so,' Hillary answered. 'There was just the one person who pushed that particular button in him.'

Neill's face cleared. 'Yeah. That's what it was. I just saw him answer the phone, get that look on his face, and I'd think to myself, Oh no, it's the pest again. Not that he ever said anything like that, don't get me wrong.'

'You ever hear him lose his temper on the phone to whoever that was? Use a specific name, or sound scared?'

'Hell, no.' Neill shot upright in his chair. 'Don't get me wrong, it was nothing like that. I don't want to blow it up out of all proportion or anything. If you hadn't been so interested in it, I wouldn't have even mentioned it. It was never any big deal.' Or Felix Olliphant made sure that it hadn't seemed like one, Hillary mused silently, and wondered if Varney had traced all of Felix's phone calls for the past year of his life. She made a mental note to herself to check it out, and if Varney hadn't, to start doing so. Although, after fifteen years that was going to be a pain in the backside. Most of the numbers would probably be dead ends by now. People would have moved, died, upgraded their phone lines or got new numbers.

Still, that was what she had Zoe Turnbull and Jake Barnes for, wasn't it?

'You socialize with him much, Mr Gorman?'

'Please, call me Neill. And no, not really. Not much. Me and the wife, and Felix and his girlfriend…oh good grief, I can't remember her name.'

'Rebecca Morton?'

'Becky, that's it.' Gorman snapped his fingers. 'Pretty girl. We'd go out for the odd dinner sometimes, at Browns, or the Eagle and Child, somewhere like that. The Trout, once, at Wolvercote. You've been?'

Hillary admitted that she had. 'You see any tension between him and his girlfriend?' she asked blandly.

'Can't say that I did. They seemed well suited.'

'He drink much?'

'Not at all. I assumed he was teetotal to be honest. But then, whenever we met up, we'd be driving, so neither of us drank a lot.'

Hillary nodded. 'You ever see him upset about anything? Thinking back, can you remember a time when he played really badly on court, when he obviously wasn't concentrating on his game?' 'Well, only that time he had the car accident. He was sort of cut up and bruised so he wasn't as limber as he normally was. And that poor little boy…that really upset him. And then, after he'd got over that, there was that one time he played like a girl, and I called him on it, and felt really bad when he'd told me he'd been at a friend's funeral earlier that day.' Hillary nodded. Hadn't somebody else mentioned that he'd lost a close friend? 'But nothing untoward happened just before he died? Say in the month running up to it?' 'No. No, he was pretty much the same as usual.' Hillary kept on for another ten minutes or so, but whilst Gorman was able to paint more or less the same picture of the man as Mitchell Harris had, he came up with nothing new.

Once Hillary had thanked him, and they were walking back to the E-type, Hillary gave Jake a list of instructions.

'This is the second time we've heard about a funeral for a friend. Find out who it was, and when, and if there's anything about it that rings alarm bells.'

'Guv.'

'And find me a copy of Felix's will—it wasn't in the original files I had. Things can go missing, so if you can't track it down, apply for another copy from his solicitors. Varney would have seen it, and the fact that it didn't feature in his notes probably means there's nothing in it to raise our eyebrows, but I don't like not having it to hand.'

'Guv.'

'But make Olligree Interiors your first priority. And when you've done all that, run a background check on Querida Phelps.'

'Guv.'

They were now back at the car, and Jake opened the

passenger door for her and stepped back to let her in. Hillary caught his eye for a moment and smiled blandly. Jake nodded, and when she was seated, closed the door for her like the gentleman that he was.

BACK AT HQ, Hillary gave Zoe the onerous job of tracing all of Felix's phone calls in the last year of his life. 'I want you to concentrate on the evenings when he was at the squash courts. See if you can find out who was pestering him, if anybody. It may turn out that he was just getting the odd call or two from legitimate friends or relatives, and that our witness was reading more into it than there was. On the other hand, it's our job to run down any leads that Varney missed. You'll get the details from our reports on the Harris and Mitchell interviews, which will be in the murder book by tomorrow morning. Right, Jake?' she added archly.

Jake Barnes, already busy at his keyboard, smiled without breaking his lightning-fast fingerwork. 'Yes, guv.'

'Right. Before that, Zoe, you're with me. I want to start reinterviewing some of the people at the party. We'll start with the finders of the body.'

'That'd be the twins, guv?' Zoe said eagerly. 'I've got their latest address. One of them lives in Bladon. Isn't that where Churchill's buried?'

'It is. Call her, see if she's in.' Felix Olliphant's body had been found by identical twins girls, who'd been the first to decide to leave the party, just after one o'clock, and had gone to retrieve their coats. Roberta and Thomasina Gregory had just turned eighteen at the time, and according to Varney's notes had both been semi-hysterical by the time the first responders had arrived. Normally anyone finding the body is looked at very closely by any SIO, but Varney had been able to find no connection between the Gregory twins and the victim. Besides, his notes had made it pretty clear that he thought the idea of the girls murdering Olliphant to be all but laughable.

Hillary liked to make up her own mind about such things. As she was thinking this, Zoe hung up the phone, her blacklined eyes shining avidly. 'That was Roberta Gregory, guv. She's not only at home but her sister's with her—karma or what? They're planning their parents' golden wedding anniversary or something, and she says we're welcome to come over and chat any time.'

'It wouldn't matter if we weren't,' Hillary pointed out with a small smile.

'We may not be official police officers but we do carry a certain amount of weight,' she reminded her. It was time the girl learnt that they were in a serious job, and start getting used to dealing with authority—and that included wielding it when necessary, as well as submitting to it from the top brass.

'Because of what we do, we carry a certain amount of gravitas around with us, so get used to it.'

In response, Zoe grinned and held up a thumb. A skeleton ring on said thumb winked back at her out of two red-garnet eyes.

Hillary sighed.

ROBERTA GREGORY LIVED in a small Cotswold-stone cottage on the outskirts of the village. The garden had the slightly overgrown look of a not particularly keen gardener and was a riot of messy colour.

When Hillary rang the bell, she wasn't totally surprised to hear the old-fashioned ding-dong peal echo within.

The door was opened quickly by a tall, dark-haired woman, who was almost painfully thin and dressed in a lime-green tracksuit. 'Hello, come on in. I'm Bobby, this is Tommy.' The woman looked over her shoulder as she spoke, and Hillary found herself looking at another painfully thin woman, dressed in a buttercup yellow tracksuit. Their style of hair and make-up were identical. They both wore absolutely no jewellery.

'Hello, you're the policewomen right?' Tommy said.

Her voice had the same, throaty resonance as her twin, and Hillary had them both down as heavy smokers.

Hillary agreed that she was, flashed her ID card, introduced Zoe, and followed the witnesses into a small but charming lounge.

French windows led out to a similarly overgrown back garden and were thrown wide open to let in the late-afternoon sunshine and blackbird song.

'This is about that man we found, right?' Tommy said, sitting down on a sofa. When her twin joined her, Hillary could have been looking at a double negative from a photograph, and found herself relieved that they were wearing the different-coloured tracksuits. Otherwise, she'd never be able to tell them apart.

Identical twins had always made Hillary feel just a little uneasy. What must it be like to stand beside someone, look in a mirror, and see two of you looking back? From what little she'd read on the subject, some identical twins went out of their way to appear and act differently from their siblings—colouring their hair, maybe, dressing different, even sporting plain-glass spectacles in order to differentiate.

Others seemed to go down the opposite route and revel in their sameness, dressing identically and getting a great deal of fun out of other people's inability to tell them apart. These often formed an almost uncanny bond. In extreme cases, she'd read that identical twins sometimes, in childhood, formed their own language or a unique way of communicating in order to isolate themselves further from the outside world.

Although they probably hadn't gone that far, Bobby and Tommy obviously belonged to the latter category, for, consciously or not, they sat close together on the sofa, all but holding hands and looking uneasy, instantly creating a them-and-us atmosphere and looking like exact replicas of themselves.

Hillary quickly began to put them at ease.

'I'm sure you were surprised to hear about this out of the blue, as it were. But I'm a retired DI, now working cold cases. And we're taking another look at the Felix Olliphant file. We do that occasionally. It's nothing to be concerned about.'

'Like that show on the telly?' Bobby Gregory named a popular BBC cop show that featured a cold-case squad.

'Yes, just like that,' Hillary lied with a smile. 'Zoe here is a probationer, who may join the police force later on. So, you see, this is nothing like a formal interview or anything. We're just hoping that, after all this time, you might be able to tell us something that didn't come out during the original investigation. Sometimes people remember all sorts of things years later. Things that, for one reason or another, never got mentioned at the time. We never close a murder file, you see,' she added, sure that the twins would appreciate the drama of that last statement.

As indeed they did.

Tommy nodded, looking a little happier now. 'Oh good. I mean, not good. Nothing about that time was good. But I'm glad you're doing it this time around. We didn't much like that man in charge much, did we?'

'Varney,' Bobby said flatly.

'No. But there's not much we can tell you. And we were both really out of it that night, weren't we?'

'Utterly blotto.'

'So I can't really remember much. Except when I rummaged around to find my coat and I saw his face, I got the fright of my life,' Tommy continued.

'Squealed like a rabbit,' her twin put in helpfully.

'But I thought he was asleep.'

'We laughed.'

'Only he wasn't. When Bobby lifted her coat off him we saw the blood.'

'Tommy was sick in the corner.'

Tommy blushed. 'Sorry.'

Zoe Turnbull, struggling to get down this tennis match of a conversation, wondered if these women were for real. They must be now, what, in their early to mid-thirties, so why did she feel as if she was dealing with someone her own age, or even younger?

Hillary nodded and smiled encouragingly. 'Did either of you know Felix?'

'No, never met him,' Tommy said.

'But he was a dish,' her twin added.

'Bobby!'

'Well, he was. We'd both clocked him at the party. Old Ma Querida had introduced him to us as the divine man who'd feng-shuied her house, whatever the hell that meant, and we both fancied him rotten.'

'True,' her twin conceded.

'But you never approached him?' Hillary put in, trying to corral the two women into giving at least the beginnings of a coherent statement.

'Oh no. He was old. Well, to us he was old. Bit out of our league. Besides, his girlfriend was there,' Bobby said, 'and she gave us the evil eye whenever we went near him.' She giggled helplessly.

'Or any other woman for that matter. Old gorgon eyes we called her,' Tommy agreed, with a giggle that utterly matched that of her twin.

Zoe blinked. They were having her on, right? This had to be a wind-up. She looked at her boss, who sat blank faced beside her.

Hillary no longer wondered why neither of the Gregory girls had married, and resigned herself to this odd two-way conversation.

'Did you see him drinking much?' she asked Tommy.

Both girls shrugged. 'Only Mr Olliphant had a high level of alcohol in his bloodstream,' Hillary persisted doggedly.

Bobby giggled. 'Didn't we all? The foxy bartender was kept busy all right.'

'Oh yes. The foxy bartender!' Tommy put her hand on her twin's arm and the women burst out laughing again.

'So he must have been drinking at some point.' Hillary kept them firmly on track. 'Did you see anyone maybe spiking his orange juice?'

'Nope.'

'Nope.'

'Did you notice Felix arguing with anyone at the party?' Hillary gamely soldiered on.

'Oh no,' Tommy said.

'Oh no,' Bobby said.

'OK.' Hillary bit back a sigh. 'When you went to the bedroom for your coats, did you see anyone hanging around outside?'

'Nope, it was just us. We had to leave early; we promised Mummy and Daddy we'd be back by one,' Bobby said. 'Well, half past anyway.'

'That's the only reason they let us go to the party in the first place. That, and because old Ma Querida was, like, Mummy's oldest friend ever, and we were eighteen by then,' her twin added.

'OK. Well, thank you for your time, Miss Gregory.' She nodded at the woman in lime green, 'And, er, Miss Gregory,' Hillary added to the other woman in buttercup yellow.

Both of them smiled brightly back at her.

'I hope we helped,' Tommy said brightly. Or was it Bobby?

Once they were back outside, Zoe burst out laughing. And after a moment or two, Hillary simply had to join her.

SIX

THAT EVENING, ZOE TURNBULL drove to the nearby village of Bregbroke where she was currently renting a small flat. Well, she liked to call it a flat but in reality it was a converted two-car garage with a clever mezzanine level with just about enough room for a double bed.

As she pulled her Mini off the busy dual carriageway that bisected the little community, she glanced at her watch: 5.30, not a bad time to be rolling home, she thought, pleased both with her working hours and how the day had gone. It had been nice to finally see some proper police action instead of being assigned boring office work again.

She parked the car under a rather inadequate carport and let herself into the small combined living area/cooking/dining room. 'Hello, gorgeous, you home yet or am I the first?' As she called out, a small face, almost hidden by a river of straight, jet black hair, appeared over the top of the mezzanine railing, confirming her suspicions that Lui had been skiving off her lectures again.

'Hello, Miss PC Plod, I wasn't expecting you back yet.' Lui raced down the spiral stairs towards Zoe, her arms already out in welcome. The Chinese student was barely five foot two, slim as a reed, and was currently dressed in ragged denim cut-off shorts and a white T-shirt.

The two women kissed warmly.

'Not so much of the sarcasm, if you please,' Zoe said with a grin, glancing towards the kitchen area—which was, not surprisingly, devoid of any culinary activity. 'What, no dinner on the go for the triumphant, returning breadwinner?' Zoe said, a shade sarcastically.

Lui's pretty face flushed. 'I've only just got back from college myself. That Professor Carter is a slave-driver. I have to do the essay on Donne all over again, he says.' Zoe sighed. Lui was a looker all right, and had that oriental mystery vibe thing going for her in spades, but ever since she'd moved in with her, Zoe had come to realize that she was also a chronically lazy little madam.

'I'll start a stir fry going,' she said, with exaggerated long-suffering patience, earning a smile from her lover.

'At least you don't giggle,' Zoe said, then found herself giggling instead.

Lui looked a little put out, not to mention puzzled. 'I never giggle.'

'No, gorgeous, I know,' Zoe said, and found herself talking about the Gregory twins. As she did so, she had the vaguely uneasy feeling that Hillary Greene wouldn't have approved. She'd been read the standard lecture by Sexy Steven on her first day, of course, that you never discussed work, especially an ongoing investigation, with anyone outside of the office—and that included your nearest and dearest. But surely it didn't matter in this instance? She was sure—well, almost sure—that Hillary didn't seriously suspect the twee twins of bumping off their murder victim.

Besides, Lui loved hearing all about Zoe's adventures which, since she'd started working for the Thames Valley Police, always seemed to be so much more interesting than doing a boring BA in English lit.

As the two girls helped and hindered each other in their tiny kitchen, Zoe was careful not to mention any other details of the case. Which wasn't easy, since Lui was fascinated, and quite clearly jealous, to hear that Zoe's very first case with her 'proper' boss had turned out to be a matter of murder.

As Zoe teased her lover by withholding information, Hillary Green was busy updating *her* lover on every detail of the case so far.

They were at Steven's house on the outskirts of Kidlington, also in the kitchen and preparing a meal. In her case, however, she had a view of the willow trees at the back of his garden that lined the Oxford canal as it meandered south towards the city. And her shop talk was not only permissible, but essential.

'So, nothing striking you so far then?' Steven concluded for her as he chopped the carrots and watched her sprinkling something herb-like over the stewing steak she'd bought on her way home.

'Not really. The whole is-he-or-isn't-he-gay thing is a bit of a curiosity, but not necessarily relevant.' She poured stock into the casserole dish and shoved it in the oven. 'I mean, if he is gay, why would he be in the closet? It would hardly have affected his job prospects and his father didn't seem the kind to be shell-shocked about something like that. From the way he talked, I don't think his mother would have cared overmuch either.'

'No one suspect standing out?'

'Give me a chance, we've barely started,' Hillary

said with a grin. She reached out for the carrots he'd finished chopping and tumbled them into a saucepan of salted water, asking casually, 'So, what did the great silver shark want?'

Steven grinned. 'As opposed to the great white, huh? I take it you're referring to our beloved commander and leader?'

Hillary grinned. 'That's him all right.'

Steven took the small glass of wine that he'd been sipping at meagrely all night, watching her carefully over the rim. 'It's like we thought. He wanted to offer me promotion. Well, not outright promotion, not yet anyway. I'll stay superintendent. But Oxford's setting up a new task force targeting rings that are grooming young girls, mostly from care homes, into enforced prostitution, and they want experienced officers to head it up.'

Hillary let out a long slow breath. 'I thought it might be something like that.' Ever since high-profile cases throughout the country in the past couple of years had highlighted the plight of young girls being abused in this way, the public demand that something be done about it had made it almost inevitable that such task forces would be created.

And people like Steven would be needed to oversee them.

'You'd be top banana, I take it?' Hillary probed gently.

Steven took another careful sip. 'I would. And, in due course, providing the new team gets good results, a promotion within a year, two at the tops, is almost certain to follow.'

Hillary nodded. 'Something that's not going to happen at CRT,' she said matter-of-factly.

'No. Donleavy congratulated me on setting it up and getting it running and starting to produce good results. But now all it really needs is someone to run with the ball for a few years to really establish it.'

'And Donleavy thinks somebody else can do that.'

'He does. Someone who needs to put in a few years and learn what running a small team is all about, before moving on. He thinks I'm wasted staying on there now and that it's high time I let the brass see what I'm really capable of. His words, not mine.'

'But you agree?' Steven sighed and rubbed his forehead.

'Six months ago, I'd have agreed like a shot. It's a bit of a no-brainer, isn't it? Stay in CRT and stagnate. Or move onward and upwards to an exciting new job where promotion, provided I don't royally screw it up, is almost guaranteed.'

Hillary turned down the saucepan under the now-boiling carrots and looked at him thoughtfully. 'Six months ago you'd have thought that? What, but not now?' she asked sceptically, one eyebrow rising.

Steven smiled. 'Now, all I'm saying is, there are other things to be considered,' he corrected her quietly. He was no mug—he could see that she wasn't taking this as calmly as she appeared to be. And the last thing he wanted to do was get on her bad side.

Hillary leaned back against one of the worktops and slowly folded her arms across her chest, unaware that her body language was now screaming caution and wariness to the man who was watching her so intently over his wine glass.

'Such as?' she asked calmly. 'If it were me in your position, I wouldn't hesitate. You're clearly up for a new challenge and Donleavy just as clearly rates you. You'd be mad to turn it down.' Steven sighed gently. She obviously wasn't in the mood to make it easy for him. 'If I leave CRT, I won't be your boss anymore.'

He stated the obvious boldly, getting the big fat elephant in the room out there in the open where they could both take a good, long hard look at it.

Hillary shrugged one shoulder casually. 'No doubt that's one of the reasons why Donleavy offered you the job in the first place,' she said flatly. 'Like most of the top brass, he doesn't feel comfortable having two senior officers on the same squad also sharing a personal relationship. And yes, I know, technically, I'm a civilian now, so it shouldn't count. But we both know that it does.' Steven nodded wordlessly.

'So, what does it matter if you stop being my boss?' Hillary went on calmly, reaching for a glass and pouring out some wine of her own. Unlike Steven, however, she took a hefty swig. 'Does it really matter?'

Steven Crayle heard the aggression behind the words, and sighed again. 'Not to me,' he said levelly. 'There's no reason why it should affect us at all. Right?'

Hillary Greene smiled. 'Well, then, problem solved. Take the new job and get the promotion. It's what you want, and what you deserve. Now, do you want rice with the beef, or a baked potato?'

AS HILLARY GREENE pretended that nothing was wrong, in his north Oxford mansion Jake Barnes was about to order a takeout. The telephone rang just as he approached it.

He picked it up, moving with the cordless handset towards a large Chesterfield sofa that sat squarely in front of an original Adams fireplace. He sat down and smiled gently at the familiar feminine voice coming over the line. As he listened, he stretched his long legs out in front of him and rubbed the back of his neck wearily.

'I'm fine, don't worry,' he said. 'Everything's going more or less as I thought it would.' He listened to the worried voice, a small frown creasing his dark brows. 'No, I told you, you're worrying about nothing. Yes, I've met her now, she's back off holiday.' He paused, listened, and sighed again. 'Like I said, she's smart, very smart. Which is actually good. For us, I mean. We want her to be smart. If I can get her on side, she's going to be very useful to us.' He glanced out of the window to where a small green garden backed on to Five Mile Drive, a leafy, cherry-tree-lined avenue on Oxford's exclusive northern edge.

'Well, she's more wary than I had hoped,' he admitted reluctantly. 'I don't know if I've done something to make her particularly suspicious or whether she's just got a good nose for trouble. But she's certainly giving me the impression that she's keeping an eye on me. It's not going to be easy getting her to trust me.' He listened to the somewhat indignant tone of the woman on the other end of the line, and laughed gently. 'Now, that's hardly fair, is it? As far as she's concerned, I'm the new boy with everything to prove. And it makes sense that she doesn't trust me yet. Let's face it, it's her job to be cautious. And having a rich kid forced on her isn't going to make her feel exactly happily predisposed towards me, is it? I think she's just expecting me to be a know-it-all smart-arse, and I'll just have to be patient and show her my good points, that's all.' He took a long slow breath, and for a few minutes let the caller give free rein to her feelings. Finally, though, he interrupted her.

'Look, it's like I told you at the start. Nothing is going to happen quickly—we always knew that. And now that I've met Inspector Greene for myself, I can tell you that's definitely true,' he added ruefully. 'And while she's keeping an eye on me, and trying to find out what my angle is, I'm going to have to be even more careful than we thought. You know, keep my head down, do the work, take my time and pick my moment. But that's OK too, because the more I learn about the job, the better. That'll only help us in the long run. What?' He listened, and shook his head, although he knew his caller couldn't see him. 'No, even that's to our advantage really. Hillary Greene was a really successful copper, and after only working with her for a day or so, I can see why. And that's what we need too, right? Someone really good being on our side. Besides, I'm going to learn a lot from her, and the more she teaches me, the better my chances are of finding something out that we can use. And the better I get at police work, and the more she sees that she can rely on me, the less wary she's going to be about things. And then, when she's not constantly watching me, I can start making my move.' He reached forward and lifted up the TV remote, pressing the mute button and then selecting the BBC1 news programme. As he watched the silent images, he listened intently to the woman on the other end of the line.

'You let me worry about that,' he said sharply. 'She's smart but she's hardly a mind-reader. She won't find out what I'm really there for because I won't let her. I'm smart too, remember?' He laughed softly at something she said, then nodded.

'Exactly. Besides, don't forget, she'll want to be on our side anyway when she knows the truth. So even if she does figure it out eventually, by then, with a bit of luck, she'll be willing to actually help. And if not... well—' Jake Barnes shrugged graphically.

'I've still got a lot of money and a lot of clout. And Hillary Greene isn't a serving officer anymore, which makes her vulnerable.' Jake's eyes narrowed on the television screen.

'Which means that, if I have to, I can either work around her or get her taken out of my way. So stop worrying, OK? Yes, I'll talk to you soon. Love you too.' He disconnected the phone and for a moment or two tapped it thoughtfully against his lips. Then he shrugged and turned up the volume on the television.

THE NEXT MORNING, Hillary woke up rather late on her boat after a long and disturbed night's sleep. Consequently, she felt heavy-eyed and vaguely depressed as she got dressed and headed in to work.

Her mind, which should have been on thoughts of Felix Olliphant, and how to go about finding out who'd killed him and why, kept straying instead to Steven Crayle, and it was annoying her. Mightily.

In spite of what she'd said to him, asserting that things wouldn't change between them, how would it really feel to drive to work knowing that he wouldn't be there at the office waiting for her? And once he was working from Oxford, how often, realistically, would they see each other? Especially if he was working hard for a promotion, which meant long hours, as she well knew.

For all their talk that the new job wouldn't change things between them, they both knew that it would. So where did that leave them?

Her sense of vague depression thickened suddenly, and she found her throat starting to ache as she swallowed back something hard that had settled just below her sternum.

So when she stalked into the HQ lobby entrance, the desk sergeant took one look at her closed, pale face, and bit back the cheerful insult that had been hovering on his lips.

So the rumours that Superintendent Crayle was on his way up and out of Kidlington HQ looked like they might be true, he mused. He'd have to call his mate in records and see what he knew.

Hillary, unaware of the speculation and gossip that was already beginning to trickle its way through the Big House, made her way to her office, where she forced herself to read the murder book for any updates. Although both her new recruits had diligently kept it concurrent, there was nothing in it yet to attract her attention.

Which needed to change. Get your mind off your precarious love life, my girl, and concentrate on the victim, she snarled grimly at herself. And in that frame of mind she marched towards the communal office. There, she looked around the small room, her eyes hesitating over Jake Barnes, before turning to Zoe.

'Zoe, you have the latest address for Felix's girlfriend?'

'Yes, guv. She's since married and has a couple of

kids, but they're still living locally. Well, Middleton Cheney.' She named a large village on the other side of the market town of Banbury, about twenty miles away to the north.

'Well, fairly locally.'

'Right. It's time we got her perspective on things. You can drive.'

'Guv,' Zoe said, playfully shooting the finger at Jake Barnes, who watched the two women leave with a thoughtful look on his face.

Was it his imagination or had Hillary Greene got a rather white, spiteful look about her this morning? He glanced across at Jimmy Jessop and was rather disconcerted to find the old man watching him alertly.

'My advice, son, is don't ask,' Jimmy said with a bland smile. Jake Barnes grinned but made a mental note not to underestimate the old codger again. He obviously didn't miss a trick either. He wasn't Hillary's right-hand man for no reason, and if Jake wanted to slowly take over that role from the old man then he'd better keep his wits about him.

'Got it, Jimmy,' he said with a cheerful smile.

BECKY LESLEY BANKS, now Mrs Rebecca Morton, hadn't changed much from her photographs in the file, Hillary thought a little while later, as the housewife and mother showed them through her attractive and spacious house into the kitchen.

She was a little plumper maybe, and with a few more lines, but she was basically the same vaguely pretty woman, with the same short blonde hairstyle and large blue eyes.

'Poor Felix,' she said now, as she poured them out a

mug of coffee each in her well-appointed kitchen and pushed towards them a milk bottle and a bowl of sugar.

She was wearing a pair of tailored lilac slacks that did their best to hide the bulge of her stomach, and a silvery-coloured loose-fitting top. A pair of dangling amethyst and silver earrings completed the outfit. Her nails were well manicured, as were the lawns outside in her garden.

She looked calm and at ease but Hillary could sense the tension emanating from her. Her smile, when she indicated a pair of tall stools and invited them to sit, was just a shade too brittle to be genuine.

Hillary was well aware, from what she'd read in DI Varney's notes, that Rebecca Morton had not always been this calm or collected. Or so sure of herself, and her position in life, as this woman seemed to be. So this was Becky Banks mark two—the Becky that emerged from the ashes after Felix's death.

Interesting.

Most of Felix's friends, when questioned by Varney or a member of his team, had intimated that Rebecca, or Becky as she was widely known then, could be a touch manic, possessive or needy, depending on the witness being interviewed.

So apparently marriage to a successful advertising executive had had a calming effect on her.

'As I explained, we're taking a new look at his case,' Hillary began, glancing around the modern kitchen diner in the new-build detached house. There was scant evidence on show of her children, who must presently be at school, and Hillary wondered what the woman found to do with herself all day to pass the time. According to Zoe's background research, Rebecca Morton didn't hold down a job of her own.

'Oh, it was so awful,' Rebecca said now, sitting on her own high stool and looking across the central marble-topped island around which they all sat. She held her own mug of coffee but was making no effort to drink from it, Hillary noticed. 'I don't mind saying, it utterly devastated me. It took me years to get over it. Felix was…well…' She managed a shrug and a smile that was half shamefaced and half defiant. 'He was the love of my life. He always will be. Mike is…well, don't get me wrong, he's great. The twins adore him.' But you don't, Hillary thought silently, and nodded. Yes, below the outwardly calm wife-and-mother exterior, there still lurked something of a drama queen. Which could be played up to.

Hillary smiled with every appearance of sympathy. 'It must have been made so much worse, to be treated like a prime suspect as you were. I think from the notes it's very clear that the officer in charge gave you a hard time.'

'Oh, he did. He was a horrible man. I told him that I loved Felix, and that we were going to be married, but I don't think he believed me,' Rebecca said now, her face flushing with remembered resentment. 'I got the feeling that he thought that Felix wasn't as much in love as I was, and that I was jealous and possessive.' She shook her head sadly, her short blonde hair, from which all traces of approaching silver had been carefully dyed, clinging slightly around her chin. She pushed the strands back impatiently. 'He was a stupid man. I told him, he shouldn't listen to the others—they were always jealous of Felix and me.' For a second her eyes flashed with some intense emotion that was too fleeting for Hillary to categorize, before dulling again. 'I wasn't surprised when he never found out who killed Felix. He simply didn't have the brains for it. It makes me angry to think of it. The person who killed my poor Felix should have spent all these years since rotting in jail! It makes my blood boil to think of them just going on, blithely living their life as if nothing had happened.'

'I'm sure it does,' Hillary said, believing her. For the woman facing her across the vast expanse of cold black marble was almost radiating the heat of thwarted rage. 'Tell me about that night. It was a big party, and such a momentous moment in time. You must have been happy to be invited.' From what she'd read, Becky Banks had been the fifth child of working-class parents, who'd still been living with them in their council estate in a rather run-down area of Cowley.

Zoe, busy scribbling down in her notebook what was being said, looked up at Hillary briefly at this point, and then across at Rebecca Morton. It was clear to her that her boss was taking a very different approach with this witness. And it was so fascinating to listen to her manipulate the other woman that she had to keep reminding herself to make clear notes.

'Oh, I was. It was a really big flash house. And our hostess was quite something,' Rebecca said, a large, pleased smile crossing her face. 'Have you met her?'

'Not yet.'

'Oh, well, you'll see what I mean when you do. She really loved the job Felix made of redecorating the house—well, she would, Felix was marvellous. Greer too, I suppose,' she added somewhat grudgingly, 'but it was Felix who made Olligree Interiors the success that it was. That's why she invited him—Querida Phelps, I mean. Isn't that a wonderful name? I'd never met anyone like her. She was real class, you know what I mean? It was a really swish do—all those fancy costumes—I went as Marie Antoinette, it was a gorgeous outfit. It cost a bomb to rent it, but I was glad that I did. Everyone complimented me on it. And the food, and the champagne.' She sighed suddenly, and looked around the large, attractive kitchen, as if surprised to find herself there. In her mind, clearly, she was back once again on that last evening of December 1999.

Hillary wondered how often she found herself living there, instead of the here and now.

'Of course, since marrying Mike we have champagne from time to time so it's not quite so special,' Rebecca sighed. 'But back then, I was still so young, and it all felt so, well…sophisticated, you know? Like something you see in the films?'

Hillary nodded. 'But Felix ruined it, I suppose, by getting so drunk?' She determinedly ruined Rebecca's pink-tinted view of the night in the hope of jolting something useful out of her.

'Oh no! And he wasn't drunk,' Rebecca said, her face flushing a dull ugly red. 'Felix hardly ever drank.'

'But the post mortem showed that he had a high level of alcohol in his bloodstream that night,' Hillary pointed out gently.

'I don't know about that,' Rebecca Morton said sullenly. 'I was with him all night, and I never saw him drink much. He started off with orange juice, for pete's sake! And then when I teased him about it a bit—I mean, it was New Year's Eve, and the brand new millennium was only a few hours away, after all, and if you can't let your hair down then, I told him, when can you? But even then, he only asked for the odd half a pint of cider shandy from the fox serving at the bar. So I don't know how you can keep on saying he was drunk. And he certainly never made a scene. I didn't even know he'd gone off to lie down until I suddenly couldn't find him anymore.'

'That was just before the countdown, right?' Hillary put in.

'Yes.'

'Did you see him arguing with anyone that night, Rebecca?'

'Oh, please, call me Becky. And no, of course he didn't argue with anyone. Felix wasn't the sort to argue. Besides, who would want to argue with him? Felix was a lovely man. Really lovely.' Reaching for a roll of kitchen towel, Rebecca tore off a couple of squares and began to sob into them.

Zoe shifted restlessly on her stool. Hillary simply let the witness cry and then, when she'd finished, said softly, 'He must have been very popular. I mean, from what you say, he must have had many friends.'

'Oh, he did,' Rebecca said, a shade challengingly. 'But he was *my* boyfriend. We were going to be married. There were no other women, if that's what you're getting at.'

'Of course not,' Hillary said soothingly. And because she didn't want her becoming truculent, she decided to steer her back to something less contentious. 'Tell me about this friend of his who died. I understand that Felix had gone to his funeral, and several people have mentioned it, and how much it upset him.'

'Oh, that was Harry Fletcher,' Rebecca said offhandedly. 'Yes, Felix was a bit quiet and moody for a while after that. But then he was the same age as Felix, so it's always a bit of a shock when someone you know dies, isn't it? I mean, you don't expect it.'

'Do you know when he died, or how?'

'Not really. Felix didn't want to talk about it.' Zoe's lips twisted as she rapidly turned a page on her notebook. She'd already long since written off Felix Olliphant's girlfriend as shallow and clingy. No wonder everyone said that Becky had been far more keen on their relationship than Felix.

Personally, Zoe doubted that he'd ever meant to marry the woman. From what she'd heard about their murder victim from other people, he'd been the sort of man who would have wanted someone with a bit more substance to her than this airhead.

Hillary was thinking much the same thing. And wondering. Did Rebecca's healthy ego prevent her from realizing that Felix was unlikely to take their relationship to the next stage? Or had she guessed how things truly were, and felt outraged enough to do something about it? Had Felix tried to end it, even? People like Becky, in Hillary's experience, could be very volatile and unpredictable when crossed. She could see her lashing out in a moment of rage and fury. But did that equate with how Felix had been murdered?

Hillary wasn't sure. It was hard to pin down exactly the modus operandi in Felix's case. It smacked in some ways of opportunism, and in other ways of very careful planning. And it was the careful planning part that didn't go with Rebecca's personality type.

'Were you aware of any phone calls that Felix was

having that were making him anxious, say, or impatient?' She changed tack again.

'Oh, Felix was always on the phone,' Rebecca said dismissively. 'Talking to clients, mostly, but to friends too. I didn't really pay much attention when he was talking on the phone.'

No, Hillary thought, you probably wouldn't. 'And you never noticed anyone acting in any way strangely that night? Perhaps watching Felix closely, or fiddling with his drinks maybe?'

'I would have said if I had,' Rebecca Morton said huffily.

'Now, if there's nothing else?' There was, of course, plenty, but Hillary was in no hurry to push it. She could always return to this witness later. Besides, she knew the petulant type. If she tried to carry on questioning her now, Rebecca Morton would only turn uncooperative and mulish.

'No, thank you, Mrs Morton, you've been very helpful,' Hillary said, with a bright, bland smile.

Rebecca sniffed slightly and pushed her untouched mug of coffee away. 'Yes, well, I only hope you catch who did it. You can't do any worse than that stupid man, Varney.' And then she reached for more kitchen roll again. 'Poor Felix!' she wailed.

Zoe and Hillary silently left her to her sobbing, and showed themselves out.

Once outside, Zoe shook her head. 'Another bimbo. First the Bobsy twins, now her. It's getting depressing, guv.'

Hillary grinned. 'Cheer up. And team up with Jake and find out all you can about this Harry Fletcher.'

'The dead friend? Why, guv, you don't think he

came back from the grave and killed Felix, do you? It was New Year's Eve, not Halloween,' Zoe pointed out cheekily.

'Because there's no mention of him in Varney's files, which means it's an avenue that he never followed up,' Hillary said patiently. 'Granted, it'll almost certainly lead nowhere,' she sighed, 'but when you've got a case this cold, you have to pick over every tiny little thread. So find out exactly when he died, and how, and if you can, why it seemed to affect our murder victim so much.'

'Guv,' Zoe said.

'You really get a kick out of saying that, don't you?' Hillary mused, a tad sourly.

Zoe grinned widely. 'Yes, guv.'

SEVEN

WHEN THEY GOT back to HQ it was lunchtime, so Hillary, Jimmy and Sam trooped up to the canteen. The Boy Wonder was busy on his computer, as always, and Zoe said she'd bought some sandwiches and would eat them at her desk. She was keen to see what she could dig up on Harry Fletcher, and wanted to impress the boss with her efficiency.

Hillary hoped that such enthusiasm would last for at least a month.

But doubted it.

In the canteen, Sam spotted a friend of his who'd recently joined the traffic division, so took his shepherd's pie off in his direction, leaving Jimmy and Hillary to snaffle a table near a grimy window and tuck into their own choices of tomato omelette and bangers and mash.

Hillary forked a rather rubbery mouthful of egg and tomato into her mouth and chewed without really tasting it. After years of eating police canteen food, it was a skill she'd acquired and nearly always gratefully appreciated.

'So how's things your end?' she asked.

'Good, guv. We're going to get Knocker Clarke this time, I'm sure of it.' Hillary grinned. 'Bit of a crusade, is it, Jimmy?'

The old ex-sergeant grinned and speared a sausage. 'Too bloody right. I never was able to feel his collar when I was in uniform. And you know what they say—better late than never. And if we *can* link him and his tribe to the latest crime-wave, we'll clear so many cold cases as well, the super's crime statistics will make even the chief constable smile.' Hillary, who knew the chief constable slightly, rather doubted it.

'But he's still small fry compared to what you're doing. How's it going?' Jimmy asked curiously.

'You've been reading the murder book.' She stated it as a fact, and Jimmy, busy chewing on his sausage, nodded.

'Well, then, you know,' she said flatly.

Jimmy chewed and swallowed. 'Early days yet, guv. You'll get there. You always do.'

'Thanks for the vote of confidence.'

'How are the two newbies coming on? And have you seen what that girl is wearing?' Presuming Jimmy was referring to Zoe, who today was wearing a ragged black skirt and top that reminded Hillary of something one of the Addams Family might have worn, smiled.

'You don't approve, Jimmy?'

'She looks like something from a horror movie. One of the walking dead or something. And all that black eye make-up. Ugh!'

'I rather think that's the point,' Hillary said, although she could see the old man's eyes were twinkling.

'You like her,' she accused, and then smiled. 'So do I. She's got a way about her, I grant you. A certain zest for life that's appealing. But whether or not she's serious enough to make a go of it in this job…' She waved an egg-laden fork to encompass the canteen and the coppers all around. 'I'm not so sure. She's bright enough, and enthusiastic enough. But does she have the staying power?' She shrugged. 'Time will tell.'

'And the Boy Wonder?' Jimmy asked.

'He's always on that bloody computer of his, but that seems to be the way the job's going nowadays. And Sam keeps telling me how clever he is.'

'Oh, he is that,' Hillary said neutrally. 'Of that I have no doubt.'

'Ah,' Jimmy said, reaching for his mug of tea and washing down his food with a few mouthfuls. 'You don't rate him then?'

Hillary frowned over a sodden tomato. 'It's not that. I think he's sharp enough. But what's he really doing here, Jimmy? That's what's bugging me.'

'According to Sam, he has a social conscience. Whatever the hell that is.' Hillary grinned. Trust Jimmy to share her cynicism. 'Exactly. We're supposed to believe he made his millions early, feels guilty because it was such a fluke, and now wants to contribute something back to society by becoming a policeman. Jimmy, when was the last time you ever knew somebody do something out of the goodness of their heart?' Jimmy Jessop's old eyes sparked a bit more. 'It has been known to happen, guv. Leastwise, so I've heard.'

Hillary grinned. 'Right. I heard the same rumour.'

Jimmy finished his last sausage and put down his fork thoughtfully. 'Seriously, guv, you think he's up to something?'

'Maybe. Or maybe I'm just being paranoid,' Hillary admitted.

'Either way, if he *is* up to something, I'd rather know just what kind of a snake he's let loose in the grass so that I can stomp on it before it has a chance to rise up and bite me in the arse.'

'Words of wisdom if ever I heard 'em, guv,' Jimmy agreed with a grin. 'You want me to keep an eye on him, I take it?'

'Absolutely,' Hillary Greene said.

AFTER THEIR FLIRTING-WITH-INDIGESTION MEAL, Jimmy and Hillary returned to the bowels of the building where Zoe had just finished writing up the notes on the Rebecca Morton interview and was adding them to the murder book.

Jake Barnes looked up as Hillary walked in. 'Guv, I have those financial reports you wanted. Nothing really stands out, either at Olligree Interiors, or with Colin Harcourt's double-glazing company. Although the latter has been doing surprisingly well, given the economic downturn. Which does suggest that he might have another income besides the one he's filing tax returns on. Also, he's not long sold up and retired. I've got feelers out,' he added, before Hillary could tell him to follow it up. 'I'll know more in a couple of days.'

'Right,' Hillary said, accepting the folder of facts and figures from him with a sigh of weariness. Fascinating bedtime reading, she didn't think.

'I'll go over these tonight,' she said, with a distinct lack of enthusiasm.

'I've done a summary at the back, in layman's language, guv,' Jake said, a small smile tugging at his lips.

'Suck-up!' Zoe said softly.

Jake shot her an affable finger.

'OK,' Hillary said. 'Well, as a reward for all that number crunching, you can come with me on the next interview. We're going to talk to the hostess of the party.'

'Oh no, not Querida Phelps!' Zoe wailed. 'Oh, guv, I was hoping I could get to do her. After what Rebecca Morton said about her and all, I'm all agog.'

'I'm sure Jake will be able to paint you a picture with words,' Hillary commiserated.

'Have fun,' Zoe muttered somewhat mendaciously, watching them leave with a wistful look on her face.

'So, where does this wonderfully named individual live, guv?' Jake asked, as they trotted up the stairs and into the daylight of the lobby.

'You tell me,' Hillary said.

Jake grinned. 'Still testing me, guv? According to the notes, she's still in the same house that our murder victim died in. Just the other side of Headington.'

'Find that odd at all?' Hillary asked thoughtfully, as they stepped out into the car park and paused to let a convoy of patrol cars speed past them on the way out. Probably a pile-up on the M40, Hillary guessed gloomily.

'What? That she didn't sell up and move out, you mean?' Jake interrupted her dark thoughts.

'I suppose, in a way. After all, it can't be nice knowing that someone was murdered in the place where you're living. I think most people would sell up and move, if they could. And Mrs Phelps certainly could. I did a quick financial check on her too, and she still is, and always was, wealthy enough to buy a place somewhere else if she'd wanted to.'

Hillary nodded thoughtfully. 'Perhaps she's just not the sensitive type.'

'My car or yours, guv?' Jake asked, rattling his car

keys in his pocket. This morning he was wearing black designer jeans and a mint-green shirt, with a casual white and black summer jacket that had probably cost more than her car had.

Hillary, with a guilty glance at Puff the Tragic Wagon, kept on walking towards the gleaming racing-green E-type Jag. 'Oh, yours, I think,' she said, with no intonation at all.

Jake Barnes grinned. 'Yes, guv.'

QUERIDA PHELPS'S HOUSE, 'Spindlewood Grange', missed being within the boundaries of the suburb of Headington by at least a good mile or so. Set in the rolling hills that would eventually stretch on into the Aylesbury Vale, there was not another house in sight of it.

Furthermore, it could only be reached by an unadopted tarmac road that led you down past centuries-old large oaks and towering horse chestnuts, to a small tributary of the River Cherwell. It looked to Hillary as if at one point it might have been a working water mill, although there was no trace of a big wheel remaining. However, weeping willows ran the length of the garden, indicating a stream, and lush water meadows stretched as far as the eye could see. Grazed now by black and white cows, in the spring, when they were full of buttercups, they must have looked stunning.

As Jake parked the car on the gravelled forecourt and they stepped out and looked at the late-seventeenth-century Cotswold stone building, Hillary gave a long, slow whistle.

'No wonder she didn't want to move, guv,' Jake said, looking at the beautiful old building in front of him. He noted the newly installed expanses of darkened glass and the modern extension to one side, and nodded. 'A mix of old and new. I bet it's got every mod con inside that you could think of. I bet our man had a great time decorating it.'

'Fancy living here yourself then, Jake?' Hillary asked, then realized, with something of a jolt, that this enigmatic young man beside her actually *could* have afforded to buy a place like this had it been up for sale.

'Bit too out of the way for me, guv. I like cows and all that, but I'd rather have some people for neighbours as well.'

'Apparently our Mrs Phelps doesn't share your social leanings,' Hillary said, and began to look forward to meeting the woman herself. No doubt if she'd had Zoe Turnbull by her side now, she would have been fairly bouncing on her toes in excitement. A seventeenth-century water mill was just the sort of gothic background for a murder that would have had her salivating.

'Let's just hope the lady of the house is in,' Hillary said, as she walked past the well-manicured lawns, the colourfully frothing flower borders and, most delightfully of all, a wooden bridge that crossed the stream as it wound in front of the house.

The front door was, naturally, a double expanse of oak, with ancient-looking wrought black iron garniture. An old-fashioned round-handled bell pull took pride of place, and as Hillary rung it she had a sudden vision of the door being opened by a Lurchlike figure, who would, naturally, tell her that the lady of the house had died two years ago but if they'd like to come in, he'd go and see if she would see them.

She was fighting back the urge to laugh when the

door was abruptly thrown open, making Hillary take an instinctive step back.

No seven-foot tall, cadaverous-faced butler stood there, but rather a striking woman with waist-length silver-white hair and eyes the colour of aquamarines. She was Hillary's height but seemed taller, probably because she was as thin as a rake. She was barefoot and wearing a single, floor-length kaftan in a green-blue colour that almost perfectly matched her eyes. Although she could have been aged anywhere between sixty and eighty, she was still stunningly beautiful, with prominent cheekbones and a taunt jawline. She was well tanned too, and had the stained yellowish fingers of a cigarette devotee.

'Yes? If you're Jehovah's Witnesses, you can bugger off,' the vision said, in a perfect Sloane Ranger accent that would have made royalty feel common. The blue eyes sharpened on Jake like a predator, and a wide smile played with the woman's somewhat over-generous mouth. 'Although you can come on in, if you like. I'd be more than happy to corrupt *you*.'

Jake blinked, then instantly rallied and grinned. 'Thank you, I'd be honoured. But not while I'm on duty.'

'Oh, bloody hell, not the rozzers? I only grow a bit of weed for my rheumatism, Officer,' she mock-whined.

Hillary reached for her ID. 'Relax, we're perfectly harmless. We're not even real coppers, and have no teeth.' She instantly fell in with the game. 'Civilian consultants only, see, and honestly, we don't give a damn about what you might be growing in your greenhouse. You're Mrs Phelps, I take it?'

Querida Phelps rolled her eyes. 'For my sins. After the bastard died, never married again.'

'So you're a widow, Mrs Phelps?'

'Dunno, darlin', I divorced the sod before he popped his clogs. Does that make me his widow anyway?'

'Not technically,' Hillary said, vastly amused.

'Damn! I rather like playing the role of the merry widow. Oh well, come on in. By the by, if you're not here to bust me for possession, just what have I done to bring the constabulary to my door? It's ages since I streaked at that rugby match at Twickenham, and besides, I deny it utterly. No matter what evidence the centre forward has to the contrary.'

As she talked, she showed them into a mind-blowing hall. The floor, Hillary realized, was made of reinforced glass, allowing them a view of the river which actually flowed under the house, proof that this had indeed once been an old mill. Back in the day, she suspected this vast space had housed the wheel. Above them, the space rose two storeys up to the rafters, the massive oak beams of which had been carefully preserved. A grandfather clock of impeccable heritage tick-tocked impressively against one bulging, lathe-and-plaster egg-shell-blue wall.

'Wow,' Jake said, looking around. A vast array of copper- and lemon-coloured chrysanthemums stood on the floor in a massive Arts and Crafts beaten copper jug, at least three feet tall.

'Like it?' Querida Phelps said, waving a hand around. Rings sparkled on every finger, showing off huge stones that ranged from diamonds to rubies to emeralds and the inevitable aquamarines.

Oh yes, Zoe Turnbull would have loved her, Hillary thought, and half regretted not bringing her.

'I had it re-done yonks ago and never could bring

myself to have it changed since. The young man who did it all died, and—' Suddenly Querida Phelps stopped speaking, and shot a quick, assessing look at them. 'I'm being frightfully dim, I do apologize. This is all about Felix, isn't it?' she said, all playfulness suddenly leaving her.

Hillary nodded, and explained yet again who they were and what they were doing.

'Right,' Querida said solemnly. 'And about time, if you ask me. In that case, let me show you around the ground floor. You can see Felix's work for yourself. That'll probably tell you more about him than I ever could. After that, I intend to open an award-winning bottle of Napolean brandy and get thoroughly drunk. And you're welcome to join me.' Hillary looked at the older woman thoughtfully. 'Still hurts, does it?' she asked softly.

'Oh yes. Oh no,' she added, laughing suddenly as she caught the speculation in Hillary's eye. 'There was nothing like that going on. Not that I'd have said no, mind you. Felix was a lovely man. But alas, not into older women. I lent him a video of *The Graduate* but it was no go, I'm afraid. Ah well. It's just that I got to know Felix really well in the time he did all this for me. And we realised we were kindred spirits, in a way. It made us grow very close.'

Hillary looked at the vast wall of floor-to-ceiling windows that overlooked the meadows, the plaster scrollwork on the ceilings around the centre rose where a large chandelier hung, the huge stone-built fireplace, and the ancient oak and peg flooring.

'Felix made this place come alive, somehow, but without pickling it in amber, or making it look like something from a film set.' Querida walked towards a drinks cabinet, disguised as an old globe of the world, and did indeed break open an impressive-looking bottle of brandy.

She brandished it in the air at them, but both Hillary and Jake declined. 'He and I just saw eye to eye on everything. From the colour scheme—' All three of them looked around at the pale walls, the colour of ripe corn '—to the furnishings—' She indicated the art deco mirrors, the old Chesterfields, the intricately carved ebony tallboys and tables '—and everything in between.' Querida took a sip of brandy and eyed the heavy lined velvet curtains in the palest of turquoise brocaded in old gold. 'It was like magic. He seemed to know exactly what I wanted, and make my vision come true, even when I couldn't see it for myself.'

'It sounds as if you got on well. Is that why you invited him to the New Year's Eve party?' Hillary brought her around to the point.

The older woman shuddered suddenly, her long white hair rippling as she threw herself down onto the nearest armchair with thoughtless disregard for her clothes, person or the bulbous glass of brandy. Hillary was amused, but not surprised, to see that she never spilt a drop of the precious liquid.

'Yes. That bloody party. If only I'd known... Well, of course, we never do know what fate holds in store for us, do we, I'm glad to say. Cheers!' She took a good slug of the brandy. 'Oh yeah, that really hits the spot,' she said with an almost feral grin. Her teeth, Hillary noted, were still all her own, and not particularly even or white, but somehow that imperfection only added to her overall glamour.

With her eye-watering jewellery and her cut-glass accent, added to her over-the-top personality, it was easy to see why the likes of Rebecca Morton had been so impressed with her. She was a lady, the real deal, the kind who wouldn't have dreamed of making any apology for themselves, or the way they lived their lives. Now she sipped her brandy, and stared up at her crystal chandelier with a brooding, fading, decadent loveliness about her that would no doubt have had Zoe Turnbull worshipping at her feet.

Hillary eyed the older woman thoughtfully. She was obviously bra-less, for the old silk kaftan clung to her revealingly, but she would have bet her next month's salary that Querida Phelps was genuinely unaware of the figure she created, and wouldn't have cared less if she had been.

She glanced across at Jake Barnes, who was watching the performance with a man's typical approval, and Hillary bit back a smile. Time to get down to work.

'What can you tell me about that night, Mrs Phelps?'

'Oh, call me Querida, darlin', everyone does. And that night? That night was wonderful and hellish in about equal measure. It was wonderful in that it was the last day of an old millennium and everyone was in an almost feverish party spirit. I had ordered so much champagne that we were awash in it. I had gone overboard, as usual, in deciding to make it fancy dress. So retro but there you go. Although in my defence, it hadn't been my own original idea, but when my pal suggested it I leapt on it like a panther. I mean, what else could you do for the millennium but go over the top? Everyone turned up looking a scream—we had grizzly bears, spacemen, tarts and vicars, tramps, and of course milkmaids and women who would insist on coming dressed like something from the bloody French Revolution!'

She laughed dismissively, and Hillary couldn't help but wince for poor Becky Banks, who'd been so proud of her Marie Antoinette outfit. 'I was dressed as Lady Godiva, of course,' she said, and eyed Jake hopefully. 'I was younger then, let me say in my own defence. And the long blonde wig I wore *was* very long, and very bushy. Oh, all right, I had a flesh-coloured body stocking too. I admit it.'

Jake grinned at her. 'I wish I'd been there.'

'Me too. And of course, Felix came as a romantic poet. Well, he would, wouldn't he, he had just the looks for it. That sort of too-good-for-this-world, delicate male beauty that you see when you look at those engravings of Keats and the rest of that crowd. He looked good enough to eat, let me tell you.'

'But you and he weren't lovers?' Hillary pressed.

'No, worse luck.'

'Do you think he was gay?' Hillary asked. 'Only we keep getting mixed views on that.'

'Gay? Well, I suppose he could have been,' Querida said vaguely, taking another sip of her brandy 'Mind you, I'm not so vain as to think that any man who didn't want to shag me had to be bent, mind. But no, I don't think so. He came with a girlfriend. Some vapid blonde, I seem to remember.' Again Hillary had to fight back a small wince on Becky's behalf.

'Did you see him getting drunk?'

'No. I was surprised, to tell you the truth, when that came out at the inquest.' Querida shifted her position slightly on the Chesterfield. 'He'd had ample opportunity during the months he worked here to make full use of the wine cellar, or the good old globe over there—' She wafted her exquisite, balloon-shaped brandy glass towards the liquor cabinet '—but he never indulged. And I never saw him with a proper drink in his hand during that night, either.'

'That's just it,' Hillary said. 'Neither DI Varney, the original investigator, nor myself, can seem to find anyone at that party who admits to seeing Felix drinking heavily. The DI made a point of asking your bartender for that evening, the very good-looking…' For a second, Hillary couldn't remember the man's name, and Jake smoothly provided it.

'Peter Goodman.'

'Right, Peter Goodman. And he said in his original interview that the few times that he remembers serving Felix drinks, it was either a fruit juice or some sort of shandy. Which ties in with what his girlfriend said he was drinking,' Hillary carried on.

'Peter, very good-looking?' Querida Phelps snorted inelegantly. 'Whoever told you that needs glasses,' she laughed, making Hillary wonder just how potent the brandy was that she was drinking, and whether or not their wild-child of a hostess might have a surprising inability to hold her liquor. 'Peter's a lovely boy, and the nephew of a great friend of mine. She helped me set the party up, as it happens. But he's hardly what you'd call an Adonis!' She laughed, then yawned hugely. 'Sorry. Pardon me. Manners of a navvy, my old nanny always said. And Peter bunked off right after midnight in order to go to a party of his own. Not that I minded; by then everyone was more or less as pissed as the proverbial newt and helping themselves anyway. Much less conventional that way, I always think.'

'Mrs Phelps…'

'Querida.'

'Sorry, Querida. Did Felix ever talk about himself much? While he was doing all this for you.' Hillary indicated the huge living area. 'Did he tell you about losing a friend, for instance, Harry Fletcher?'

'Oh, I knew he was sad about that. He came here after going to the funeral, and I could tell he was down. He even flirted with the idea of fern-patterned wallpaper so I knew something was drastically wrong with him.' She opened her eyes dramatically wide. 'I mean, ferns! Of course, he ditched the idea and apologized, and that's when he told me that he'd just been to a friend's funeral and obviously wasn't thinking straight. I offered him whisky, vermouth, gin, you name it, but he would only drink tea. But then, that was Felix,' Querida said, with a sleepy sigh.

'You know, I think I'll take a nap now.'

'Just one more thing,' Hillary said hastily. 'Did you see Felix leave the room that night?'

'No. I told that man that I didn't. The one who came when it all turned hellish, and those silly little identical twins started to scream. And I learned that Felix was gone. That man…you know…'

'DI Varney?'

'Yes. Him,' Querida said, draining her brandy glass and then frowning over towards the globe, as if she could will it to come within touching distance. She glanced down at her feet, sighed, then smiled at Jake and waved the glass at him. 'Be a darling man for me, would you, poppet?'

Jake obliged, but took the glass slowly, and walked slowly, giving Hillary plenty of time to get some more questions in before the witness became utterly blotto and incapable of answering anything coherently.

'Did Felix ever say that he was getting threatening phone calls?' Hillary continued rapidly.

'Ah now.' Querida Phelps waved a finger at Hillary, on which a gigantic Ceylon sapphire sparkled. 'Funny you should say that. I did notice once or twice that he would get phone calls and seem unhappy. He'd take his mobile into the conservatory and…oh, you should see the conservatory and what he did with it! Hanging wicker basket seats and these huge majolica jardinieres and seats that… Oh, thanks.' Querida took the refilled glass from Jake and winked at him. 'You really are gorgeous, aren't you?'

'Yes, I am.' Jake winked back. 'Now be a pet and concentrate. These phone calls. Did you hear the name of whoever it was that made Felix unhappy?' Hillary, somewhat taken aback at the smooth hijacking of her interview, nevertheless had to admire the smoothness of the man. No two ways about it, the Boy Wonder was proving useful.

'No, sorry. Like I said, when he got this funny look on his face, and I knew it was one of *those* phone calls, he always took the phone into the conservatory where I couldn't hear. And afterwards he'd be sort of quiet for a while. Maybe even angry. But he never said what it was about,' she added, waving another finger at him, 'so don't ask me. I wish I knew. You think whoever it was killed him?' She sounded genuinely distressed now.

'That's what's always been so hard to deal with, you see. I must have invited whoever it was that killed him.' And two tears ran down her cheeks. Hillary couldn't help but compare this woman's genuine if slightly drunken grief with Rebecca Morton's more self-centred tears.

'I'm really sorry, Mrs… Querida. You were obviously very fond of him.' 'I was. I never had kids. Four husbands, but none of them…. Or maybe it was me. I dunno.' She'd made good inroads into the new brandy now, and her upper-crust voice was beginning to slur. 'But if I'd had a son… Oh well. I suppose that's why I never sold up this place and left. It still has echoes of him. Besides, I do love it so. And apart from all that, I mean, where else would I go? My immediately family are all dead. Oh hell, now I'm getting maudlin.' She blinked and, with a little effort, managed to focus her lovely aquamarine eyes on Hillary once more. 'You need to get the man who killed him, you know. It isn't right that he's still walking about free. It isn't fair.' And again, two more tears rolled down her cheeks. One dripped off her chin and landed on her hand, and she looked down, obviously startled. Then a look of disgust crossed her lovely face, and she wiped her hands vigorously across her cheeks.

'Bloody tears, I ask you. At my age. Now, sure you don't want to join me in a brandy? It's a bloody good year, I can tell you.' Once again, Jake and Hillary declined, and left Querida Phelps to her beautiful home, her Napoleon brandy, and her memories.

'Think she was in love with him, guv?' Jake asked quietly as they made their way back through the beautiful grounds to the gravel forecourt and his classic car.

'Maybe. Or maybe she really did see him as a sort of surrogate son, like she said. Or a confused amalgam of both.'

'Psychology's not really my bag,' Jake said. 'But

aren't those mixed, messy feelings the kind of thing that could have led her to kill him, maybe?'

'Possibly,' Hillary said. 'And nobody gets crossed off the suspect list until we get some kind of proof, one way or the other. Although, personally, I'm not putting Querida anywherc near the top of my list.'

'No. Me either,' Jake agreed, feeling absurdly relieved. 'I rather liked the old tart.'

Hillary laughed. 'Mind you, of them all, if the murder was premeditated, she was in the best position of all to set it up. When we get back, I want you to look out the bartender's current address. We need to speak to him at some point.'

'Yes, guv.' As they drove back to HQ, Jake Barnes wondered if tonight would be a good time to see if he could find Hillary's password that would allow him to access her computer files.

EIGHT

BACK IN THE OFFICE, Zoe Turnbull looked up as Jake passed her half of the desk. Her gaze, though, went straight to Hillary.

'Don't tell me. She was something, right?' Hillary smiled. 'Read Jake's report,' she advised her unhelpfully.

She was about to turn and go back to her office to catch up on her paperwork when Zoe said urgently, 'Guv, those telephone records that you asked me to find. You know, one of his friends at the squash club said that Felix had got a few that upset him, and you wanted me to see if I could track down some possible candidates?'

Hillary regarded her with a small smile. 'Yes, I remember. I'm not quite senile yet,' she chided gently.

Zoe flushed. 'Sorry, guv. It's just that the original team *did* keep a record of all his calls and they went through them, but didn't find any that rang any warning bells. So when I went through them, I got the same result. They were all tracked down to either work, clients, friends, family or what have you. But when I just did the background check on Harry Fletcher that you wanted, I realized that some of the calls Felix got while he must have been at the sports club came from Fletcher's number. Now that might just be a coincidence, but…'

Hillary nodded, already ahead of her. 'OK, so what

have you learned of interest about Harry Fletcher? He didn't have a record for violence, I suppose?'

Zoe laughed. 'No such luck, guv. He worked for an engineering company, and didn't even have any outstanding parking tickets. He was one of Felix's friends from school, so they were the same age and went well back. Harry was a bit of a high flyer, did well and got a scholarship to Oxford—Brasenose College—but for some reason, he dropped out in his second year without getting his degree in engineering. He died nearly six months before Felix, in a fall from a roof.'

'Oh?' Hillary said, perking up.

'No, guv, I know what you're thinking, I thought the same thing,' Zoe said with a small sigh. 'It was a bit of a eureka moment, or so I thought. You know, finally something meaty to get our teeth into. But the accident was witnessed by Harry's mother, one Eileen Millbright. Apparently, she was living at the time in a small block of flats, and had the top, fourth floor. She was having trouble with her television reception or something and he went out onto the balcony to see if he could see what the problem was, and apparently climbed on the rail to unhook a caught wire or something and…well, splat.' Zoe shrugged graphically. 'The coroner's court returned a verdict of accidental death, so there was nothing iffy about it.'

'Hmm. Still, a friend dying young in such a stupid accident would account for it affecting him so badly that most of his friends remarked on it,' Hillary agreed. 'And as you said, the fact that he was in touch regularly with our murder victim doesn't necessarily mean anything. On the other hand, Neill Gorman seemed a reliable witness, and he was pretty sure that Felix got at least some phone calls that he didn't like. Even if they weren't from Harry, he might have known who they were from. Pity we can't ask him.' Hillary checked her watch. It was not yet quite four.

'I know a good medium, guv,' Zoe said, and clearly meant it.

Hillary bit back a smile and said solemnly, 'If we get desperate, I may ask you for her number and hold a séance.'

'*His* number, guv,' Zoe said. 'Don't be sexist.'

'Perish the thought.'

'Mrs Millbright lives in Kidlington, guv, just down the road, in the Moors area. Posh, eh? And only five minutes away,' she wheedled shamelessly.

Hillary smiled. 'All right, we'll go and see what she has to say. Good work,' she added.

Zoe winked at Jake as she passed, and Hillary followed the girl out, musing that she could hardly look more like a pleased puppy if she'd had a furry tail to wag.

EILEEN MILLBRIGHT LIVED in a large, semi-detached house on the northern outskirts of the town. As Zoe had indicated, it was an affluent area, as the large gardens, tree-lined avenues and the quality of the cars parked outside the residences clearly indicated.

As they walked up a narrow, flag-stoned path, bordered by gaudy marigolds, Zoe found herself wishing that she could afford something similar. Hillary, who was thinking both fondly and sadly of her old boss, Mel Mallow, who had also once lived in the area, barely gave the evidence of well-heeled suburbia a second thought. Her old boss and long-time friend had been shot down right in front of her, and it took a considerable amount of willpower to thrust the miserable memories aside and concentrate on the task in hand.

Zoe rang the doorbell, which was quickly answered by a tall, flat-chested woman with a straight-up-and-down boyish figure. She was dressed in black trousers and a grey hip-length, tunic-style top. Short-cropped, no-nonsense grey hair topped a bony face with a strong nose and chin and wide, somewhat watery blue eyes. Although both Zoe and Hillary knew her age to be nearly seventy, she looked a good decade younger, with the kind of lean, wiry build that made Hillary wonder if she was the sort who still ran marathons for charity.

'Yes, can I help you?' To go with her rather androgynous body, Eileen Millbright had a deep, mannish voice that was very pleasant on the ears. Her hands, Hillary noticed, were entirely devoid of jewellery or ornament, as was the rest of her. She wore not a scrap of make-up on her bony, distinguished features.

Hillary produced her ID and once again went through the familiar routine of explaining what CRT was all about, and why they were now on her doorstep.

'Oh yes, of course. Felix. Harry's friend. Yes, I remember. It was awful. Well, you'd better come in.' She led them through a cool and dim hall into a much brighter lounge, with French windows opening out onto a regimentally neat back garden. 'Tea?' she asked crisply. The carpet looked as if it had been recently vacuumed, and Hillary got the feeling that not a speck of dust would be allowed to settle on Eileen Millbright's furniture, and that the tea would be good quality and served piping hot.

Hillary accepted for both herself and Zoe and took

a seat in one of the chintz-covered armchairs that were grouped around a low, oak coffee table.

Mrs Millbright was back in quick time, with a neatly laid-out tea tray, and quickly dispensed the milk and sugar.

Hillary, taking her cue from the no-nonsense manner of her witness, plunged right in. 'I understand your son Harry was a good friend of Felix Olliphant, Mrs Millbright?'

'Yes, he was. They'd known each other since school.'

'First of all, let me say I'm sorry for your loss. I understand that Harry passed away a little while before the incident with Felix? Is that him?' she added, nodding towards a photograph on the mantelpiece opposite her.

'Yes, that's him,' Eileen confirmed, standing up and bringing the photograph over. It showed three men, two of them older, and one man in his mid-twenties. The younger of the trio was a good-looking boy, with a mop of dark hair and soulful dark eyes. He was dressed casually in white jeans with a pink shirt, and a knitted white sweater tied carelessly around his shoulders.

'Who are the others?' Hillary asked, to be polite.

Eileen pointed to the man on her son's left. 'That's my second husband, Harry's stepfather Jonathan, and his brother, Martin. My first husband, Harry's father, died when he was just a baby. I divorced Jonathan not long after I lost Harry. Things just fell apart between us. I read later that that often happens, when there's been a traumatic event in the family. You'd think it would bring people closer together, wouldn't you?' Eileen said, stirring her tea absently. 'But it doesn't. Anyway, about six years afterwards, I met and married my current husband. He's semiretired now, but still works one day a week.' Hillary nodded, her eyes still on the photograph. She passed it on to Zoe. 'He looks as if he was fond of his stepfather,' she mused.

'Oh yes, he was. I have no complaints about that. Jonathon did right by him.' Hillary's sensitive ear picked up a certain hesitation in her tone, and something of it must have reflected in her expression because Eileen Millbright smiled crookedly.

'Jonathon was very…conservative, shall we say, in his views. And as Harry got older, and his proclivities became more obvious, Jonathon wasn't always as understanding as myself. But then, I was his mother, and I think it's easier for us, isn't it?'

Hillary looked at Zoe, who handed the photograph back, and picked her way carefully through the older woman's cleverly weighed words, nodding gently.

'Yes, I see,' she said gently. 'Your son was gay, I take it?'

Beside her, she could almost feel Zoe's interest suddenly perk up.

'Yes, he was,' Eileen said, a certain amount of defiance in her deep voice now. Then she took a long, slow breath, and her shoulders slumped slightly. 'Alas, he was not altogether happy with the fact,' she carried on as she glanced briefly and pensively out of the French windows. 'Harry was in the closet for a while, right up until he was in his first year in Oxford. I think Felix always knew, mind, and of course didn't care. He was a very supportive friend and I was glad of that. Harry relied on him a lot for help and advice. But in what was to turn out to be his last year at university, Harry went through some sort of crisis. He wouldn't tell me what.' Eileen shrugged her bony shoulders helplessly, causing her flat chest to rise and fall beneath the grey tunic. She spread her hands graphically.

'Sometimes we mothers are the last to be told anything. I can only imagine that he embarked on some sort of tentative love affair that went badly wrong. Anyway, it resulted in him dropping out of college. Felix was a great help during that time. He got Harry a job with an engineering firm, even though he didn't have his degree. It wasn't very high-flying, obviously, but Harry seemed to settle down there, and after a couple of years he seemed to get himself into some sort of shape again. Worked his way up to a promotion, and even found himself a steady boyfriend, Rob. A nice man.' Eileen sighed. 'And then one day, he was visiting me at the flat where I used to live and I mentioned the television wasn't working. Something as simple and as stupid as that, and it can change your whole life,' Eileen said bitterly. 'Harry said he'd take a look, and I thought he meant at the television. I was in the kitchen, making tea, and I remember him calling something about the aerial, but I had no idea… I was just coming through with the tray when I saw him out of the window. He had one of his feet on the edge of the railing on the balcony, and he was leaning his top half over the roof. I can still see it quite clearly now whenever I close my eyes—a white trainer, balancing against a grey steel railing. Perhaps it didn't have the best of treads, or maybe the railing was wet, I don't know. My heart went into my mouth, as you can imagine, and I remember starting to call his name, to tell him to come on down from there. I was furious. You know, like when he was four years old and I was reprimanding him. It struck me as absurd at the time and then….'

Eileen swallowed hard and looked away. 'Well, then his foot just slipped, and he yelled out something, but it was all over in a flash. There were concrete paving stones in the courtyard beneath. If there'd been grass or better still trees or bushes to break his fall…who knows? But there wasn't and that was that,' Eileen said flatly. 'He was my only child. More tea?'

Hillary accepted another cup, and Zoe did the same. For a moment, all three women were silent. Then Hillary stirred slightly.

'We have records of Felix's phone calls, and noted that Harry used to call him a lot.' She left it deliberately vague and open-ended, with only the slight rise in her voice at the end to make it into a question.

'Yes, like I said, Harry always relied on Felix, ever since they were boys together. He always said that Felix understood him and never judged him, so I daresay he did call him a lot.' Hillary nodded. She was getting the feeling that the poor dead Harry had been a needy sort.

'I was so sad when I heard about what had happened to Felix,' Eileen Millbright added, her face turning grim. 'But bad things happen to good people all the time, don't they? You must see a lot of that in your line of work especially.'

'Yes,' Hillary agreed, just as grimly. 'Mrs Millbright, did Harry ever talk to you about Felix? Perhaps Felix confided in and relied on Harry too? Did he ever mention to you that Felix was worried about something or in any kind of trouble?'

'Not that Harry ever told me. I can assure you, had he ever done so, then I'd have contacted the police the moment I heard about Felix's death,' Eileen Millbright said firmly.

And with that, Hillary knew, she'd just met yet another dead end.

'Well, thank you for your time, Mrs Millbright. If you do think of anything Harry might have said, no matter how insignificant it might have sounded at the time—' Hillary handed over a card with her contact details at CRT '—please get in touch.'

'I certainly will, Officer,' Eileen said, rising and showing them out with that same calm dignity that she'd shown throughout.

Outside, Zoe let out her breath on a long, slow exhale. 'That poor woman.' Hillary smiled grimly. 'I doubt Mrs Millbright would approve of pity, Zoe,' she said.

'No, guv,' Zoe said quietly. 'I don't suppose she would. She's the competent, suffer-in-silence sort, isn't she?'

Hillary sighed heavily. 'OK, back to HQ. At least if nothing else, we've now nailed down where the Felix-is-gay rumours probably originated.'

'What, his being friends with Harry, you mean?' Zoe said.

'Yeah, I suppose so. I mean, Harry was openly gay, and he had that sort of look about him. You could tell, even from his photograph.'

'Right. And his mother said Felix was the one he went to when he needed help. And I got the feeling he needed it often. People would have seen them together, and if Harry was being emotional, and Felix was comforting him, they would have put two and two together and come up with five.'

'So it has nothing to do with his death then,' Zoe said, getting behind the wheel of her Mini. 'That Felix might have been gay, I mean.'

'It doesn't look like it, does it?' Hillary said practically, doing up her seatbelt. 'I think it's clear now that he never was gay, so we can rule out any connection with either a hate crime or a gay-lover scenario.'

'Right. Because everyone knows that old chestnut about gays being more vicious when crossed in love than anyone else, right?' Zoe said lightly.

'There's an element of homophobia everywhere, even now,' Hillary agreed, equally lightly. 'And that includes institutions such as the police force. I don't like it but I'd be a fool if I didn't acknowledge that it still exists.' As Zoe reached forward and turned on the ignition, Hillary continued gently. 'Despite the strides that gay groups are making, if I were a young officer starting out today, especially being a woman, I would think very carefully about just how militant and in-your-face I'd want to be about it. At least until I'd got myself firmly established, had a good group of friends around me, and had gained the rank of sergeant,' she added.

Zoe slowly put her car into gear. 'So in your view there's no place for gays in the Thames Valley?' she asked tightly.

'That's not what I said. And personally, I don't give a monkey nut what an officer's sexual orientation is,' Hillary said.

'If someone's good at the job and willing to do it well, that's all the criteria I need. But I'm not the top brass. Nor am I one of the lads, already feeling slightly miffed that some bit of skirt has managed to be cleverer than I am, work harder than I have, and been awarded a promotion that I think, by rights, should have been mine.' Zoe snorted. 'Who cares what those sort of wankers think?'

'All I'm saying is… I'd be careful to pick my battles. And be sure I could win them, without too much cost to myself.' Zoe blinked hard for a moment, then slowly nodded, indicated and pulled out. 'Interesting. Thanks, guv.' In the passenger seat, Hillary said nothing. They were driving past the road down which her old friend Sergeant Janine Tyler had once lived, and she was once again back in the car park at HQ, with the sound of a sniper's bullet echoing in her memory.

Grimly, she shrugged the sound away and said abruptly, 'Zoe, turn right at the main road. You can drop me off in Thrupp. It's home time anyway, and Steven can drive me in in the morning.'

'Guv.'

Zoe knew her boss lived on a narrowboat (and just how cool was that?) and that she kept it moored in the tiny hamlet, right on Kidlington's doorstep. She wondered what Sexy Steven made of it, and bit back a giggle at the thought of the tall, elegant super on a cramped narrowboat.

Still, it obviously worked for them, so who was she to knock it?

STEVEN CRAYLE, IN FACT, liked staying on the narrowboat well enough. He found the confined space comforting rather than oppressive, and since he was sharing it in such close quarters with Hillary, the enforced intimacy was all the more appealing. Consequently, as he drove to Thrupp later that evening, he was feeling a mixture of pleasurable anticipation at the thought of spending the night with Hillary, along with a low-level unease at the thought of telling her that he'd reached a decision concerning Donleavy's job offer.

She was just putting the finishing touches to a salad as he walked through to the narrow kitchen/dining area, and the aroma of warming garlic bread filled the air.

'Hello. You're home at a reasonable time for a change,' Hillary said lightly, ignoring the way her spirits lifted at the sight of him, and laying the table in her usual haphazard dash.

'Budget meeting finish on time for once?' His lips twisted wryly. 'Wonders will never cease. I think the majority of them must have had golf matches that they needed to get to.'

She watched him as he shrugged out of his jacket, removed his tie, and unsnapped his gold and onyx cufflinks, leaving them carelessly on top of the tiny fridge. How to go from prim and proper executive to hunky casual stud in two seconds flat, Hillary mused. She smiled and poured out a glass of his preferred white wine, then handed it over.

'Thanks, sweetheart. By the way, I've made an appointment to see Donleavy tomorrow.' Steven was a firm believer in getting baggage out of the way first. He took a sip, and sighed.

'Lovely.' Chilled just how he liked it. He sat down in one of the tiny space's two comfortable chairs and slipped off his shoes. He wriggled his toes, then leaned back, the lines of his face easing as he looked at her.

Hillary fought back the urge to go and sit in his lap and start nibbling on his earlobes, and instead poured herself a glass of wine and leaned back against a tiny cupboard. 'Oh? This is about the move to Oxford?' she said casually.

'Yes.'

'You're going, of course?'

'Yes.' Hillary nodded. Steven watched her closely. 'But I don't suppose I'll be leaving CRT in any great hurry. Donleavy and the other top brass will want a long recruiting period. I don't know whether they'll want to promote in-house or look outside for someone. Either way, I'll be staying on for a while even after they've found someone, just to show them the ropes. You'll still be working for me for a few months yet.'

'Good.' Steven nodded. Yes, he thought she'd take it like this. Wouldn't give an inch. Wouldn't show that she was in any way worried or concerned. Wouldn't admit to any damn chink in her armour.

'So, what's for dinner?' he asked brightly.

'Lasagne. Don't get excited—Sainsbury's had more to do with it than I did.'

Steven smiled. 'Ah yes. But what's for dessert, that's what I really want to know?'

Hillary's lips twitched. 'Oh, I'll think of something.' She turned away from him to check the progress of the pre-packaged meal, a tight feeling in her chest. No matter what he said, before the year was out, Steven Crayle's presence in her life would be all but minimal. And they both knew it.

Why didn't he just come out with it now and say that they might as well call it a day? They both knew that once they weren't seeing each other professionally every day then nights like this would become rarer and rarer. Eventually, they'd be down to seeing each other every other weekend for a quick physical fumble, until even that no longer appealed.

Which was fine, after all, she reasoned. Relationships came and relationships went—that just seemed to be the nature of the modern beast. It had been good while it lasted, and now it was adios and hasta la vista, baby.

And let's face it, she thought, catching a warped reflection of herself on the small sink's corrugated steel draining board, he was a good few years younger than herself, and gorgeous and sexy as hell. And clearly his professional star was rising as well. What had she expected? To be with him forever? All stars and roses and happily ever after? She was fifty-one, not some naïve 20-year-old.

Best just to enjoy it whilst it lasted. And to hell with the tight hard knot that was forming in her chest cavity and seemed intent on making her want to scream.

It wasn't as if it was the first time a relationship had gone belly up on her. She could do this standing on her head, right?

'Poached pears and elderflower ice cream OK for dessert?' she asked brightly.

She then began to feel slightly sick. Which was her own damn fault, of course.

She really should have known better than to eat canteen food.

'Sounds good,' Steven said softly. Then, 'Hillary, come here and let me kiss you.'

JAKE BARNES GLANCED at the white plastic clock on the office wall. It was nearly six, and only Jimmy Jessop remained in the office. But Jake could wait him out.

He was just putting the finishing touches to his report on the Querida Phelps interview when Jimmy called goodnight on his way out the door.

Jake waited ten minutes then printed off the file, put it in the murder book and slipped into his jacket. At the door, he glanced up and down the narrow, twisting corridors and listened.

Nothing, as he'd expected.

He knew that the main bulk of the CRT offices, which contained the computer geeks, forensics specialists and paper crunchers, kept strict office hours. Since overtime was now almost unheard of, he wasn't surprised by the almost total silence that greeted him.

He slipped smoothly from the office and down and around the next corner, coming to rest outside an anonymous door. He wondered why Hillary Greene never had her name put on it, and couldn't help but speculate that it was because she no longer had a rank to put in front of it.

After researching the woman who would be his day-to-day working boss, he'd found himself dissatisfied with the official reason for her retirement. The woman had a record that was literally second to none, and must have worked like a demon to maintain it. She must have been proud of what she'd achieved, and fiercely ambitious in the first place to rise so high and be so respected. Her reputation, even now, was fearsome and near-legendary in the Big House. And in his experience, people like that didn't just throw in the towel early. Just because she'd put in the years and earned the pension didn't necessarily mean that she *had* to take early retirement.

He was sure that there was some other story behind her decision to leave. Maybe something to do with the Janine Mallow incident. Still, finding the skeletons in Hillary Greene's cupboards was not his top priority, and so he shrugged and tried the door. It was, as he'd expected, locked.

But that was not a problem. A man with nearly unlimited means such as himself could easily afford the most illegal of gadgets, and within a minute or two he was pushing open the door and slipping inside. Not wanting to get caught out, he left the door slightly ajar so that he could hear anyone coming, just in case there was still someone out and about down here in the depths.

He grimaced at the tiny, windowless space. He'd heard Hillary mock-complain that her office had once been a stationery cupboard but he'd thought she'd been either joking or exaggerating. Now he could see that she hadn't been doing either. He could even see the screw-marks in the walls where the shelves had once been, which had no doubt held paper and envelopes.

Surely a woman of her previous standing and record could have been given a better office? And he'd thought that having to share the other cramped office with three others was the pits. In the commercial sector, nobody would have put up with this working environment.

Still, he thought with a sudden philosophical grin, it made it easier to search.

He sat down in the single chair behind the tiny desk and booted up Hillary's computer. He wasn't anticipating too many problems figuring out her password, and began to run a programme that he'd previously set up that used a combination of possible numbers—her date of birth, National Insurance digits, old telephone numbers, house addresses, etc. Plus names and words that might be relevant to her life.

While that was running, he began to search her desk. Most people, especially those who chose to use a random set of letters and figures for their password, as he suspected someone as smart as Hillary would choose to do, had trouble remembering it, and wrote it down somewhere to remind themselves.

But there was nothing taped beneath her desk or in the drawers, or under the console itself, or underneath the mouse mat. He watched the programme run, to no avail, and reluctantly shut it down.

He sighed.

The hard way it was then.

As he began to type quickly and expertly at her console, Jimmy Jessop, holding his shoes in his hand and standing barefoot outside the door, peered through the crack created by the hinges and watched thoughtfully.

He nodded once, then slowly tiptoed away, only pausing to put his shoes back on once he was almost at the foot of the stairs leading out.

THE NEXT MORNING, Hillary was in early. Even so, Zoe Turnbull was ahead of her, and as she walked past the communal office, the goth called out a cheerful hello in greeting. She was reading Jake's report on Querida Phelps, and wishing that she'd seen the beautiful converted mill house for herself.

Hillary went to her office, hung up her lightweight jacket on the back of the door and walked to her desk.

And stopped dead.

The chair behind her desk, a standard black swivel chair, was facing slightly to the right. And her last action every night, in a purely habitual reflex, was to tuck it straight and hard beneath the knee-hole in her desk.

Slowly she sat down and looked around. The items on top of her desk were exactly as she'd left them, as was the order of her paperwork in her in and out trays.

She leaned slowly back in her chair and booted up her computer. As she did so, there came a soft knock on her door and she looked up to see Jimmy Jessop in the doorway.

'Jimmy, some sod's been in here,' she said at once.

Jimmy grinned, not at all surprised by her perspicacity. 'Yup, I know. Good job you asked me to keep an eye on him.'

'The Boy Wonder?'

'Last night, he was too careful to be the last one to leave. Rang the old alarm bells in here.' He tapped his forehead.

'What was he after?'

'Not sure, guv, but I think he wanted your password.'

'Makes sense. None of my paperwork on the current case seemed to be touched. Did he get it?'

'Can't say, guv. I didn't want him catching me watching him. But he's a whizz on IT and all that, isn't he? So I expect that he did. Eventually.'

Hillary sighed and pushed the hair back off her forehead. To Jimmy she looked tired, as if she hadn't slept well. 'So, for some reason the Boy Wonder wants deeper access to the police database.' She knew that, as a civilian and a newbie, none of the others, including Jimmy, had any high-level access to sensitive records.

She herself had more, due to her past rank, and Donleavy's backing. But even she was still, technically, a civilian, and her clearance didn't go exactly sky-high, as Barnes must have guessed. So what good would having that limited access do him?

'You going to call him on it, guv?' Jimmy asked.

Hillary thought about it, then shook her head. 'No. Not yet.'

'You could get him kicked off the team, easy as,' Jimmy pointed out.

'Not until I know what he's after,' Hillary said stubbornly.

'That might come back to bite you if he pulls something major off,' Jimmy warned her, not that he was second-guessing her or even thought that she was playing it wrong. He'd come to know her too well to doubt either her gut feeling or her thought processes.

'What, you think he's out to rip off our evidence lockers or gain info so he can start up a blackmailing ring?' Hillary said with a small smile. 'You seem to forget, he's already got more money than he can spend. I might be wrong, of course, but I don't think he's a criminal mastermind out to rip us off.'

Jimmy grinned. 'So whatever it is he's after…' He shrugged.

'Dunno. Something personal, most likely? A private vendetta.' Hillary nodded. 'Seems our best bet, yes. And whatever it is, I want to know about it. So we'll just have to play along, act dumb and keep an eye out. In the meantime, we can assume that whatever I have access to he now has access to.'

Jimmy nodded. 'Even so, I don't like it, guv. You're going to tell the super, right? Cover your arse?'

Hillary smiled bleakly. 'Soon it won't be the super's headache either, Jimmy. He's leaving us.'

She told him about the transfer and watched his face fall. 'So we've got to break in a new super, as well as try and figure out what the Boy Wonder is after? Great.'

Hillary smiled grimly. 'Well, you can always retire, Jimmy. Again.'

Jimmy Jessop grunted. 'Tried that once, guv. Didn't like it.'

'Ditto,' Hillary said drolly. 'And speaking of getting on with work....' She got up and followed the old man back to the office. Now both Sam and Jake Barnes were in but it was to Zoe that Hillary turned.

'Greer Ryanson. Where does Olligree Interiors hang out nowadays?'

'Oxford, guv.'

'Right. It's about time we talked to Felix's business partner, don't you think?'

Zoe didn't need asking twice. 'Right, guv.'

'Jake, you too. I want a successful businessman's eye view on how our murder victim's company is doing nowadays.'

'Guv.'

NINE

GREER RYANSON HAD elected to keep the company name after losing her partner, probably because by then it had earned such a good reputation for itself that she didn't want to advertise the fact that the Olli part of the firm was no longer extant.

Presumably she had had to take on a new partner, though, and as Zoe drove towards the city, she had Jake Barnes do his stuff and fill her in on who that was.

Within a few minutes of opening up the laptop he took everywhere with him, he came back with the news that Greer Ryanson's husband, Guy, had taken over. He had, of course, known all about that from doing his financial research but it made him feel better to have the digital proof of it in his hands.

'It all seems above board, guv. He was an advertising executive in some Saatchi and Saatchi wannabe firm in High Wycombe that went belly up not long after Felix was killed. He's been written in all nice and legal, and has been claiming a salary since. Nothing too extravagant. But from the looks of it, all of Felix's shares stayed with her.'

'So she's kept all the power for herself?'

'Looks like it, guv.' Which made Hillary wonder whether bringing in her spouse had been a case of simple expediency, or whether Greer Ryanson, on finding herself in sole charge of the enterprise, had simply not wanted to give up her hold on the reins of power to anyone else. No doubt an unemployed hubby would be more easily manipulated than an outsider.

The office was located in the Osney Mead area of Oxford, which had probably suffered some flooding a few years back, when a particularly soggy summer had rendered large parts of the city underwater. There was no sign of that now, however, as they parked up outside a rather elegant, converted Edwardian house with large sash windows. Olligree Interiors had the entire top floor to themselves. On the bottom floor was a staffing agency, and a firm of quantity surveyors, but as they climbed the stairs and emerged into the large, initial reception room, she could see that someone had made sure that the décor now represented a good advertisement for their wares.

Light and spacious, in neutral earth tones that were pleasing on the eye, several large ferns competed for attention with a single, stylish piece of modern art on the far wall. Behind an art-deco-inspired desk, an ash-blonde in her early fifties, dressed in an impeccably tailored power-suit of powder blue, rose and smiled at them, with a question in her eye. The question clearly had something to do with them not having an appointment.

Hillary, suppressing the urge to sigh impatiently, reached for her ID, and went into her usual spiel. As she did so, the look on the receptionist's face went from politely puzzled to something far more human.

'This is about poor Felix, isn't it?' she said, when Hillary had finished and asked if Mrs Ryanson and/or her husband would be free for an interview.

'Yes. You knew him? You were working here when

he died?' Hillary asked, never loathe to talk with someone who knew the victim.

'Oh yes. I'm Joyce Weatherspoon. I was here nearly from the beginning, when the firm first started. It was Felix who got me this job, bless him. I was a neighbour of his parents, and when my husband left me when my youngest was only ten, he recommended me. He was such a thoughtful, nice man. It's not fair, what happened to him.' Hillary nodded. So far she hadn't yet been able to find a witness who had a bad word to say for their murder victim, and she wasn't yet so cynical that she simply couldn't believe that everyone had been fooled. In fact, she could see no good reason to suppose that Felix Olliphant had been anything other than a good and decent human being.

And yet somebody, somewhere, had wanted him dead. Unless it was a case of mistaken identity? He had been attending a costume party, after all. But even as she thought it, she dismissed it. He had not been wearing any kind of a face mask that night, his costume not calling for one.

'I don't suppose you know of anyone who might have wanted to do him harm?' she asked quietly.

'Felix? Oh no. No one would want to hurt Felix,' the receptionist said with clearly misplaced confidence, given the circumstances.

'I understand that Olligree was doing well at the time of his death?' Hillary asked smoothly.

'Oh yes. The company's always been strong. Well, perhaps lately things have fallen off a little. In this economy, with money tight for nearly everybody, even the well-heeled aren't spending like they used to. But I'm sure we'll ride it out. But back in Felix's day, oh yes, we were very successful. Felix was such a wonderful designer and decorator, you see. So is Mrs Ryanson, of course,' Joyce Weatherspoon added quickly, but rather perfunctorily, Hillary thought.

Nor did Hillary miss how it was 'Felix' but his partner, even now, was 'Mrs Ryanson'.

'Did he get on well with Greer Ryanson?' Hillary asked next, careful to keep her voice strictly casual.

'Oh yes. Felix got on well with everyone.' Joyce's face finally broke into a small smile. 'Not everyone gets on with Mrs Ryanson, mind, but she's as nice as pie with the clients, which is what matters, isn't it? And Felix always said that she was good at networking. So with Felix's flair, and her contacts, they made a good team.'

'And how are things now?'

'Well, perhaps Olligree Interiors is more known for being a safe pair of hands rather than being…well, innovative or original. That was one of Felix's strengths as a designer. But there's a market for safe but up-to-the-minute, and Mrs Ryanson and her husband are usually good at predicting the next big trend. It keeps us ahead of most of our main rivals.'

Hillary nodded. 'So you never heard any arguments between Felix and Greer Ryanson?'

'Oh no.'

'And did Mrs Ryanson have any money worries that you know about? Perhaps that Felix wasn't aware of, even?'

But that was obviously going a step too far because Joyce Weatherspoon's face closed down to a polite smile, and Hillary could feel the woman withdraw back into her polite shell. 'I'm sure I couldn't say. I only answer the telephone, make the bookings, and fetch and carry. I have nothing to do with the financial side of matters. Mrs Ryanson saw to all that. So I'll just buzz through and see if she's available, shall I?'

Hillary smiled gently. 'Yes. You do that.' Greer Ryanson, it seemed, was available, for after a moment's silence when Joyce had announced the presence of the police, they all heard her instruct the receptionist to show them straight in.

If the woman was surprised to see a deputation of three arrive in her office, nothing on her face showed it.

According to the files, Greer Ryanson had been thirty-nine at the time of her business partner's death, which now put her in the near mid-fifties. But it would have been hard to guess at her age without those pointers. She was still very slim, with a chic jet-black geometric-shaped haircut. She had big, near-black eyes, and her face was carefully made up to look as if she was wearing no make-up at all. She had probably had a nip and tuck in the recent past. She was wearing a long, loose-fitting white dress of a deceptively simple and no doubt breathtakingly expensive cut, and a string of amber beads that reached nearly to her waist.

Hillary noticed that she wasn't wearing a wedding ring, but that fact didn't surprise her. She rather thought she knew who wore the trousers in the Ryanson relationship.

'Police, Joyce said?' Greer Ryanson asked coolly, as she rose from behind a large green marble-topped desk. On the desk there was no computer or paperwork of any kind, only a large green old-fashioned angle-poise lamp, and a vase of flowers containing a riot of sweet-smelling, multi-coloured freesias.

Très chic, Hillary mused.

In fact, everything in the room was très chic, from the plain white walls, steel-grey deep-pile carpeting, and the green and turquoise accents, via the curtains, chair covers and the series of Arts and Crafts framed mirrors lining the walls, reflecting the already bright daylight.

'Yes. We're taking another look at the murder of Felix Olliphant,' Hillary said, with deliberate bluntness.

'Oh. Right,' Greer said, a shade blankly. Then added somewhat stiffly, 'Please sit down.' Her eyes went to Zoe and took in the goth hair (blue-tipped today) and her black leather bustier over what looked like a cobweb-draped multi-layered black skirt and chunky black granny boots, and dismissed her totally.

Her gaze lingered longer on Jake Barnes, and there was no doubt in anyone's mind that she liked what she saw. Young, fit, good-looking and dressed in expensive designer-labelled gear from top to bottom, what was there not to like, Hillary mused, feeling, for some reason, suddenly vastly entertained.

'We were hoping you might have some insights for us,' Hillary began, as she and the others drew up several jade-green painted chairs and sat down in front of Greer's impressive desk.

'I'm sorry, but I have no idea who killed Felix. Or why. I didn't understand it then, and I don't now. Coffee?' she offered briskly.

'Please.' Greer leaned forward and spoke into the intercom, ordering coffee for four.

'From what I've been able to learn, Felix was very greatly liked and admired by nearly everyone who knew him,' Hillary began neutrally. 'Tell me, how did you and he come to meet and form Olligree Interiors?'

'My best friend graduated from the same uni at the same time as him. We met at one of her parties. We found that we both wanted to do interior design, but didn't want to work for a boss or a big conglomeration that was only interested in making cash. Oh, we wanted to earn money, don't get me wrong,' Greer laughed, a tight, hard sound that sat oddly with her elegant image, 'but we wanted to do it on our own terms. Anyway, we got to talking and realized that we were chasing the same goal, but had different strengths and ideas, and decided to see if we could make a go of it together. I had some capital to put into it—from my parents—and Felix had some too—from the same source, I expect. And so we gave it a go. We formed the company name from a mix of our names, and decided to give it six months and see.' Greer paused for a moment, and frowned at a freesia that had dared to drop one of its petals onto the marble-topped desk. Hillary could practically hear her debating whether or not to pick it up and drop it in a wastebin or leave it.

She decided to leave it.

'I don't think, to be perfectly honest, we ever really thought it would become as successful as it did,' she carried on smoothly.

'But we seemed to complement each other wonderfully. I was very good at organization, overseeing workmen, that kind of thing. And Felix was good at understanding exactly what it was the clients wanted, and finding a way to make their vision come true.' Greer paused for a breath, and then laughed again—that same hard, tight, unattractive sound. 'Not that that was always easy. The ideas some of our clients had—well!' She threw up her hands in despair. They were well-manicured hands, Hillary noticed, with clear polish on the nails.

At that point, Joyce came in with a coffee tray, left it on the table with a brief, all-encompassing smile, and promptly left. Hillary poured for herself and the other two members of her team, leaving Greer to see to her own.

The other woman, though, didn't seem interested in a caffeine fix, for she made no move towards the tray, and carried on talking instead. 'After a while, our reputation grew, and more and more people came to us. And Felix gradually got to do more and more of the stuff that *he* wanted to do, since more and more people trusted him and gave him carte blanche. And I kept the cash flow going, did the PR, made sure our name spread, and before long, we were riding high.' She turned and glanced out of the window, where anonymous traffic flowed beyond the windows. 'I never thought it would end,' she said flatly, sounding, even now, faintly aggrieved. 'It shouldn't have ended. Not like it did.' Her lean, not-quite-attractive face suddenly clouded and she looked positively angry. 'Whoever killed Felix should rot in hell.'

It was not the first time someone had said that to her during the course of the investigation. But in Greer Ryanson's case, Hillary thought that the sentiment probably had more to do with the fact that she was angry that someone had killed her goose that had been laying the golden eggs for her rather than out of any sense of empathy. Or justice.

'You were at the party that night, yes?' Hillary brought things back on track.

'Yes. Querida had invited both me and Felix—and

our plus ones, of course. I brought my husband, and Felix came with that vapid woman he was seeing at the time. I can't remember her name.'

No, I don't suppose you can, Hillary mused. 'Did you see him drinking heavily that night?'

'Felix? The original goody-two-shoes? Good grief, no. I was as surprised as I'd ever been in my life when it was read out in the coroner's court that he'd been drunk. After that awful car crash, I never knew Felix to have more than a single glass of wine at most. Not that he was exactly a boozer before then, either.'

'Did you see him arguing with anyone?'

'Felix wasn't the arguing sort.'

'I understand that you had an insurance policy that paid out in the event of Felix's death?' Hillary threw in casually, seeing that questioning the likes of Greer Ryanson on what she had seen or heard at the party would be virtually pointless. If the woman had seen anything significant, she was obviously not going to say so at this late date.

Greer flushed slightly. 'That was strictly standard business practice, I can assure you. If I had died, then Felix would have got the payout, and my share of the company. It was all completely above board, and overseen by our solicitors.'

'Yes, I'm sure. But the money must have come in handy?' Hillary persisted.

Greer gave the woman opposite her a long cool look of dislike. 'I would have preferred Felix alive and well and earning good money for us. We were doing well, with every prospect of doing better. I can assure you, Felix was worth far more to me alive than dead. I'm sorry if that sounds heartless, but it's also undoubtedly true. Besides, I liked Felix. He was a friend, and I don't really have many of those.' No kidding, Zoe Turnbull thought, and had to bite her tongue to stop herself from saying so out loud. Beside her, she could sense Jake Barnes smiling.

'Tell me what you remember about that night.' Hillary tried a more open-ended approach to finding out what this woman might know, but wasn't holding out much hope.

As she'd expected, Greer sighed heavily. 'I'm sure I went through all this with that man Varney.'

'I'm sure you did, Mrs Ryanson. But please indulge me.'

'Well, Felix was already there when we arrived. I saw him dancing with Querida—she was dressed as Lady Godiva of all things! Some women have no… never mind. Of course, it was a fabulous party—that type of big country house just lends itself to that sort of thing. Some of the costumes were really theatrical-quality stuff. And the food was good, and the drinks were varied, as you might expect from someone like Querida. You could order anything from some of that ghastly alco-pop stuff to vintage champagne. As time went on, people got louder and more drunk, as you'd expect, and then midnight came and we had the countdown. I think the fox who was tending the bar left around about then because everyone started helping themselves, which is typical of that sort of party. The hostess certainly didn't care about being conventional! And then, at some point, that pair of young identical twins came running in, all hysterical, and we realized that some sort of crisis had occurred.' Greer's lips thinned ominously. 'Of course, we had no way of knowing then that it concerned Felix.

Then the rumours started to circulate that someone was dead, and then the police came, and an ambulance. We all had to give our name and details. I still didn't know for ages that it was Felix who was dead. Or that he'd actually been murdered. I think we were all thinking maybe one of the older guests had had a heart attack, or one of the young silly set had taken some bad ecstasy or something like that. You hear about that sort of thing all of the time, don't you? But no, it was Felix, and he'd definitely been murdered. It was all just so...unbelievable.' She spread her hands in a helpless gesture.

Hillary sighed. 'Yes. And you saw nobody who was acting oddly that night?'

'No. Well, to be honest, we didn't know that many people there. Querida Phelps knew all sorts of people, from the titled aristocracy down to, well, near down and outs, it almost seemed. One man there I swear had been living on the streets! But that was what she was like. Duke or pauper, if she liked you, you were in. She was the arty type, you know? I think she used to do a bit of modelling in the late sixties, and never got over being a sort of hippy. Comes from a fabulously rich family and all that. Well, one way or another, we didn't really socialize in the same bracket, as it were. So how could I tell who might have been acting "oddly", as you put it?'

Hillary ignored the attempt at one-upmanship, and kept on track. 'So Felix didn't know anyone there either?'

'No, I don't think so. He certainly didn't act as if he did. That didn't mean that he wasn't being friendly though, and getting on with people. But then he was the gregarious sort.'

'You must have met up and talked to him a bit. He

never mentioned anyone there coming on to him, or maybe acting weird around him? Pressing drinks on him maybe?'

'No. Nothing like that. And the only one that I saw getting him drinks was that limpet of a girlfriend of his. And then, the few times I noticed, it was only fruit juice—Felix's usual tipple.'

'Right.' Hillary sighed. 'Well, thank you, Mrs Ryanson. We may have to get in touch with your husband at some point, just in case he can shed any light on things.' Greer Ryanson's delicately arched, plucked dark eyebrow rose sharply to show just how unlikely she thought that scenario might turn out to be.

BACK IN THE CAR, her two newest team members were unusually silent, which gave Hillary plenty of time to think. Zoe didn't seem to find it difficult to handle Puff, so she let the goth drive while she sat in the passenger seat, watching Oxford's remote and beautiful colleges pass by the window.

She did a quick mental review of their progress so far, and had to conclude that they'd learned nothing new. Or so it seemed. Yet somewhere at the back of her mind, Hillary felt a nagging little worry that someone, somewhere, might have said something significant. Nothing mind-blowingly obvious. But important. And she rather thought that it might have been Querida Phelps. But try as she might, Hillary couldn't bring it to the forefront of her mind.

She sighed, and decided not to push it. With a bit of luck, if she ignored it, her subconscious would chew it over and eventually spit out whatever it was.

As Zoe negotiated the Banbury Road roundabout,

Hillary continued to let her brain mull over the case. The business about Harry Fletcher had cleared up the Felix-might-be-gay rumours, and also solved the problem of the worrisome phone calls and why his friend's death had upset him so much. Which might be satisfying to know, but didn't help them get any closer to solving Felix Olliphant's murder.

Everyone's memories of the party seemed to tally. Everyone said that Felix was not a drinker, and yet he'd drunk well that night. Which reminded her—she needed to talk to the good-looking bartender at some point in the near future. If someone had been slipping alcohol into Felix's fruit juices then a bartender was an ideal candidate—a fact that DI Varney had not overlooked.

But the fact was, the foxy Mr Peter Goodman, who'd tended the bar that night, had had no connection with their murder victim at all. 'Didn't know him from Adam' was how he'd put it to Varney, and the original SIO had not been able to find any evidence to contradict that. So why would a man with no criminal record, who'd been asked to serve drinks at a fancy New Year Eve's bash, have been spiking the drinks of a complete stranger?

Unless someone had paid him to?

Hillary knew from Varney's notes that Goodman had left the party shortly after a quarter past midnight, to go on to a party that one of his own friends had been throwing, and he had left with Querida Phelps's knowledge and blessing. Why shouldn't the young man have had a good time, along with everyone else, had been her attitude. Besides, by then, midnight had come and gone, and her guests (those that were still upright and capable) were perfectly happy to pour their own drinks.

This had meant that Varney had had to track down Goodman and question him the next day, but the costume he'd been wearing that night had shown no traces of the victim's blood, or any DNA evidence that put him anywhere near the bedroom where Felix Olliphant had been killed.

So that had led to another dead end. But still, Hillary needed to follow it up herself, if for no other reason than to tick it off her to-do list.

What else? Well, Hillary had saved till last the questioning of the widow of William Brandt, DI Varney's favourite suspect. Mostly because, with Brandt already deceased, there was no hurry to get around to that aspect of the case. If it turned out that Brandt had killed Felix, what exactly could they do about it? Unless Zoe wanted to throw a séance so that they could posthumously arrest him.

So what *did* they have? Hillary mused restlessly.

A very nice man, that everybody liked, and yet somebody had wanted dead.

A man who everybody said didn't drink, but who'd been drunk as a skunk when he died.

A man who felt guilt about a dead child in a road traffic accident that wasn't his fault.

A man who'd mourned the loss of a gay friend in a tragic accident.

A successful businessman, with a rather cold-hearted business partner who nevertheless had no reason to want him dead.

A somewhat needy girlfriend, who had gone on to marry someone else and successfully start a family.

And something significant that Querida Phelps might have said, although what that was, who the hell knew?

'Where do we look next, guv?' Zoe asked, as she pulled into the car park back at HQ.

Hillary pulled herself from her blue funk and took a deep breath. 'Well, you have a report to write and add to the murder book, and I need to check in with Steven. After lunch, we need to speak to the widow of William Brandt, so look out her particulars, will you? Oh, and find out where our foxy bartender hangs out nowadays as well. We'll be wanting a word with him.'

'Right, guv. And you will take me along to see the fox, won't you? I do like good-looking men.'

Zoe grinned. 'Jake can have the stuffy widow.'

'Now there's a surprise,' Jake Barnes drawled from the back seat. 'And thanks a lot.'

Hillary, wondering if she'd read Zoe Turnbull wrong after all, said that she'd think about it, and the three of them separated at the bottom of the stairs.

Steven looked up at the knock on his door, then smiled as the door opened and Hillary walked in. Today, she was wearing a wheat-coloured two-piece jacket and skirt combo, with a deep chestnut-coloured blouse that matched the colour of her hair and complemented her sherry-coloured eyes.

He'd been up early that morning and had left her sleeping. Now, vivid memories of their energetic night spent pressed close together in her tiny bed flashed through his mind, then flashed out again, as she sat in the chair facing him and began to bring him crisply up to date on her latest case. Quickly he turned his mind to the business at hand.

When she'd finished, he leaned back in his chair with

two fingers forming a steeple together under his chin, and a small frown tugging his dark brows together.

'So, getting nowhere fast then?' he summed up succinctly.

Hillary wrinkled her nose at him. 'So far. And I wouldn't say exactly nowhere. We've cleared up a few loose ends that Varney never bothered with. The trouble is, they didn't really lead us anywhere.'

'No. I thought when I looked through it that it was a bit of a stinker,' Steven admitted with a cheeky grin. 'And I said to myself, if anybody can make anything out of it, then it was you.'

Hillary smiled grimly. So he was down to grovelling, was he? Paying her compliments as a sweetener? Why didn't he just come out and say that he was ready to call it quits on their affair? He must know she was half expecting it. It wasn't as if she wasn't capable of reading the bloody writing on the wall.

'But nobody expects you to work miracles with every cold case that passes your desk. If you want, you can write it up and toss it back into the pile,' he offered magnanimously.

'Not just yet,' Hillary said, feeling her hackles rising. 'I still have other witnesses to see.'

'OK, as you like,' he agreed amiably. Was it his imagination or was she trying to pick a fight? 'Anything else?' he asked mildly.

Hillary sighed. 'I need to discuss the team. As you know, Sam will be starting his last year at uni in September, and he needs to concentrate on getting good exam results. That's my idea, by the way, not his. I imagine he would want to keep on working in his spare time, but it's just not on. I'm going to have a chat with him about it. He's enjoyed himself here, and I think it's almost certain that he's going to apply to join up when he graduates. So I'm going to tell him that I'm going to write him a glowing recommendation, providing he does well in his finals. The lad's got a good head on his shoulders and he's made of the right stuff. He's learnt a lot since he's been here, and toughened up enough to make me hopeful that he'll last the course.'

Steven nodded. 'OK. And if he comes to the interview panel with a recommendation from you, no recruitment officer is going to turn him down. Anyone you sponsor is someone they're going to want on our side.'

Hillary waved the compliment away with the grimace it deserved, and Steven frowned. 'Come on, I mean it. You must know how high your star's in the ascendant round here,' he pressed.

Hillary again waved the compliment away, but it made her wonder. Did he resent, even now, her so-called popularity with the top brass and the rank and file alike? Was he, maybe even unknowingly, just a little bit jealous of her? Had she somehow turned herself into a rival for him? Is that why he was leaving her?

She suddenly heard the pathetic, self-pitying tone in the way her thoughts were going, and cut off the whinging instantly. The last thing she was going to do was make a scene over this. She didn't do messy, emotional break-ups. When the time came, and he finally worked up the nerve to tell her like a man that he was dumping her, she'd just take it on the chin and send him on his way with a goodbye drink at the local. What the hell else could she do?

Her hands for some reason began to feel cold, and she resisted the urge to rub them together for warmth.

'Jimmy is good to go for another few years yet,' she carried on, 'so there's no change there.'

'You just want to keep him on as your wingman,' Steven said with a grin. 'Go on, admit it, he's your enabler and enforcer all rolled into one.'

'Damn right!'

'He's Tom to your Jerry, Bodie to your Doyle, Dr Watson to your Sherlock Holmes…'

'Laurel to my Hardy more like,' Hillary corrected, grinning back. 'Now, Zoe Turnbull.' She scratched her chin, frowning at the coldness of her fingers. Damn it, was she coming down with a summer cold? That was just what she needed. 'I think she's probably gay.' And then she thought about the goth's seemingly genuinely statement that she liked good-looking men, and amended slowly, 'Or maybe bi-sexual would be a better guess.'

Steven blinked, thought about it for a moment, and then shrugged. 'Not a problem, surely?'

'Not for me, no,' Hillary said. 'Her private life's none of my business. And naturally, my first reaction would be to say to her, fine, no problem, stick two fingers up to the establishment if you want and go for it.' Then she sighed heavily. 'But, of course, better sense prevails. We both know that even now she'd take some flak if it became common knowledge. Not that we don't need the pioneers to push the boundaries and drag all the troglodytes screaming into the modern world. But we both know it's not that easy. In the end I sort of hinted that, if I were her, I'd put some time in, make some friends and get a bit of rank behind me before sticking my head above the parapet for them to start taking pot shots at.' Steven listened, nodding, and understanding immediately where she was coming from. But would a newbie like Zoe?

'Think she heard you?' he asked curiously.

Hillary shrugged. 'Who can say. It's still early days yet—she's still getting to know me, to figure out her place in life, as well as in the team. She might be willing to take advice, or she might not. Besides, I'm not sure yet that she's a keeper.' Hillary tucked her hands under her thighs on the seat, and frowned. 'Oh, she's very keen and clever enough. But she might just burn out early. We'll have to wait and see.'

'OK.' Steven, as ever, trusted her judgement without question. It was part of her job to train and guide the potential recruits under her care, after all. So he wasn't about to interfere or second-guess her. He wouldn't dare! She'd probably hand him his head back on a platter if he tried, baked to perfection and with an apple clenched between his teeth. 'So a tentative question mark over Zoe Turnbull. What about Jake Barnes?'

'Ah yes. The Boy Wonder. Zoe's pet name for him seems to be sticking. Besides, it sort of suits him.'

'OK. I can see how he might have earned it,' Steven said with another slow grin. 'He does seem to be something of a golden boy, doesn't he? Donleavy and the top brass were all but salivating over him when they thrust him my way,' he concurred. 'Did you know he's already sponsoring several community youth initiatives and drug rehabilitation programmes?'

'Doesn't surprise me,' Hillary said neutrally. Jake was nobody's fool, and would have made sure to earn himself serious brownie points before even approaching Thames Valley's recruitment officers.

'He's also set to give a series of interviews with the media that the PR department has set up. You can imagine the hook they're using? Millionaire businessman backs the boys in blue, and how. Why he's joining the force, and all that jazz.'

He stretched wearily in his chair and bit back a yawn. 'As you can imagine, the ACC loves him.'

'That doesn't surprise me either,' Hillary repeated laconically.

'But? Come on, sweetheart, I know you too well not to hear the but in your voice by now.' Hillary's smile twisted slightly. He knew her so well, did he? And if she was his sweetheart, why… Hillary stopped herself right there and forced herself to keep on track. She had always been able to rely on herself to be professional, damn it.

'He's up to something,' she said flatly. Briefly she told him about her doubts, which had led to her asking Jimmy to keep an eye on him, which in turn had led to Jimmy spying on Barnes's little foray into her office last night. As she spoke, she could see her soon-to-be-ex-lover and boss getting more and more tense.

'And you're sure it was your password that he was after?'

Steven said finally, sitting up straighter behind his desk now, his eyes narrowing angrily. 'Did he get it?'

'I presume so.'

'You have changed it, right?' he demanded shortly.

Hillary hesitated. Then admitted cautiously, 'Actually, no. And that's what I want to talk to you about.'

'What do you mean? The little sod's out on his ear,

as of right now. I'll escort him from the building myself, and apply my boot to his rear end, Donleavy's golden boy or not.'

Hillary held up a hand. 'Hold on, not so fast. Like I said, I want to speak to you about that. Don't you think it makes more sense to see what it is that he's after?'

Steven stared at her for a few moments, his mind racing. He'd always found the cunning way her mind worked to be fascinating, sometimes frightening, and, yes, he thought with a wry inner smile, more often than not downright sexy.

'What did you have in mind, exactly?' he heard himself ask warily.

'As I said to Jimmy, my password isn't going to get him access to anything vital. And what's the likelihood, really, of him being interested in pulling off some sort of a financial scam anyway? I mean, that's what you're really worried about, right?' She outlined to him the same thoughts that she'd shared with Jimmy.

'So, it looks far more likely at this point that the Boy Wonder has a personal bee in his bonnet. Maybe he's got a pet crime that he wants to investigate and solve for himself; or more likely, he wants to find out more about a specific cold case that touches on his life somehow.'

'Has it occurred to you that he might have committed a serious crime and now he's joined up with us in the hope that he can somehow cover it up? Erase vital evidence from the database or something?'

Hillary nodded. 'One of the first things I thought about. But let's face it, it's not likely, is it? If he's already got away with it, why jeopardize that by calling attention to himself?'

Steven thought it through, and didn't like it. 'Maybe.

Or maybe he's just big-headed. Thinks no one can touch him, or no one would be smart enough to figure out what he's doing.'

'Sure. But if that is the case, then it makes even more sense for us to keep him on, and find out what he's up to. That way, if he is trying to cover up a past crime, either for himself or somebody else, we can nail him for that, and probably solve the original crime, whatever that may be as well.'

Steven slowly nodded. 'I can see where you're going with this. But it's a dangerous game. If Barnes manages to pull a fast one on you, the brass will want your head.'

Hillary smiled. Well, that wouldn't be his problem for much longer, would it? If the brown stuff ever did hit the fan, the chances were that the newly promoted Superintendent Crayle would be long gone and out of the line of fire.

'True. You want to pass it on up the chain, don't you?' she said, and before he could defend himself, swept on quickly. 'But have you considered the downside to that? Believe me, Donleavy isn't going to thank you for scuppering Barnes without knowing all the whys and wherefores before you do. Besides, as far as the top brass is concerned, it's far better for us if we have a neat little solution all ready and packaged and waiting to go. Besides, say we do chuck him out on his ear, that's no guarantee that he'll stop trying to achieve whatever it is that he's up to. And he's rich enough, and well connected enough, to try and ride roughshod over the lot of us to get what he wants. He might even sue us. And that we need like we need a hole in the head.'

'So it's better to have him inside the tent pissing out, then outside pissing in.'

Steven nodded slowly. 'That's still a risky strategy.'

'I know it is,' Hillary admitted reasonably. 'Which is why I want to put a trace on my password. You can ask one of the boffins in the lab to do that, right? Every time my password is logged in, make a note of whatever it is that's accessed? That way, I can try and figure out what his angle is.'

Steven sighed heavily. 'Yes, I can arrange that, I suppose. But Hillary, I want you to promise me, the moment it starts to look really iffy…'

'We pull the plug on him. Sure. And hopefully, by then, we'll have some real evidence to show Donleavy, and cover our own backsides. Because right now all we've got to show the brass are my hunches, and an old ex-sergeant's word that he's been snooping. Which, quite frankly, m'dear, they wouldn't give a damn.'

'Funny, I never saw you as Clark Gable,' Steven said, with a distinct sparkle in his eye. Why was it this woman, even when she was being outrageous, could make him smile?

Hillary saw the warmth in his eyes, and felt her heart contract. Then she took a deep, shaky breath, and forced a smile on to her face. 'I always saw myself as the James Cagney type, personally. You dirty rat.'

TEN

'RIGHT, IT'S TIME we talked to Mrs Brandt,' Hillary said, walking into the communal office later that afternoon. 'Zoe, where's she living nowadays?'

'Just outside Bath, guv,' Zoe replied promptly. 'She left within a year of her husband dying. I don't suppose she could stick it there, what with all the memories and what have you. I can't say as I blame her for wanting a new start. None of what happened could have been easy for her. Besides, her daughter lives out that way, so I suppose she wanted to be near her and her grand-kids. The ones she's got left, that is,' she added grimly.

Hillary nodded. 'OK. Jake, you're driving.'

Jake nodded and shut down his personal laptop. At first, she'd assumed he preferred to use it because it was both familiar to him and was no doubt the latest, all-singing and all-dancing example of its kind. And to be fair, Hillary had to admit, the police-issue computers down in CRT for Steven's team tended to belong to the megalithic age, in IT parlance. It was only the boffins and forensics experts in the main office that got the very best on offer.

Now, though, she couldn't help but wonder if Jake preferred to use his own machine in order to ensure privacy. She knew that she herself wouldn't stand a chance of hacking her way through his passwords and security programmes.

At some point, she might have to see if she could sneakily part him from it, and let the boffins in the technical department loose on it.

Which was, of course, strictly illegal.

So she'd have to be careful. And pick her man for the job carefully. He'd either have to owe her a favour, or be happy to have her owe him one. She began to mentally review the other staff in the building, when Jake interrupted her thoughts.

'My car, guv, or yours?' he asked, with a perfectly straight face. Hillary, who was well aware that he knew damned well just how much in love she was with his E-type Jag, childishly contemplated telling him that they'd take her car. But then she took pity on Puff, who might not be happy with the fairly long haul to the Roman spa town, and shrugged.

'Sure, your car. Why not?'

Zoe shot Jake a snort and an eye roll. 'My Mini's a classic as well, you know, guv. We could take her.'

'I thought you wanted to be in on the foxy bartender interview?' Hillary grinned. 'Which, by the way, we'll get around to tomorrow, so make sure you know where he's gonna be all day. He can't still be bartending at his age, unless he's made a career of it.'

'Oh, right. OK, guv, I'll find out what he's doing now.' Jake shot her a cheeky wave as they went.

'Nice to see the troops getting on so well,' Hillary commented dryly as they walked down the winding labyrinth of corridors towards the main stairs.

'She's a nice girl,' Jake said, and meant it. He hadn't realized, when he'd applied to join the civilian ranks of the Crime Review Team, that there would be any other newly installed probationers as well as himself, but he couldn't see Zoe Turnbull presenting any problem. She was bright enough, certainly, but still young and wet behind the ears, so he didn't think she'd be likely to cotton on to what he was doing. And thankfully, she didn't seem interested in him romantically, either, which meant that she wouldn't be constantly watching him or looking over his shoulder in any attempts to catch his attention. Which was just as well.

'And how are you getting on with Jimmy?' Hillary asked as they reached the top of the stairs and emerged into the lobby.

'Fine. He's obviously…'

'Hey, Hill,' the desk sergeant suddenly called out, and she motioned Jake to go on without her and detoured towards the chunkily built fifty-something currently manning the desk and drinking from an outsized mug of coffee.

'Sarge,' Hillary said, with a smile and a nod.

'What's all this I hear about your guv'nor taking off for parts unknown, then?'

Hillary sighed. 'You lot must be slipping. Donleavy only approached him a couple of days ago. You're falling down on the job.'

The desk sergeant's slightly florid face creased into a grin, making his rather irregular features crumple into something resembling a boxer dog. And a rather grizzled, battle-scarred specimen at that. Hillary would have bet money that the old-timer had got most of his battle scars policing football games, and volunteering for riot duty.

'Well, you know how it is. You can't get the staff nowadays, can ya?' He grinned at her over his coffee mug. 'Mick got it from the cleaner that does Donleavy's secretary's office.'

'Oh, an impeccable source then,' Hillary countered dryly.

'So he's really going?'

'Looks like it.' The desk sergeant took another noisy gulp from his mug and looked at her casually. 'So you'll have to break in another super then?' he asked, perfectly straight-faced, and making no attempt to hide the double entendre.

Hillary grinned widely at him. Cheeky bastard!

She let her face become woeful. 'Somebody's gotta do it, Sarge,' she said with a heavy sigh and a confiding hand on his arm. 'Let's just hope the new boss, whoever it is, doesn't have as ugly a mug as you. I might be willing to give my all for Thames Valley, but there's a limit, even for me.'

Some uniforms from traffic, who'd come in just in time to hear all this, broke out in raucous laughter, and the desk sergeant, who'd just taken another gulp of coffee, began to choke in a most satisfactory and spectacular manner.

Her work done, Hillary left the now scarlet-faced and still-hacking desk sergeant to his duties, nodded sombrely at the uniforms, who went mock-respectfully silent as she passed.

She knew, of course, that now that she had confirmed the rumour of Steven's departure, it would be all over the Big House before she got back. Just how many of them would be feeling pity for her, guessing that the writing was on the wall for her and her personal relationship with her boss, as well as the end of their professional one? She knew the Big House fed on gossip like sea lions on fish, and anyone and everyone was a legitimate target.

She also knew that she and Steven had been a nine-day wonder, back in the beginning, mostly because her private life had been practically non-existent for so long that the gossip mongers had had nothing to gnaw over. So when she'd come back, and become an item with a superintendent over half a dozen years younger than herself, they'd had a field day.

Oh, she knew it hadn't been malicious—she was sufficiently self-aware to know that she was well liked and that most of her comrades wished her well.

Even so, she'd always hated the thought of being the object of gleeful gossip. Or, worse still, become an object of pity.

She walked rapidly across the car park, unaware that she was scowling ferociously. It was only when she passed a startled-looking Sam Waterstone, a sergeant from her old office back when she had still been a DI, that she realized what she must be doing. She forced herself to smile and greet him, but deliberately didn't linger. They swapped a few reminiscences and general good wishes, and then she carried on. She wouldn't have been surprised, had she turned around, to see her old colleague was watching her with a mixture of curiosity and slight anxiety.

By the time she'd reached the Boy Wonder's beautiful E-type Jag, however, her face was as neutral and composed as it usually was.

'Right then. You've got the address from Zoe?' she

said, slipping in to the weirdly low-down depths of the leather-lined bucket seat.

Jake started the car with a classically throaty roar of the engine. 'Yes, guv.'

It was a beautiful afternoon, sunny and bright, and Hillary watched the impressive scenery pass by as they crossed the Oxfordshire border and headed towards the beautiful spa town most famous for its Roman baths and Georgian architecture, epitomized in The Crescent.

It turned out, however, that the small market town where Margaret Brandt now lived was on the right side of the county for them, which meant that they didn't actually have to go through Bath itself. Instead, the sat nav directed them to turn off about six miles from it, which would no doubt help them avoid the worst of the rush hour when it came time to leave.

Pulling out the file from her case, Hillary re-familiarized herself with the witness statements the Brandts had given to DI Varney. From the file photographs, William Henry Brandt had been sixty-one years old at the time of Felix Olliphant's murder. At five foot ten, he'd been a heavy-set man, round faced and balding, with deep-set brown eyes and the florid broken-veined face that sometimes denoted a heavy drinker.

There was no photograph of his wife.

William Brandt had died of alcohol-related natural causes in the autumn of 2007. And if Varney had not been able to break the couple's alibi or prove their involvement at the time, Hillary had no real hopes of being able to do so now. She was not a bloody magician, she thought, a shade mutinously. So she had no real hopes of anything solid coming from the next hour or so.

Unless, of course, the Brandts *had* been guilty, and after all this time the widow was willing to confess. It was extremely unlikely, but such things had been known to happen.

Looking out of her window to check if there were any squadrons of flying pigs whooping it up outside, Hillary saw that there weren't, and went back to the paperwork.

Billy, the little boy who'd been killed in the collision with Felix's vehicle, had been the oldest son of the Brandts' son Matthew. Matthew and his wife had also had a little girl, aged two at the time.

Hillary sighed and put the paperwork away. As a young constable, she'd done her share of attending RTAs—road traffic accidents—and didn't need to call on her imagination to understand how just a split second in time had managed to explode the Brandt family apart.

Not only would they have lost Billy, but his parents' lives would have been shattered too. And William Brandt had gone to jail, and all but drunk himself to death afterwards. And what of the grandmother? Would her loyalties have been with her shattered, stricken, guilty husband? Or with her grieving, probably angry and resentful son? Either way, the emotions would have run deep. Shame. Guilt. Anger. The desire for revenge.

So far, of all the people she'd talked to, the Brandts were clearly the ones with the best motive for wanting Felix dead.

Sure, she could see the greedy and ambitious Greer Ryanson being happy with the big insurance payout due on her partner's death. Felix's demise would also mean that she'd have the company to herself, and could bring in her spouse to take Felix's place, leaving them in marital bliss to enjoy the big monetary reward that would ensure their future.

But would she kill for it? And risk prison, if caught? Somehow, Hillary thought Greer was too careful of her own comfort and skin to be inclined to chance it.

And OK, Felix's girlfriend, Becky, had obviously been the needy, clinging type, and might well have realized that while she was fathoms deep in love with the good-looking interior designer, Felix hadn't been half so keen.

But again, would she kill him because of that?

Hillary couldn't really see it. You needed to be either pathologically egotistical or clinically desperate for attention and love to do that. And she hadn't seen any signs of that in the housewife and mother she had then gone on to become. Which didn't necessarily mean she hadn't been that mentally ill at the time of the murder, of course. But she was fairly confident that Varney would have spotted it. From all she'd read of his case notes, the man had been competent and thorough and experienced.

'This is the place, guv.' Jake Barnes's voice interrupted her darkening thoughts, and she gave a mental head shake as he turned off the engine. Time to concentrate on the task at hand.

They were parked outside a modest, semi-detached house in a small cul-de-sac of similar council houses, which had probably been built in the early sixties. Uniform, small front gardens fronted grey-clad houses that had been painted various hues of pastel colours, signalling that most of them were now privately owned.

The house Jake pointed at, however, still retained

the original, somewhat ugly and dismal grey colour, and the same type of doors and windows as three of the other grey-clad houses. Which meant that Margaret Brandt hadn't been one of the lucky ones who'd been able to buy their own home. It made sense: her husband had been a labourer all his life and Hillary doubted that he'd had any big insurance policy to see her through to her old age after his death As if reading her mind, Jake said, 'I think Zoe mentioned that she has a part-time job, guv, working in a newsagents. Even though she must be in her early seventies by now. So if she's not in, we might have to have a wander down the high street and chat to her in the shop.'

Hillary gave a silent grimace. 'Let's hope not.' Having to talk to the woman while she sold fags, magazines and chocolate bars to her customers wasn't exactly conducive to a good interview.

However, after they'd walked up a narrow flagstone path, bordered on both sides with a sparse square of lawn with no floral representatives at all, the door opened quickly after Hillary's first knock.

Margaret Brandt was a small, round woman with short grey hair that had been permed into tight, neat curls. She wore one of those loose, floral-printed dresses that was tied in the middle with a belt of the same material, and she was wearing warm and comfortable-looking blue slippers on her feet.

'Yes?' Hillary showed her their ID and explained what they were doing there. Margaret's button-brown eyes darted quickly around the street, checking no doubt for nosy neighbours, and stepped aside quickly to usher them inside.

'Better come in then,' she said. She didn't sound particularly surprised or resentful to find them on her doorstep. Nor was she particularly welcoming either, but then Hillary supposed she didn't have any reason to be.

Margaret Brandt had probably been brought up working class and respectable all her life. She'd married, produced children, held down jobs and done the best she could, and probably never imagined she'd have anything to do with the police or the judicial system in all her born days.

'Come into the kitchen, if you don't mind. I don't use the living room much and I was just about to get my tea on.'

'That's fine. We're sorry to interrupt you, Mrs Brandt,' Hillary said politely if not strictly truthfully. 'We'll try not to keep you too long.'

Margaret nodded, and showed them into a small kitchen with a view of an equally flower-less back garden. One dismal tree sat in a square of lawn and was even now in the act of shedding its leaves. Hillary wasn't sure whether that was because it was a variety that dropped its leaves earlier than most, or whether it was dying.

Predominantly blue and yellow, the room was small but clean, and a tiny table by the far wall had been set for one. It had two chairs tucked under it, and the woman of the house nodded to them briskly. 'Better sit down. Want some tea then?'

'Please,' Hillary said.

Margaret looked at Jake, her eyes running over him thoughtfully, no doubt taking in the superior quality of his clothes and the aura of easy money that Jake Barnes seemed to generate without even trying. She frowned very slightly, but said amiably enough, 'And you, young 'un? Tea?'

'Yes, thank you, Mrs Brandt,' Jake said, and took the seat opposite Hillary. She was pleased to notice that he didn't try to tape this conversation, but instead reached into his jacket pocket and withdrew a neat notebook and a tiny retractable pen. It was, of course, gold, vintage and a Parker.

Hillary watched the old woman make tea, then open a packet of oven chips, sprinkle some on to an old tin plate, and put them in the oven and turn it on. She opened a can of peas and whilst the kettle was boiling, emptied them out into a saucepan, but made no move to heat them up. An unopened tin of Spam sat on the sink draining board.

When the tea was made, she brought two cups over to the table and put them down, one each in front of them, and then withdrew to the sink, where she pulled out a battered yellow-topped stool. She dragged it over to the table and sat down with a weary sigh.

'So, how can I help you?' she asked. As she blew across the top of her own cup to cool the liquid down, Hillary glanced at her own brew and saw that it was as dark as ink, the kind of tea that dried up your mouth and left the bitter aftertaste of tannin lingering on the tongue.

She turned the cup in its saucer but made no move to drink any of it. She could see that Margaret Brandt had brought out the best china for them, a pretty, rather fussy set that had gild-edged pink roses on it, and felt a momentary pang of pity.

Then she smiled gently across at the stiff-backed old lady watching them.

'We're taking another look at the Felix Olliphant murder, as I said, Mrs Brandt,' she began quietly, but without any sugarcoating. 'We were wondering if, after the passage of so many years, you had anything new that you wanted to tell us about that? Now that your husband has passed on, you might feel more able to talk freely, perhaps?'

Margaret's brown eyes blinked rapidly in succession, and then her rather chubby face gentled into a near-smile.

'If by that you mean you want me to tell you that my Willy did it, then no. I don't have anything new to tell you,' she said uncompromisingly. 'I can only tell you what I told that other inspector before. Neither of us had anything to do with that man's death. We didn't know where this party was that he was living it up at, and if we had, we had no way of getting there. We stayed in all that night, and watched the New Year in on the telly. Then we went to bed.' She took a small sip of her tea, and said, 'You want a biscuit, love?'

'No, thank you. It was a very special night, though, that night, wasn't it,' Hillary pressed on. 'Not just any old New Year, was it?

A whole new millennium. Everybody was pushing the boat out a bit.' Margaret sighed and definitely smiled this time. But it was a sad, infinitely weary smile. 'So they kept on saying. Everybody you'd meet in the streets said it, and them telly people, what do you call 'em? Presenters? All going on about how unique it was and all that. And I remember everyone was going on about how all the computers were going to go haywire, and there'd be pandemonium.' She gave a sudden chuckle. 'Not that *that* happened, did it? Not that we'd have known if it had. Willy and me never owned a computer in our life. Of course, the kids all did.' Margaret shrugged and took another sip of the inky brew. 'But for us, it weren't nothing special. So it was a new millennium, whatever that was supposed to mean. For us it was just more of the same.' Margaret took another sip of tea, then went off in search of a digestive, and came back with it, munching it slowly before carrying on as if she'd never left the table. 'Yes, just more of the same old thing. Willy couldn't get a job after he came out of prison. I was working in the garage then, behind the till. It was all we could do to pay the bills. Didn't have no money to go partying or making a fuss. Like I told the inspector, we stayed in, watched the telly and went to bed. I don't know who killed that man, or why.'

Hillary nodded. It was the second time, she noted, that Margaret Brandt had referred to Felix as 'that man'. Did she hate even his memory so much that she couldn't bring herself to use his given name? Or was that just how she'd always thought of him? As that anonymous, maybe even nightmarish figure, who had ruined her life and that of her husband and son?

'I understand that your husband blamed Mr Olliphant for the crash, even though it was clearly proved that he'd been drinking and had been on the wrong side of the road at the time of the collision?' Hillary said, careful to keep her voice level and free of accusation. 'Did you believe him, Mrs Brandt?'

And here the widow surprised her, because, after taking yet another sip of her tea, Margaret sighed and said, 'Of course I didn't. It was as clear as day that he'd been drinking, and going too fast.' She sighed and took another bite of her biscuit, meeting Hillary's gaze head on. 'I'd been in the car with him many times, Mrs Greene. He was a good driver, very competent, like. You know, when someone's been driving for years, they just get good at it. My Willy was like that. But I ain't daft, nor blind, and I could tell he often drove too fast, and was sometimes too confident that nothing bad would happen to him.' She sighed, drained her cup and put it down firmly onto the saucer in her hand. 'I often said to him that he should take more care. There were other folks on the road, I'd say, and plenty of bad drivers too. But he wouldn't listen. He was a good man, my Willy, but he was a *man,* you know? Couldn't be told nothing. Especially by me.'

Hillary nodded. Yes, she knew that sort of man all right. 'Did you know he'd been drinking that day?'

'No. Not so's I'd notice. But then Willy always could hold his drink. You don't think I go over that day in my head all the time? Wishing I'd stopped them from going?' she demanded, some animation finally coming into her voice.

'Of course you do,' Hillary said softly. 'I can't imagine how bad it must have been for you. And I'm sorry to have to drag it all up again. But we have a job to do, you know. And I don't approve of murder.'

Margaret Brandt blinked at her, then her rounded shoulders slumped a bit. 'No. No, course not. Me either. Nobody deserves to be done to death, do they? And that man had a mum and dad too, didn't he? So I know how they must have felt. Our Mattie blamed us, of course. His dad most of all, of course, but me as well. I could tell. At Billy's funeral…' Her voice trailed off, and she swallowed hard. Then her shoulders stiffened again and she leaned forward and put her cup, saucer and half-eaten biscuit on the table.

'By the time Willy got out of jail, Mattie had stopped coming over to see me altogether. He said he didn't want to see his dad at all. He never visited him in jail, not even when he got moved to an open prison. So when Willy died, I decided there was no point staying on in the old house, so I asked the council for a transfer. My girl, Betty, lives in Bath—she's our youngest. She never blamed me, not like the others did. And, well, she was always Daddy's little girl, so she was pleased to have me near. She's got kids so I come in useful as a babysitter. Maybe even be the babysitter when they've got young 'uns of their own. Always provided I'm still alive then, touch wood.' She leaned over and patted two chubby fingers on top of the table, which was Formica, but had been patterned to look like wood.

Hillary found herself wondering, inanely, if that counted.

'So, here we are. Mattie and his wife had another little boy, you know. Six, seven years ago. I haven't seen him. I wasn't invited to the christening.' The last simple statement, said without pity or surprise, hung in the air for a moment, and Hillary wasn't surprised to see Jake Barnes shift uncomfortably in his seat.

'So you didn't blame Felix Olliphant for the accident that killed your Billy?' Hillary pressed gently.

''Course I didn't, love. Weren't his fault, was it? He was just in the wrong place at the wrong time. If it hadn't been him coming in the opposite direction it would have been some other poor sod. I saw him during the court case, you know. Seemed like a nice enough lad. And it had cut him up rough, like, what happened to our little Billy. You could see it on his face.'

'But your husband *did* blame him,' Hillary said. 'In fact, didn't he accuse him of paying off the other witness to the accident, a Mr Colin Harcourt?'

Margaret Brandt shrugged her well-padded shoulders helplessly. 'That was just Willy's way of trying to cope with it all. Inside, he knew it was his fault. We all did. But he couldn't live with it, see? So he had to make it somebody else's fault, and the only one he could blame was the other driver. See?'

'Yes,' Hillary said simply. 'Mrs Brandt, are you sure your husband didn't go out that evening?' Margaret Brandt turned sad, defeated brown eyes on Hillary Greene and said simply, ''Course I am, love. He was as drunk as a skunk long before midnight. I had to practically drag him up the stairs myself. He was snoring and dead to the world before I'd even managed to get him undressed. So you see, he was in no fit state to even get out of bed, let alone find and kill that man.'

'SO THAT SEEMS to be that,' Jake Barnes said a few minutes later, as the early evening sun began to mellow and they drove back towards Oxford.

'If you believe her,' Hillary pointed out.

Jake took his eyes off the road long enough to take a quick glance at her. 'I thought she was telling the truth, guv. Not that I'm saying my instincts are always right, mind, but she didn't strike me as the killing type.'

Hillary sighed. 'No, I'm not saying that she is. Or even the aiding and abetting type, come to that. And for what it's worth, I believed her too. But it's not about what we *think*, is it? Besides, for all we know, Margaret Brandt might be such a good actress, she could put Dame Judi Dench to shame.'

Jake grinned. 'Guv.'

'It's all about what we can prove.' She carried on the lesson grimly. 'And remember, always keep an open mind. So, although we put her and her now deceased husband to the bottom of the pile, we don't rule them out altogether. Got it?'

'Got it, guv.'

AS THEY DROVE back towards HQ, so that Hillary could pick up her ancient Volkswagen and head on home, Steven Crayle was just being shown into Commander Marcus Donleavy's office.

It didn't take the two men long to conclude their business. Steven found himself agreeing to be interviewed by a selection panel by the end of the month. But they both knew that was a mere formality—barring any major snafus.

'So how's Hillary taking it?' Donleavy asked, as the two men rose and shook hands on it.

Steven looked at him sharply. Now what the hell sort of a question was that? 'She's all for it, sir. She's happy for me, and wants me to get the promotion. As you'd expect.'

Commander Donleavy nodded, not a flicker of expression crossing his urbane face. 'Good, good. Well, I'll let you get on.' Steven left his office stony-faced. If the commander had been angling to be let in on the state of their relationship, he could bloody well angle as much as he liked. It was none of his damned business how he and Hillary were coping.

Or not.

Besides, he had his own ideas on that.

ON THE WAY to Thrupp, Steven pulled off to pop into Tesco and collect the makings of a nice dinner. When he arrived at the *Mollern*, he was a little surprised to see that he was the first to arrive. It was gone five, and he'd have expected Hillary to be back by now. But he wasn't worried, and it would give him time to get the dinner under way.

He put the pre-made coq-au-vin dishes in the oven and put it on, and washed the mange tout and baby carrots. He set the tiny table with the best china, and folded some paper napkins inside two wine glasses. He had a little trouble finding a vase to take the mixed bunch of flowers that he'd bought, but when he set them in the centre of the table they looked suitably romantic.

He was just setting the coffee machine to percolate when he felt the narrowboat rock a little and heard her coming down the metal stairs in the stern.

Hillary followed her nose, which had picked up the delicious scent of cooking chicken, and her eyes went at once to the table.

Even as she did so, he was reaching out to light two candles that he'd found in her emergency storage tin, in case the batteries on the boat ran down. She felt her mouth go dry.

So this was it then, she thought fatalistically. The now almost legendary breaking-up dinner. Although she'd never had to sit through one personally, she knew how it went all right. First, the big romantic scene—hence the candlelight and flowers. A lovely meal to follow. Plenty of wine, get them nice and squiffy. And then the gentle let-down. That's how it went, wasn't it?

She shrugged off her jacket and tossed her case under one of the armchairs. Her spine was stiffening and her face was forming itself into a bland smile when he said, 'I thought we'd celebrate. I accepted the job offer. Donleavy's set up the interview, but he all but promised me the job, and promotion in due course.' Hillary let out a long, slow breath. So, it was to be a stay of execution then. But that made sense. As he'd pointed out before, it would be two months at least before he left. Why risk pissing her off by dumping her before then, when they still had to work together for another eight weeks?

'That's great,' she said, reaching out for a wine glass and unceremoniously dumping the napkin inside it onto the table.

'Let's drink to your success.' She waggled the glass at him.

Steven looked at the napkin lying haphazardly on the table, and then at her slightly tight, forced smile.

'Red or white? I bought both,' he said quietly.

ELEVEN

JAKE BARNES WAS also drinking wine that night, but he was sitting behind a large, antique inlaid walnut desk as he did so. And his glass was full with the offering of a certain vineyard in Bordeaux that was rather famous for the quality of its product.

After a few appreciative mouthfuls, he reached down to one of the drawers on his right, which had a much more sturdy and complicated lock than the original builder of the desk would have envisaged. Reaching into his pocket, he withdrew a gold Albert watch chain, and from a collection of keys on this chain he selcсted a small, ornately carved one, and unlocked the desk drawer.

Putting his hand inside, he picked out a heavy and bulky folder and put in on top of the desk. He was not normally into hard copies of anything, like much of his generation, preferring cyberspace, but some things he simply didn't want on computer files. Knowing first hand just how vulnerable they could be, he had to concede that paper and ink still had its uses in the 21st century.

He took another sip of the expensive but exquisite wine and contemplated the idea of installing a proper safe. So far he hadn't done so, but then so far there hadn't really been a reason too. He didn't keep real valuables in the house, and nobody knew about the contents of this particular folder, so nobody had any reason to be afraid of it, or steal it.

But, in the months to come, that might all change. He thought about it for a moment, wondering if he was being melodramatic, and then gave a small smile and a shrug. Perhaps he was, but then again, perhaps he wasn't. Besides, as his old gran had always said, it was better to have something and not need it than need it but not have it.

Taking out a small Dictaphone from the unlocked drawer above the one already open, he made a note for his private secretary, a tall, very attractive Dane, who came in twice a week to see to his personal correspondence. And anything else they might mutually feel the need to take care of.

'Trude, I want you to find me a capable security or locksmith company that can install, hide and monitor a safe for me. It can be in any room in the house, set in the floor or walls, or any other smart place of their choosing. It doesn't have to be big, no more than say…' Here he switched off the tape, thought about it for a second, then switched the button back on and gave his roughly calculated measurements. 'There's no great hurry but I do need it installed within a month. You can promise them a bonus if that's too short notice for them. Naturally, I rely on you to be discreet about this.'

Here he grinned rather wolfishly. 'As always. Ta, love.' He switched off the machine and left it on his desk where she'd be bound to see it and check it the next time she came in.

Pushing the half-empty glass of wine aside, he pulled the folder to him and began to go through its contents. Nothing in it was new to him, of course. He'd been through it all before. Sometimes many, many times, and he knew that it wasn't good to be this obsessive. Which didn't stop him from looking through it again now.

The bulk of the file was taken up with copies from newspaper articles. Some papers were the transcripts from court cases that were in the public domain and the rarest of all were the files he'd commissioned from three various firms of private inquiry agencies over the years.

For a while, Jake Barnes sat and stared down at the photographs of a man, which the private eyes had taken with long-distance lenses. Not that he could blame them for taking the photographs from a long way away. The man depicted in them was dangerous. Very dangerous. And everyone knew it, including Jake. He'd had to pay the private agencies vast sums of money to do even the tentative amount of investigation that they had agreed to do. Even then, he was not sure just how diligent they'd been. After all, nobody in their right mind wanted to get on the bad side of this particular individual, and if he'd found out that somebody was snooping into his life, personal or professional, the consequences would no doubt be very dire indeed.

Now he sighed as yet again he burned the image of the man into his retinas.

'Soon, you bastard,' Jake murmured, reaching for his expensive glass of wine and sipping it slowly. 'Nobody's untouchable. Not even you.' This he truly believed, but he would have been less than honest if he hadn't acknowledged that his heart thumped just a bit harder with suppressed fear.

Not that he'd let his own cowardice stop him. And now that he was in at the CRT, and had access to Hillary Greene's computer, things could finally start to move.

But carefully. And slowly. And thoroughly.

Jake Barnes was nobody's mug, and he didn't intend

to get caught out, either by the police or by the thug in the photographs.

He closed the folder with a sigh and put it back in his locked drawer. The night was drawing in and his study-cum-library was beginning to get gloomy, but he made no move to get up to turn on a light.

Instead, he reviewed his progress so far.

For the longest while, he'd felt utterly helpless and hopeless. Despair and rage and frustration had almost eaten him alive.

Until he'd forced himself to think—which was something a lot of people had always said he did best.

And after thinking long and hard, he'd had to concede that there was no way he could take on the likes of the enemy and his gang on his own. And a direct appeal to the police had already proved useless. Luckily, that appeal had been made by someone else, so his name had never been mentioned. Which was now just as well.

So he'd started, as the saying went, to think outside the box. And outside the box, it turned out, had led to him joining the CRT.

Jake Barnes contemplated Detective Superintendent Steven Crayle's small team within a team, and weighed them up. Sam Pickles was negligible. Besides, Jake was almost sure that he'd be leaving them soon. Zoe Turnbull, likewise, was a non-starter. She was too green to be of use. And besides, there was no way Jake was going to let her stick her neck out and catch the attention of the likes of the man he was hunting. No, especially not Zoe, he mused grimly. Young, pretty, vulnerable girls were the very prey that his enemy was on the lookout for.

Not that Zoe would consider herself vulnerable, Jake thought, with a sudden brief smile. After a moment that same smile quickly fled because of course, whether she believed it or not, she *was* vulnerable.

And nobody knew that better than Jake.

Jimmy Jessop was another matter altogether. The retired sergeant was a man of vast experience, whose quiet exterior, in Jake's view, hid a vast depth of knowledge, hard-headed scepticism and cunning. There was something knowing and competent in that quiet, steady gaze of the old-timer that both reassured and intrigued Jake.

It was just a shame that he was too old. Like Zoe, Jake couldn't risk putting him in the orbit of his target. Not that Jimmy Jessop would object, Jake was sure. In fact, even though he'd only known him a short time, Jake would have bet a sizeable amount of his fortune that if he confided in the old man just who it was that he had in his sights, then Jimmy would have been straining at the leash to help. Taking down the man whose photographs littered Jake's files and nightmares would be a copper's dream come true.

But he was just too old. What if he got caught out by one of the thugs working for their quarry? There's no way he could take a beating, not at his age. He'd probably end up having a heart attack or something, and that wasn't something Jake wanted to have to live with.

Which left Steven Crayle and Hillary Greene.

Jake thought he understood Steven Crayle well enough. The instant he'd met him on the interview panel he'd picked him out as top dog. Behind the well-groomed exterior, there lurked a man with a mind like a diamond—cold, hard and probably at times quite brilliant. And a man like that had ambitions. Consequently, the CRT had to be a stepping stone for him, on his way to bigger and better things.

Which, in itself, was no bad thing for Jake. A man like the superintendent would see Jake's quarry as a glittering prize, simply because to be the man who took him down would mean instant and widespread kudos, not to mention an almost certain promotion.

But therein, probably, also lay the snag. Steven Crayle was just too ambitious to go off-grid. If he found out what Jake was up to, he'd instantly take it higher up to the top brass. And they'd pull the plug on him faster than Jake could phone for his solicitors.

No, much as he would have liked to have had Steven Crayle onside, he knew he had to work around the superintendent.

Which left him with Hillary Greene.

Jake Barnes slowly sipped the last of his wine, contemplated having another drink, and then decided it wouldn't be a good idea. He needed to keep a perfectly clear head. Like their murder victim, Felix Olliphant, Jake had never been a particularly avid drinker anyway.

The thought of his first murder case brought his mind once again to Hillary Greene. Who was, in Jake's growing estimation, little short of a phenomenon.

It was hard to imagine that he'd only known her a few days. Before joining CRT he'd spent many weeks researching her with a growing sense of hope and excitement, and thought he'd managed to get a good grasp of the sort of person she'd turn out to be. A bit of a maverick, he'd decided. She had the approval of the top brass but he'd sensed a certain reservation between her and them—on both sides. A bit of a hard nut, maybe—she couldn't win medals for bravery and close as many murder cases as she had without having iron in her backbone. And that nearly-ex, fully dead, bent copper of a husband of hers, Ronnie Greene, had intrigued him most of all. Among other things, it had led to her being investigated for corruption as well. And yet, in spite of all that, he hadn't been in the Big House for more than a couple of days before he understood that the rank and file really rated her, and regarded her as their own personal heroine. Rumours abounded about her standing by Janine Tyler when everyone else was willing to throw her to the wolves, for instance. And while nobody had truly understood the reasons behind her retirement, everyone had cheered when she'd come back.

And now that he'd finally met her, and was working with her.... Jake leaned back in his chair and stretched, linking his hands behind his head, elbows bent at acute right angles either side of his head as he regarded the ornate chandelier hanging from the library ceiling, and its pretty plaster rose.

Yes, now that he'd met her, he couldn't help but be impressed. She'd been all that he suspected she would be, and probably more. There was an inner core to her, a determination to succeed that he recognized only too well from looking in a mirror, and that caused him to feel equal measures of excitement and concern.

She clearly hated and had contempt for villains, which was a magnificent bonus. For all their quiet, seeming lack of progress so far, she was like a rat with a terrier regarding the Olliphant case. And although Zoe seemed to doubt that they were actually getting anywhere near to solving it, Jake would have bet money on Hillary Greene closing this case as well.

All of which made him very happy indeed.

Because Jake had no doubt that Hillary Greene knew all about the man whose photographs adorned his files.

What copper in the area didn't? And she would burn to take him down. Better still, she was qualified to do it. Jake had no doubt at all that the thought of taking him on wouldn't make Hillary Greene so much as blink or think twice. What's more, as a civilian, she wasn't as shackled to the rule book as their mutual bosses. And she'd already proved her willingness to cross the line when it needed to be crossed.

Which meant all that Jake had to do was find a way to let her do it. To steer her in that direction and do all that he could to help her. After all, some of the cold cases languishing in the files must have that bastard's MO written all over them, so it would be a legitimate exercise if he could think of a way to make sure that just one such file landed on her desk. She probably wouldn't even care about him manipulating it all. Providing they got to put the bastard away.

Yes, Hillary Greene, Jake knew, was his best chance, because she wasn't a young, vulnerable girl, or an old man. She was smart, and hard, and determined. And, if Jake could just figure out the best way to use her, she'd help him to get everything that he wanted.

Realizing that it was now fully dark, and that he'd been sitting alone for some time, Jake got up, carried his wine glass through to his sparkling, underused kitchen, then went upstairs for a shower.

After that, he went downtown, in search of dinner and a woman.

THE NEXT MORNING, Jake was in very early, only to find Jimmy Jessop already there ahead of him. He was a shade surprised and not a bit miffed, since he'd hoped to spend an hour in Hillary's office on her computer. It not being a portable laptop, he had no other option but to use it in situ, and although he knew he could use her password any time on another terminal, he preferred to use hers. That way, just in case there was any come-back, all links would lead back to Hillary's machine.

So seeing the old man sitting at the large, communal desk (which was two big desks pushed together) made him grit his teeth.

Jimmy looked up at him and smiled.

Jake did a quick double-take. Was it his imagination or was there a knowing glint in the old man's eye?

'Hello, Robin, you're up bright and early,' Jimmy said. 'After the worm, are you?'

'Robin? Oh, right.' Jake grinned.

'There's nothing special on, is there? Only….' He glanced pointedly at his watch, which showed it to be ten minutes before seven o'clock.

'No, not for you. Me and Sam are hot on Knocker Clarke's trail though,' Jimmy said genially. 'Hoping to nab his collar later today, all going well, so I thought I'd make sure I had all my ducks lined up in a row. The DI in Robbery is the sort who needs his hand holding. And you? It's not like Hillary to demand that anyone gets in before she does.'

'Oh no, just wanted to go through the murder book.' Jimmy Jessop nodded and watched the young man take his seat and retrieve the folder. He also noticed the slight tense line to Jake's jaw, and smiled widely, revealing straight, white, even dentures.

'Very wise,' Jimmy said mildly.

WHEN HILLARY ROLLED in at nine o'clock on the dot, with Zoe just behind her, Jake Barnes had managed to work his way into a marginally better mood.

'OK. Jake, what can you tell me about Colin Harcourt?' Hillary began, without preamble.

'This is the witness to the car crash between our victim and William Brandt, right?' Zoe piped up as she settled herself down at her own spot on the desk.

'Right,' Hillary confirmed. 'Last time we spoke about him,' she carried on, turning her attention back to the Boy Wonder, 'you were a bit intrigued by the amount of income he seemed to have?'

Jake frowned slightly. 'Sort of, guv. As you know, Harcourt owned a double glazing company at the time. Not a big outfit, just him and three employees. He worked more or less out of an office in his back garden, which was little more than a converted shed. Rented a space in an industrial complex nearby for the storage of the actual windows and doors and whatnot. A typical small business, in fact: simple, with low overheads.'

'Right. So what tweaked your antenna exactly?' Hillary asked, then added sharply, 'You have been preparing the financial assessments I asked you for?'

'Yes, guv. That's when I ran across the discrepancy. Well, if it is a discrepancy.' Zoe rose a theatrically black eyebrow, which had a gold ring piercing at one end of it. Today she was wearing a black leather biker's jacket, studded with brass tacks that formed the shape of a skull on the back, with a contrasting exceedingly feminine white lacy top underneath. With it, she was wearing a pair of velveteen bloomers that wouldn't have looked out of place at a Venetian-themed party, with a pair of white sandals that were so wispy-looking they seemed to be made almost entirely out of spaghetti straps. Her face was made up with the usual lashings of mascara and black eyeshadow.

'Sounds mysterious to me,' she mocked.

Jake smiled thinly. 'There's no sign that Felix Olliphant paid him off, guv, like William Brandt claimed. That's not what I'm saying. During the eighties and nineties, his firm did well and made steady profits. And after our victim was murdered, there wasn't any wild spending either. But as you know, since the credit crunch, things have been tight. Harcourt was—' He quickly checked a little palm-sized gizmo in his hand '—right, forty-eight at the time of the crash. And according to his tax returns, he's only just retired now. Four months ago in fact. But before that, like everyone else, his company must have begun to feel the squeeze. When times are tight, people cut back on nonessential things first—like getting new double glazing, or fitting new doors or conservatories. But from what I've been able to tell, Harcourt's company didn't go to the wall. In fact, he sold it, for a very small profit.'

Hillary was nodding. 'Right. So you're wondering why a small, not particularly recession-proof company, was able to last so long?'

'Right, guv. Plus the fact that Harcourt's personal spending doesn't seem to have decreased any. It makes you wonder, doesn't it?'

'Why he hasn't been tightening his belt like the rest of us?' Hillary said, nodding. 'Yes. It's certainly interesting.'

'What, you think Saint Felix really did bribe him to lie about the accident?' Zoe asked, somewhat irreverently.

'Nobody's calling him a saint,' Hillary said sharply. 'And remember, the man's dead and can't defend himself. And no, I don't really see how that would make sense either. From the accident report, the tyre marks, and everything else, it seems perfectly clear that Brandt was at fault. So why would he have needed to bribe Harcourt in the first place?'

Zoe, having flushed a little at the reprimand, rallied and shrugged one leather-clad shoulder. 'You'll just have to ask him, guv, won't you?'

'Yes, I suppose I will,' Hillary agreed dryly. 'Jake, where's he living nowadays?'

'Olney, guv. A town not far from Milton Keynes. Know it?'

'Aren't they famous for holding a pancake race every Shrove Tuesday?' Hillary asked, but both Zoe and Jake looked at her blankly.

'Philistines,' she muttered darkly. 'Don't you know anything about your own folk history?' Zoe grinned.

'OK, Jake, we'll go and talk to the not very skint Mr Harcourt. Zoe, track down our foxy bartender and make sure he'll be in to see us. We'll get around to him sometime after lunch—say between two and three. And don't take no for an answer. I noticed in DI Varney's notes that he mentioned that Peter Goodman seemed the nervous sort. That wasn't surprising—he was only just eighteen at the time, and probably hadn't been doing bartending for long. Suddenly finding himself in the middle of a police investigation probably spooked him. He's probably older, tougher and far more cynical nowadays, but just in case he's still of a nervous disposition, don't let him wriggle out of the interview. Tell him we can square it with whoever his employer is if he's going to be at work.'

'Right, guv,' Zoe promised. 'And I hope he's the sort who only got better looking with age. Like George Clooney, or David Tennant.'

Jake snorted and shook his head. Hillary was still smiling over the younger girl's wishful thinking as they made their way upstairs towards the beautiful Jag. Every time she saw the classic lines of the sleek sports car, she felt a pang of disloyalty towards Puff.

But damn, that car was fine.

OLNEY WAS a pleasant enough market town but Colin Harcourt had retired to a small, rather featureless cul-de-sac of new-build detached houses, that were trying so hard to all look original and individual from one another, that they only succeeded in looking uniform.

The mix of stone, brick, different coloured tiles and choice of hard landscaping made Hillary feel vaguely depressed as they located the Harcourt residence. Even though the sun was shining with late summer warmth, and the air was filled with the drone of bees and floating seeds, Hillary felt herself surprised by the lack of atmosphere in the colourful flower beds and the newly planted cherry trees that lined the roads.

Colin Harcourt turned out to be a man of medium size, with hair that was not quite white, not quite grey, and eyes that were not quite green and not quite hazel. He was neither thin nor fat, nor dressed particularly well, or particularly poorly.

He seemed only mildly surprised to see them on his doorstep, and immediately invited them in when they explained who they were and why they were calling on him.

'I hope you don't mind but I was in my workshop out back. Well, I call it my workshop—it's actually the double garage that came with this place. But the old motor has to stay outside and put up with the wind and the rain, I'm afraid,' he told them, somewhat breathlessly. 'Do you mind coming on through? Only I've got something burning and I don't want to leave it.'

'No, of course not,' Hillary said, mildly intrigued. She followed the sixty-something man through a moderately spacious hall that smelled of furniture polish and chrysanthemums to the back door and out around to the side of the house.

In the garage, both she and Jake were immediately dazzled by a display of colour that made them blink, and the acrid, unmistakable smell of burning metal.

'It's the solder,' Colin Harcourt said, as if they'd spoken out loud. 'If you wouldn't mind just waiting two minutes, only I've just got to do this…' He pointed to a section of coloured glass on his work table and Hillary quickly nodded at him to continue.

As Colin Harcourt put on a visor that covered his eyes and picked up a soldering iron, Hillary and Jake retreated and did a quick tour of the 'studio'.

'I've always admired true artisans,' Hillary said vaguely, as they looked around at the pieces on display. For although Colin Harcourt might have earned his daily bread by supplying double glazing to Britain's shivering masses, his soul obviously lay in stained glass.

She paused beside a free-standing door, in which the centre glass panel was now adorned with a Tudor rose in lovely shades of pink and red. Green leaves entwined what looked like some kind of Ionic column in the centre. A simplified version of someone's family crest of arms, perhaps?

Jake was regarding a much larger piece of work that depicted a seaside scene, with a beach hut at the centre of it. Another commissioned piece, Hillary mused. She knew that beach huts on the coast sold for ridiculous sums nowadays, but she hadn't known that the owners were so proud of their tiny plots of real estate that they were willing to order bespoke stained glass windows for the tiny residences.

'There, got it. Sorry, I didn't want St Joseph's head coming off because the lead wasn't up to the job!' Colin Harcourt's voice bought them back to his side once more.

He'd turned off the solder iron and removed the protective visor, and now all three looked down at what was obviously an ecclesiastical piece.

'My local chapel asked me to replace their old one. Some vandals had broken it beyond repair, can you believe it?' Colin shook his head, then nodded outside to a wrought-iron bench set in the garden overlooking a small patch of lawn.

'Shall we?' Leaving the hot, stuffy workroom behind, the three of them made their way towards a dwarf weeping willow, Colin Harcourt bringing with him a white-painted garden chair from the workroom. As Hillary and Jake sat on the shaded bench, he moved the chair into the full sun and sat down.

'So, you're looking into Mr Olliphant's murder again then?' he said, shaking his head sadly. 'It was a really bad thing, that. I was so surprised when I first read about it in the paper. It was his name I recognized first, of course. Seeing as I knew him—well, slightly. And it was an unusual name so it caught my eye right away. I couldn't believe it when I read about him being stabbed like that. And at a costume party too. It seemed so bizarre. But then it was New Year's Eve.' Again he shook his head. 'Some people just don't seem to have much luck, do they? Have you noticed that? It makes you think, I can tell you. First that awful car crash, and that little boy dying. And then that.'

Hillary nodded. 'The court case must have been difficult for you. Reliving it all—seeing the crash happen, and all that.'

'Yes, it was,' the older man agreed simply. 'But worse for poor Mr Olliphant, of course.'

'And Mr Brandt couldn't have made things easier. He made some rather wild allegations at the time, didn't he?' Hillary slipped in cunningly.

Colin Harcourt merely nodded. 'Yes he did, poor chap. But then, it was his grandson who died, wasn't it? And can you imagine how it must have been for him—to know that he was responsible? That it was his own fault? I felt so sorry for him, I can tell you.'

'Even when he accused you of lying? He did make the allegation that Felix Olliphant had paid you money to lie about your testimony as to what happened on the day of the accident, didn't he?'

'Yes, yes, he did,' Colin said with a sigh. 'I can't imagine why. I told the police at the time that I'd be more than happy for them to do a…whatchamacallit? A forensic audit, is it? You know, when they search your finances for something criminal. Of course, it didn't come to that. There was no question of anything of the kind having happened.'

He stopped suddenly, and looked at them a shade more sharply. 'You don't think that Mr Olliphant's death had anything to do with that, do you? I remember a detective inspector coming to call on me a little while after I'd read about his murder. But he never came back, and I never had to give a statement or anything. You're not saying that William Brandt killed him, are you?'

'No, sir,' Hillary said smartly. 'There's no evidence to suppose that. And Mr Brandt himself is dead now—he passed away a number of years ago. No, it's just that, sometimes, after a long time has passed, and you do a review of the evidence, new things can come to light.'

'Oh. I see. Well, actually, no, I don't,' he instantly corrected himself, and then smiled, a shade uncertainly. 'Just what do you think I can help you with, exactly?' Hillary looked at the not quite green, not quite hazel eyes and the slightly baffled face they inhabited, and decided to simply be honest. Sometimes—not often—but sometimes, she'd found it really could be the best policy.

'We were wondering, Mr Harcourt, why the recession didn't seem to hit your company as badly as it did many others,' Hillary said quietly.

Colin Harcourt looked at her, his mouth falling open a little in surprise, and then he laughed. 'Oh right. Yes, I see. You think maybe I was paid off, after all! Well, it's nothing that sinister, I can promise you,' he said, and then waved a hand at his workshop. 'When the normal work started to dry up, I had to let two of my employees go, and then, with only the one chap left, spent half my time on contracts and the other doing more stained glass work. It was enough to keep our heads afloat, until both of us were ready to retire permanently, like. You'd be surprised how many people are willing to pay for good-quality work. I think it's because in this day and age there aren't many true craftsmen left maybe. Anyway, I was lucky enough to know this fella who'd just been made redundant and wanted to start his own company with his payout. So I sold the business on to him. Nowadays I make quite a nice living with the stained glass—nothing fancy but enough for me. See?'

Hillary did. She glanced at Jake, whose lips were twitching with repressed amusement, and had to smile herself. So much for any hopes that there'd been some sort of sinister conspiracy between their murder victim and this average, nice, talented man.

Zoe *would* be disappointed.

'Well, thank you, Mr Harcourt. We'll see ourselves out,' Hillary said wryly.

'Peter Goodman's still a bartender! Would you believe it, guv?' Zoe said, the moment they walked back in to HQ. 'I thought that would be just a job he was doing whilst attending uni or something.'

'Well, some people make it a career,' Hillary pointed out reasonably. 'Where's he working nowadays?'

'In a pub in Oxford. But he doesn't start work until tonight, so he's at home at the moment. It's a small bedsit just up the road.'

'Right then, in that case you can drive,' Hillary said. 'We'll take your Mini. I wouldn't want to be accused of vehicular prejudice.'

PETER GOODMAN LOOKED decidedly ill at ease when he opened the door to their knocking. At nearly six feet tall, he had a slightly muscular frame and an attractive mop of nut-brown hair, but that was about as far as it went in the looks department as far as Hillary was concerned. The rest of his features comprised rather wide-set, grey eyes, a sharply pointed nose and a distinctly less-than-spectacular chin.

Beside her, Hillary could almost feel Zoe sag with disappointment, and smiled wryly. Obviously the goth shared Querida Phelps's assessment of him as not being particularly foxy at all. Or perhaps all the other female witnesses they'd interviewed just had very different views on what constituted good looks?

'Mr Goodman?' Hillary said, amused and annoyed at the whimsical tangent that was distracting her from the matter at hand.

'Yes. You're the police, right?' he said, with a shade of uneasy eagerness that accompanied a patently false welcoming smile.

'Well, come on in. I really don't know what I can do for you, but I'll try,' he gabbled, showing them into a small but pleasant enough room. A single bed was tucked discreetly out of the way against the far wall, and he led them past a small sink, to where a small table had been set up with two mismatched chairs placed around it.

He stood, hovering nervously, as they took a seat each, before looking around somewhat vaguely and then finally sitting on the arm of the room's only large piece of furniture, a rather shop-worn black leather settee.

Hillary saw him rub his palms on his jeans as he sat down.

'Just a few quick questions, sir,' Hillary said, careful to keep her voice calm and neutral. But if he'd been this jumpy when DI Varney had interviewed him, no wonder he'd attracted the policeman's attention. Witnesses with sweaty palms tended to ping any copper's radar.

'If you can just cast your mind back to New Year's Eve, 1999. You'd been hired by Querida Phelps to tend the bar at her costume party, yes?' she began briskly, hoping to focus his mind on something other than his own nerves.

'Yes.' Peter Goodman nodded emphatically. 'That's right.'

'You were eighteen at the time?'

'Yes. I suppose you might think that's a bit young, but I'd had a few gigs before,' he said defensively. 'Mostly at the local pub, I admit, but one time I did a two-week stint at a nightclub in Oxford. So I wasn't a complete novice or nothing.' He talked fast, like most people did when they wanted something over and done with quickly.

'Right. And during the night you must have served Mr Felix Olliphant with some drinks?' she pressed on.

'Well, yes, I must have done,' he agreed readily enough. 'But I wouldn't have known it, would I? I mean, I didn't know him or what he looked like, so I wouldn't have known who I was serving. If you see what I mean? He'd have just been another guest. And besides, everyone was dressed up as someone else, weren't they?' he rambled confusingly. He flushed a little, as if aware of it, which only seemed to highlight the very pedestrian quality of his facial features.

Hillary had a quick vision of the Gregory twins giggling over the 'foxy' barman, wondering what on earth they saw in him, and then suddenly twigged. Of course! How bloody dim she'd been.

'You were dressed as a fox, weren't you, Mr Goodman?' Hillary said, with a smile. 'That was your costume?' Beside her, she heard Zoe suppress a slight chuckle as she too caught on.

'Yes, that's right. I borrowed it from a friend, to be honest. I couldn't afford to rent one. It was a bit manky—it was an old football mascot costume—a local team. It was twenty years old if it was a day. The nap on it was even wearing thin in places. I was a fox with mange, if you like!' He tried to laugh, and rubbed his sweaty palms on his jeans again. 'It was a full outfit though, you know, like you see them wear sometimes in the London Marathon—a full body suit, padded with that foam stuff, and a big fox head. Made me look about seven foot tall, I can tell you! I was actually looking out of the mouth part of it in order to see.

Only the gloves on it were really thick and hopeless for bar work so I just wore a thin pair of orange gloves instead,' he rattled on, then paused to take a gulp of air.

'Yes, I think I get the picture,' Hillary said wryly. 'And I understand you left the party shortly after the midnight countdown? So you weren't there when Mr Olliphant's body was discovered and the police arrived?'

'Yes. I mean, no, I wasn't there. Mrs Phelps didn't seem to mind, about my wanting to leave so early, like, and a mate of mine was throwing this really awesome rave at…well, never mind about that,' he broke off suddenly, clearly flustered. Probably because he'd just realized that the rave he was on about had been illegally organized. Not that Hillary cared about that at this point.

'And you never met the man who was killed, Mr Olliphant?' she pressed.

'Didn't know him from Adam,' he said emphatically.

'Did you notice a young man at the party, dressed like poet, becoming ill or being helped out of the room by anyone?'

'No. I told all this to that other man who came asking the next morning. I wish I could have helped, but I didn't see nothing. Honest. I just served drinks.' He smiled, and looked from Zoe to Hillary hopefully.

'You didn't see anyone acting suspiciously? Slipping something into an unattended glass or something?' Hillary pressed, her eyes wandering around the room and falling on a small cupboard on which resided the almost obligatory collection of family photographs.

'No. What, like a date-rape drug or something?' Peter said, eyes going wide. 'No, we watch out for that sort of thing nowadays. Mind you, back then it wasn't so common, like.'

'No, not necessarily drugs,' Hillary said. 'Mr Olliphant was very drunk at the time of this death, but everyone who knew him insisted that he wasn't much of a drinker. Did you see anyone slipping spirits or maybe what looked like water in another glass?'

'Vodka or gin, you mean? No, I didn't. I would have said so if I had. Honest,' he added, again looking from one woman or the other, as if checking to see if he was being believed.

Hillary tried to reassure him with a bland smile. Some witnesses were just naturally highly strung. She wondered if Goodman had a long-term partner, and if he did, how she coped with his hang-ups.

'All right, sir. Did you know the victim's girlfriend? Or notice her? A rather pretty blonde woman, called Becky, or Rebecca?' 'Nah, can't say as I did. I was too busy to do any flirting, to be honest. Not that I felt in the mood for it—those outfits are heavy and make you sweat like a horse.' Again he tried to laugh. Zoe found herself thinking that it made him *sound* like a horse, though, so maybe it was apposite.

'OK, well, I think that's all for now,' Hillary said with a small sigh, thinking this was yet another dead end. Getting up, she glanced again at the array of photographs on the dresser. And as she did so, her eyes were snagged by one photograph in particular.

It showed Peter Goodman and another older man

standing proudly beside a car—no doubt a new family purchase—grinning widely and smugly at the camera.

But it wasn't the bartender that Hillary was looking at. Instead it was the older man beside him. For she'd seen another photograph of this man, just recently, and in a very different home from this.

And in that instant, it all dropped into place.

And just like that—unexpectedly and totally out of the blue—she saw it all. She knew exactly who had killed Felix Olliphant. How. And why.

She picked up the photograph and showed it to Zoe, who looked at it blankly. 'You're going to have to learn to be more observant, my girl,' Hillary told her quietly. Then she turned and looked at Peter Goodman thoughtfully. 'This is your father, is it, sir?' she asked silkily.

'Er, yes,' Peter Goodman said, going slightly pale. 'Why? I mean, what about it?'

'His name's Martin, I believe?' Hillary asked gently.

Peter Goodman's jaw dropped just a little. 'Yes. But how did you know that? What's Dad got to do with anything?' Hillary slowly put the photograph down and turned to look at the now openly sweating man in front of her.

'Oh, Mr Goodman,' she said sadly, shaking her head at him.

'You *have* been telling me lies, haven't you? Big fat porkies, in fact,' she chided.

His face suddenly and dramatically losing all its colour, Peter Goodman slowly sank back down onto the black leather settee.

'Oh shit,' he said helplessly.

'Yes, that's what you're in, all right,' Hillary Greene agreed flatly.

TWELVE

BESIDE HER, SHE felt Zoe shift with sudden tension.

'All right, Mr Goodman. I think you'd better come with us. Get up, please,' Hillary said crisply.

'What? Where are we going?' Peter Goodman asked, his voice little more than a terrified squeak now.

'Just down the road, sir. To HQ,' Hillary said, in a slightly gentler voice. She was very aware that she had no power to arrest him, and didn't want to go down the citizen's arrest route if she could avoid it. 'It's not far, as you know. You need to have a word with my superior officer, that's all,' she said, giving a small smile. 'Do you have a coat?'

'Do I need a solicitor?' Peter Goodman asked, getting to his feet and looking decidedly dazed.

'You can certainly telephone for one from the station, sir, if you think one is needed,' Hillary agreed carefully. 'But I think you'd be better off talking to Superintendent Crayle first. After all, it's not as if you've really done anything wrong, is it?' she asked, looking at him closely.

Some of the colour and a little of his nerve seemed to come back, and she noticed his shoulders relax fractionally. 'No. No, I haven't really, have I?'

Hillary smiled gently. 'This way then, sir,' she said, and with a baffled but increasingly excited Zoe Turnbull in tow, the two women escorted the not so foxy bartender downstairs to the waiting Mini.

Hillary deliberately made only small talk as Zoe drove the short distance to HQ. The moment they walked in, Hillary gave the nod to the desk sergeant, who caught on, and quickly sorted them out an interview room.

'If you'll just go with the custody sergeant for a moment, Mr Goodman, while I sort out the paperwork.' She nodded to the custody sergeant, who'd appeared to take her suspect and start processing him through the system, then inclined her head to Zoe to follow her down to CRT.

'What's going on, guv? Who was in that photograph? Are we arresting him? Did he do it?' Zoe's chatter and flock of questions skimmed mostly over Hillary's head as her mind raced, sorting out what needed to be done, and in what order of priority.

'Go and fetch Jimmy to the super's office, Zoe. I need to speak to Steven. Then you and the Boy Wonder get off to the observation room. I want you to watch carefully all the interviews we do under caution. Got that?'

'Right, guv,' Zoe said eagerly, and shot off as Hillary tapped on Steven's door and entered.

'Hillary, we need… What's up?' He took one look at her face and felt his stomach clench in reciprocal excitement. She had that look about her that he instantly recognized and which always succeeded in making his blood race.

'Sir, I need you to make an arrest. First we need a warrant—two, in fact. One for the arrest of Peter Goodman, for aiding and abetting after the fact, and obstruction of justice. For a start. There may be other charges to follow, we'll have to see how we go. And one for another suspect on the charge of murder.'

'The Olliphant case?'

'Yes, sir.'

Steven Crayle barely noticed that she'd slipped unconsciously into a more formal mode of address for him. He too was all business in that moment. 'Right. And the name of the suspect?'

She was just about to tell him when Jimmy Jessop knocked and put his head around the door. Hillary beckoned him in.

'Come in, Jimmy. We're about to make an arrest in our murder case. I've got a man, Peter Goodman, in the interview rooms. Go and keep him company for a moment, will you? If you can, get him talking about what he really did on the night that Felix Olliphant was killed. Because this is what I think he did.' For the next ten minutes, she outlined her case to Steven and Jimmy. When she was finished, Jimmy whistled silently.

'It sounds to me as if this Goodman's confession is going to be crucial, guv,' Jimmy said. 'You've not got a lot of other evidence to go on. You sure you want me to handle it?'

'Yes, I was wondering about that,' Steven said. Whilst he didn't doubt that Hillary had got it right, the lack of evidence was clearly going to be a major stumbling block for them. Getting a confession from the killer was going to be crucial. The Crown Prosecution Service wanted everything tied up in bows nowadays, and with the tricks barristers could get up to even a confession was hardly a guarantee of a guilty verdict any more. Which meant that Goodman's corroboration was essential. 'No offence, Jimmy, but you haven't even been working this case. And you're a civilian.'

'Oh, we'll need to get a serving officer in there as well,' Hillary agreed. 'But this witness is weak, and he's been carrying around his fear for years now. I think he's been half expecting to get caught all this time, and now that he has he'll be bursting his sides to tell his version of events and try and wriggle out from under. I want to strike now before he has a chance to have second thoughts. And before he wises up enough to ask for a brief, who'll tell him to zip it.'

Steven nodded, understanding her need to move fast. 'Right. Jimmy, nab DI Taylor then and have him oversee the ins and out. But you do the interviewing.'

'Right, guv,' Jimmy said. Then to Hillary, 'Any way you think I should play it?'

Hillary thought for a second, then smiled. 'I got the feeling that he was close to his dad. Likes a strong, guiding male hand, maybe. So be paternal. Explain to him how you've got his best interests in heart. Also, he's nervous as hell, so stress how the difference between serving time and maybe having a chance of getting a suspended sentence lies in full co operation. I really don't think he'll give you a hard time.'

Jimmy grinned. 'Right, guv. Everybody's favourite grandpa, that's me.' As Jimmy Jessop went out to start interviewing Peter Goodman, Steven got on the phone and wasted no time in getting the warrants needed. Then he and Hillary Greene went to arrest the killer of Felix Olliphant.

They didn't expect any trouble, and they weren't given any. When Mrs Eileen Millbright opened the door to find them on her doorstep, and Steven began the formal words of caution, she was totally docile and said not a word in response.

And it was her silence that worried Hillary Greene the most.

'BUT SHE MUST have said who it was,' Jake Barnes said impatiently, as he and Zoe finally managed to find out which interview room their guv'nors had been allocated and bundled in to the observation room.

'Well, she didn't,' Zoe said, too excited to take umbrage. 'I told you, one minute we were interviewing this bartender bloke and the next she's showing me a photograph on his dresser, or whatever, and telling me I had to pay more attention. Then we were bringing him in. And on the way in, she clearly didn't want to discuss the case in front of the suspect. I have no idea who…' Just then, the door beyond the two-way mirror opened and Steven Crayle walked in. Behind him came Hillary Greene and a tall, lean, grey-haired woman who Jake had never seen before.

'Bloody hell. That's Mrs Millbright,' Zoe said, stunned.

'Who?'

'The mother of Felix's friend. You know, the one who fell off the roof.'

'The gay one?'

'Harry Fletcher, yes. But why's she brought her in? Oh, hang on. The photograph!' Zoe said. 'Now I remember. She had a photograph of her husband—well, one of them, anyway. She's been married what, like, three times. I can't remember which one it was…'

'Shush. They're starting,' Jake hissed, and the two newbies fell silent as, inside the interview room, Steven spoke into the tape, stating those present, the time, and the fact that Mrs Eileen Millbright had been apprised of her rights and had, so far, declined to speak to a solicitor.

'Can you please confirm these facts for the tape, please, Mrs Millbright?' Steven asked politely.

Eileen Millbright cleared her throat slightly, and for the first time since her arrest, spoke. 'Yes, that's quite right. My name is Eileen Millbright, and I don't need a solicitor, as I have done nothing wrong. Nor have I committed any crime. I've been a law-abiding citizen for all my life.' And right at that moment, Hillary thought grimly, she certainly looked like it. Dressed in a pair of grey slacks, with a pale purple tunic, the older woman looked eminently respectable. No jury was going to find her unsympathetic.

Hillary felt her shoulders stiffen as she realized that there were going to be rough times ahead. It was clear that Eileen Millbright was a clever, intelligent woman who didn't intimidate easily. It was also clear that she'd chosen the path she intended to go down, and would not easily be dissuaded from it. She was simply going to deny everything, and challenge them to prove it. Which was going to be difficult. Damned difficult in fact.

Beside her, she could feel Steven's tension as he too recognized all the signs of a canny, stubborn opponent. He slowly leaned back in his chair, making it clear that, although he was the ranking officer, this was all Hillary's show. Which made sense, Jake Barnes thought, watching the body language of his two bosses with intense, interested eyes. Hillary was known for her interviewing prowess.

'Mrs Millbright. I think you should know that we have your nephew, Peter Goodman, in custody,' Hillary said, going at once for the jugular. When somebody was as confident as Eileen that her position was unassailable, it was best to get in a body blow quickly. The sooner she could put a crack in her armour, the better.

Eileen's somewhat watery blue eyes blinked, just the once. Her slightly arthritic hands, lying in front of her on the table, clenched slightly, turning her knuckles momentarily white.

'Really? I can't think what for,' she said calmly. Her low, deep voice sounded calm and unruffled.

Hillary almost felt like applauding her. She had guts, this woman. But then, she supposed, in a way it took guts to cold-bloodedly plan and execute the killing of another human being. Either that, or total cowardice.

'He's told us everything, I'm afraid,' Hillary carried on, less than truthfully. She hadn't checked in on Jimmy's progress with Peter Goodman because she hadn't wanted to interrupt whatever bond he'd managed to form with the bartender. But she had confidence in both Jimmy and her own reading of Goodman's need to talk.

'I still have no idea what you're talking about,' Eileen Millbright said stubbornly. 'May I have a glass of water, please? I can sense this may take some time, and I'm somewhat thirsty.'

'Of course. Would you prefer a cup of tea?' Hillary asked pleasantly.

'No, thank you. Some of that water would be fine.'

'Mrs Hillary Greene is pouring the witness a glass of water,' Steven Crayle said neutrally, for the tape.

In the observation room, Jake and Zoe watched, fascinated, as the unruffled white-haired woman took a drink. 'Bloody hell, it's like watching a scene from a play at a theatre,' Zoe breathed.

And Jake knew just what she meant. The tension he could feel just between him and Zoe, watching it all, was almost unbearable. What must it be like in there? The super looked totally calm but that had to be an act, right? Jake, novice that he was, could tell that if Hillary Greene couldn't crack the old woman's equilibrium they were up the creek without a paddle. So how much more uptight must Hillary Greene be feeling? Not that you could tell, from looking at her.

'I think we need to establish a few things before we continue, Mrs Millbright,' Hillary said pleasantly. 'Just facts that can be clearly corroborated. Peter Goodman is your nephew, yes? The son of Martin Goodman, your second husband's brother?'

'Yes, that's right,' Eileen agreed calmly. 'I've known Peter since he was a baby. I've always been fond of him.'

'So fond of him that you got him the job of tending the bar at the party where Felix Olliphant was murdered. You are an old friend of Querida Phelps, are you not? I have just finished speaking to Mrs Phelps,' she went on, quite truthfully this time. While Steven had been processing Eileen Millbright's admission with the custody sergeant, she'd taken the opportunity to have a quick word with the hostess of the costume party.

'It was something she said when I interviewed her that suddenly made sense,' Hillary went on, as Eileen Millbright hesitated to answer. 'She told me that an old friend of hers had given her the idea for the party. And when I spoke to her just now, she confirmed that that old friend was you.'

Eileen Millbright's lips twisted in a brief smile. Her

eyes, still level and cool, showed the merest spark of anger as they acknowledged Hillary's latest hit. 'Yes, I've known Querida for aeons. We graduated from Cheltenham Ladies' College together. We went down very different paths after that, as I'm sure you could tell, but we kept in touch. I was, and still am, very fond of Querida.'

Hillary smiled. 'Yes, Mrs Phelps has a very engaging way about her. So when she wanted to throw a big party for the New Year celebrations, you suggested that she throw a costume party.'

'I don't recall that,' Eileen denied firmly, not about to fall into the trap so easily. 'I do believe that was Querida's idea. She has always been far more bohemian, shall we say, than myself.' Eileen spread her hands in a helpless gesture. 'As you can see, I'm not the type to have much of an imagination. No, I'm quite sure it was Querida who came up with the idea of fancy dress. That's much more her line, don't you think?' Hillary smiled gently. Very good, she thought. But not good enough. 'I'm afraid Mrs Phelps remembers it quite differently. She assured me, not ten minutes ago, that she can remember you and her having lunch in Browns one day in the autumn, with her telling you that she wanted to do something big for the millennium. And after a few drinks, you coming up with the idea of a costume ball. You said that her newly decorated house would be just the setting for it.'

'After a few drinks?' Eileen pounced. 'Well, there you are then. I daresay Querida was a bit squiffy and not remembering things correctly.'

Hillary nodded. She really was good, no two ways about it. And she wasn't going to go down without a fight. Obviously a change of tactics was needed. Trading intelligent facts with her wasn't going to work.

It was time to get down and dirty.

Hillary sighed slightly. 'Ah yes. Mrs Phelps has a wonderful home, hasn't she? A converted water mill, I believe. Felix Olliphant and his company really did her proud on fitting it out, didn't they? I thought it was quite spectacular when I visited it.' Eileen Millbright's lips tightened, almost imperceptibly.

'I believe Felix was very good at his job,' she said blandly.

'Certainly, Querida was happy with his work, which is all that matters.'

'I'm surprised she didn't invite you to the party,' Hillary slipped in smoothly. 'You being such old friends, and it being your idea and everything.'

'I'm not the partying type, Mrs Greene,' Eileen said primly.

'And although I do believe that she did invite me, she knew that, and wasn't surprised, or offended, when I turned her down.'

'Ah yes, she said something of the kind to me just now,' Hillary agreed. 'She also told me that you offered her the services of your nephew to tend the bar for her.' She waited to see if Eileen would also deny this, but wasn't particularly surprised when the other woman, after a fraction of a second's thought, nodded. She was far too wily to be caught out in a needless lie.

'Yes. Peter was only just getting into bartending at the time and needed the money. The young always do, don't they?'

'Yes. So you arranged for Peter Goodman to tend bar that night?'

'I believe I just said so.'

'Did you also arrange his costume for him?' Hillary pressed gently.

'I...his costume?' Eileen reached for her glass and took another sip.

Hillary smiled. 'Yes. His costume. It was that of a fox, I believe. An old football mascot, I believe he said.'

Eileen's eyes flickered for a moment and Hillary knew she was on to something. Maybe nothing big but every little helped in moments like this. 'It won't take us long, I imagine, to find out where and how he came by it. After all, the people who had been in possession of it would probably remember loaning it out.'

'Yes. I believe I did get it for him,' Eileen reluctantly admitted. 'My husband, my second husband, that is, used to play in a senior league for his local village team. The Ferrington Foxes, I believe they called themselves. When it became obvious that Peter would need a costume, I thought it would save the lad some money if he didn't have to rent out something.'

'But that's not the true reason you arranged to take possession of the fox outfit, is it, Mrs Millbright? You really needed it because it was the type of outfit that fully covered its wearer, from top to toe. Unlike some of the costumes there, that required only an eye mask, or a carnival mask, the fox outfit would completely hide and obliterate the identity of whoever was wearing it. Isn't that so?' Eileen Millbright shrugged one thin shoulder. 'I really can't remember.'

'We have plenty of witnesses from the party who can testify that it did,' Hillary said gently.

'I dare say,' Eileen Millbright said, sounding bored.

'Which is just as well. Considering that it wasn't your

nephew Peter Goodman who was inside it that night,' Hillary continued. 'He's already admitted that he never went anywhere near Querida Phelps's house that New Year's Eve. In fact, he had no idea about the bartending job. He'd been at an illegal rave all that night. The first he knew about it was early the next morning, when you arrived on his doorstep and told him what he had to say when the police came calling,' Hillary recited the accusation in a matter-of-fact tone that made Zoe Turnbull's blood run cold.

'That's utterly untrue,' Eileen Millbright said flatly. 'And if the lad is saying anything else, then I can only imagine that you've been bullying him. The police have something of a reputation for brutality, don't they? And Peter has always been rather a nervous boy.'

Hillary let the slur pass and went straight for the relevant comment. 'Yes, I thought he was something of a weak character too. No doubt that's why you were so sure you could control him and make him do as he was told. After all, it wouldn't be hard for someone like yourself, with, if I may say, a very strong personality, to convince him that he could be in trouble if he got mixed up in a murder case. It would have been easy for you to convince him that he could be arrested for aiding and abetting, or being an accessory after the fact. Or did you simply pay him to keep quiet? I daresay he could always use some money, yes?'

'Certainly not,' Eileen Millbright said flatly. 'You really are talking nonsense, you know. Just what are you accusing me of exactly?' And as Hillary Greene looked at Felix Olliphant's killer, she knew that there was really only one way she was going to have any chance of bringing it home to her. She had to play on her emotions—specifically, her love for her son. She needed to bypass the woman's brain and go right for her heart.

But if she weathered that, Hillary would have nothing else in reserve. Which meant it was a big gamble. And if it didn't pay off....

She took a breath. 'I think you planned the whole thing, Mrs Millbright. I think you manipulated your old friend Querida Phelps into holding a fancy dress costume party that New Year's Eve night. I think you told her your nephew would tend bar, but that it was you who dressed up in the fox costume and tended bar that night. You have a lean figure, and if I may say so, a deep, rather masculine voice. There was no reason why anyone should suspect it was a woman inside the costume. It was noisy that night anyway. Who would notice? You knew that Felix Olliphant had been invited, and as the bartender you were in the perfect position to make sure that every fruit juice you served him, or his girlfriend, was spiked with large amounts of vodka or gin.' Hillary paused, but when Eileen remained silent, her blue eyes fixed unwaveringly on her, she carried on.

'I think you watched him getting progressively drunk and awaited your opportunity. You needed to catch him without his girlfriend in tow, and when that time finally came, sometime just before the countdown, I would imagine, you suggested he go up and lie down. By then he would have been drunk, and not used to being intoxicated was probably very easily persuaded and led. You took him to the bedroom where the coats were stored, got him to lay down on the bed and partially covered him with coats. He probably went to sleep straight away. Or he may just have been too confused to understand what was happening to him. You may even have taken your costume off, to avoid getting blood on it—I'm not sure. But then, with a knife, or some other implement that you had prepared beforehand and secreted on your person, you stabbed him to death. You then left. It really was as simple as that.' Eileen Millbright slowly poured herself some more water and sipped it.

'Pure fantasy. All of it,' she said. 'And you can't prove a word of it. Besides all that, why on earth should I kill Felix Olliphant anyway? He was a good friend of my son, Harry. I told you.'

'I know what you told me,' Hillary said flatly. 'But that was all lies, wasn't it, Mrs Millbright?'

Eileen's hand trembled slightly. 'I beg your pardon?'

'Your son didn't have a steady boyfriend, and he certainly didn't fall after trying to fix a television aerial, did he?' Hillary said, feeling herself tense. Here it comes, she thought. It's now or never. 'He deliberately threw himself from the balcony, didn't he?' she went on calmly. 'Because although he was deeply in love with Felix Olliphant, and probably had been for some time, Felix wouldn't love him back, would he? Not like Harry wanted him to. Not like he needed him to.' Eileen Millbright stiffened all over.

'Don't you dare talk about my son,' she said, her voice finally cracking.

'Why not? Isn't he worth talking about, Eileen? Isn't he the catalyst for all of this? Isn't he the reason Felix had to die?'

'I will not tolerate this. I'm leaving.' She made to rise, but Hillary was still talking.

'I'm sure Harry was a lovely boy, Eileen. Loving, kind, but too gentle for his own good, I expect? The world was always able to hurt him, wasn't it? Even with you there to protect and help him. But not even you could save him from getting his heart broken, could you? And when the man he loved couldn't save him either—'

'Not couldn't!' Eileen Millbright suddenly snapped savagely.

'He *wouldn't.* That's hardly the same thing.' She was breathing hard now, and Hillary leaned forward across the table, her face full of sympathy. 'It must have driven you mad afterwards,' Hillary agreed quietly, letting understanding flood her voice and her face. 'To see and hear about Felix from Querida all the time, going on and on about how her fabulous new designer was doing wonders on her house. About how he was going to attend the party, with his pretty blonde girlfriend. About how he was alive and happy in the world, whilst—'

'My Harry was dead,' Eileen interrupted flatly. 'Dead and buried and gone. Just gone. Where I couldn't find him. It wasn't fair. It wasn't *right*!'

Hillary took a deep, shaky breath. 'Did you see him actually jump?' she asked gently. 'That day?'

'No. It was like I told you—well, apart from the television playing up. It wasn't, of course, you were right about that. We'd been talking about Felix, of course. How Harry needed him to just… Oh, what's the use? When I went to make us some hot chocolate…that always made him feel better, as a little boy, when he was upset. I thought… But when I came back, the living room was empty, and the French windows leading to the balcony were open and when I went out and looked down… He hadn't made a sound. Can you imagine that? His despair was so deep, he hadn't even cried out when falling so far.'

For a moment, the room was silent. Hideously silent. And then Hillary nodded. 'I'm so very sorry. It must have been a nightmare for you.'

'You can't imagine,' Eileen Millbright said bitterly.

'No. And the funeral must have been even worse. Seeing Felix there. Knowing he was to blame.'

'The hypocrite brought flowers. *Flowers!* Why couldn't he have brought my son flowers when he was alive, tell me that?' She was almost shouting now. 'Just a kind word. Just to give him some hope that one day they might be together.'

'But he wasn't gay, Mrs Millbright,' Hillary Greene said gently. 'Felix could never have loved your son the way Harry wanted him to. Don't you see? It would never have worked out, no matter what Felix had tried to do.'

'He didn't deserve to live. Not when my son was dead,' Eileen Millbright said stubbornly.

'And so you killed him?' Hillary said flatly.

'Yes.' Beside her, she felt Steven finally relax.

'Yes. It was just like you said,' she agreed quietly, all the fight draining out of her. 'I don't mind getting caught. Not really. Harry was worth it, you see. He was all I had, anyway. I expect you want me to write it all down now?' Eileen said.

Hillary nodded, and handed over a pad and pen.

IT WAS HOURS later when the team finally met up at The Boat, Hillary's local at Thrupp. It was something of a dual celebration, for Jimmy and Sam had also managed to bring down Knocker Clarke and his gang.

'There were times there, guv, when I didn't think she was going to crack,' Jake Barnes said, after buying in his round and dispensing the glasses around their table.

'I know what you mean,' Steven agreed, with feeling. 'It was touch and go there for a while, Hillary, you have to admit. At the beginning, I thought she was going to hold out forever.'

'Yes,' Hillary said. 'She kept her nerve all right. Which is why I knew I had to bring emotion into it. And in her case, that all centred around her son.'

'I think there was something unhealthy about it, if you ask me,' Zoe put in. 'You know, gay son, domineering mother. She was a right nutter. I mean, killing poor Felix just because he wasn't gay, and couldn't be, you know, like that, with Harry.'

'Yes. I don't think killing Felix could have given her that much satisfaction really,' Hillary agreed grimly. 'I think, in her heart of hearts, it couldn't have felt like much of a victory for her. After all, it didn't bring her son back, did it?'

In the silence that developed after Hillary's comment, Jake realized that at some point he and Hillary Greene would have to come to an agreement about the reason he'd joined CRT. An agreement that would include their taking on someone far more dangerous and vicious than anyone she had ever had to deal with before. Until then, he would continue to help her on the cold cases assigned by their bosses.

A moment later Jimmy Jessop began to regale them with the look on Knocker Clarke's face when the burglary squad hauled him in. 'And can you believe, he asked for fifty-three other cases to be taken into consideration?' he crowed. 'The bosses are gonna love us!' It was late when the triumphant revellers finally left the pub, but at least Hillary and Steven didn't have far to go. Just a moonlight wander up the towpath for a hundred yards or so, and back to the *Mollern*.

As Hillary set about making them coffee, Steven, propped up against the tiny sink, watched her closely. He'd been aware for some time of the growing anger and tension in her, and he knew the reason for it, of course. His promotion and move away from CRT had brought things between them to a head far sooner than he would have liked. Or felt comfortable with. For some time now, he was aware that there was a serious question mark hanging over their heads, and it needed sorting out.

'Hillary, I think it's time we talked. Seriously, I mean. About us,' he said cautiously. Like most men, he wasn't good when it came to conversations that were likely to turn emotional and volatile.

Hillary's shoulders tensed.

'Ah.' She turned to look at him, her face utterly blank. This was it then.

Steven Crayle looked at her pale face, and thought he could make a pretty good guess at what she was thinking But would that help him, or make things worse? It was hard to say.

He took a long slow breath. Hillary swallowed hard.

'Hillary,' he said gently. 'How would you feel about getting married again?'

* * * * *